MRS. WILSON'S AFFAIR

MRS. WILSON'S AFFAIR

ALLYSON REEDY

NEW YORK

The names and identifying characteristics of some individuals have been changed.

ISBN 978-1-4549-6181-9 (paperback)
ISBN 978-1-4549-6182-6 (e-book)

Union Square & Co. books may be purchased in bulk for business, educational, or promotional use. For more information, please contact your local bookseller or the Hachette Book Group's Special Markets department at special.markets@hbgusa.com.

Printed in Canada

MRQ-T

1 2025

unionsquareandco.com

Cover design by Jared Oriel
Cover artwork: Shutterstock.com: alaver (woman);
Daniela Iga (wallpaper); Lee Charlie (paper texture);
Interior design by Christine Heun

For all the Gatsby fans and my own Gatsby,
who watched over me as I wrote this.

"Reserving judgments is a matter of infinite hope."

—F. Scott Fitzgerald, *The Great Gatsby*

CHAPTER 1

THE EYES OF DR. T. J. ECKLEBURG, blue and gigantic behind yellow glasses, were always watching her. Sure, the paint on the billboard had worn thin in places, but not around the eyes. So full of compassion, as if eternally watching a hopeful, rosy little baby lurching its first steps.

Flat but focused, those eyes cut through the gray, powdery air and rumbling sounds that haunted the minds of those unfortunate enough to live beneath them. The eyes never moved, never blinked, just towered over the trains and tracks, looking at her.

Myrtle Wilson often looked back. There wasn't much else for her to look at or do anyway. The hissing gas pumps, grease-stained garage floor, and dusty road wouldn't hold many people's interest, least of all hers.

The trio of yellow brick shops was her home, and the railroad tracks her means of avoidance and wishful desertion. She wasn't one to desert, though, which is why she was there that day in the Valley of the Ashes, staring into the eyes of Dr. T. J. Eckleburg, an optometrist in Queens who'd decided that this was the place to advertise his services.

She could see them clearly from her bedroom, which was on the second floor of one of those yellow brick buildings, hovering over her husband George's garage. They'd been up there for a few years now—the eyes; Myrtle had been suspended for much longer. So long that she couldn't remember what had been there before. Perhaps an advertisement for a drugstore or hotel. But now it was Eckleburg who blended in so casually that he may as well have been one of the passing locomotive's heavy, smoky billows.

She heard George's pounding of metal on metal ascend over the *tick-tick-tick* of a slowing train. George. So content to give all of his attention to other people's things, she thought. Fixing, mending, and adjusting what already existed. Never creating. Endlessly reliant upon the brokenness of other people's stuff.

Myrtle fixed herself in the mirror. That was her train that had just pulled in. She'd ride it into the city to see her younger sister, Catherine, but mainly to see something other than damaged cars and giant blue eyes on a billboard.

Downstairs, George was hidden by a wreck of a black Chevrolet Light Six. The garage doors were wide open to the April day, but the ashy air veiled the sun just enough to make it look like winter's stubborn dimness remained.

A face looked out from under the hood, inky grease overwhelming milky skin.

"Where you going?" he asked.

"To my sister's," Myrtle replied. "Don't ask when I'll be back. Maybe tomorrow. I don't know."

He looked back into the car's clumps of metal. They made sense to him.

She passed the open bottle of whiskey, sitting out in plain sight. Already, she thought. So pathetic. So weak. So vile. She couldn't so much as get a glimpse of the man she'd married anymore—and she tried. All that ever greeted her was a spiritless drunk, withdrawn into . . . well, she didn't know. And she'd long stopped caring enough to want to know. How can one care when feeling is gone?

The railroad tracks, road, and three yellow brick buildings ran parallel to each other, but unlike the tracks and road, there was no movement in the buildings. They'd housed the same occupants—George Wilson's garage (formerly his father's garage), Michaelis's all-night restaurant, and a third perpetually vacant spot, empty for years. While the cars and trains propelled their occupants forward in smooth, continuous lines, the yellow-bricked trio kept everyone exactly as they had always been.

Michaelis, a Greek who probably ate too much of his own food, sauntered out front when he saw Myrtle go by. He liked George and Myrtle very much, mainly because they were the type of neighbors who left him alone most of the time. He admired that they minded their own business and did not concern themselves with his.

"Mrs. Wilson!" he called, in the way he always said it. *Meesus Wheelson.* "I have an idea. To attract the ladies. There are always the men—so many men over here. We need more ladies, no? And you are a lady—a fine lady—and I want you to listen to my idea. My idea to get the lady customers."

"I'd be happy to listen to your idea, Michaelis, but I'm catching that train."

"It will only take a second, Mrs. Wilson." *Meesus Wheelson.* "My idea is this: tea and cigarettes. What do you think, as a fine lady yourself? The ladies, they like tea and cigarettes. I will sell them."

"Sounds great," she said. "Some women enjoy tea and cigarettes."

"I can put out flowers and candles and other things the ladies like. Get them all into my restaurant."

"That sounds like a good idea. I've got to catch that train though now."

"Tea and cigarettes and flowers and candles, and we will have more ladies!"

"Great! We can talk about it more when I get back, if you like."

Myrtle hurried on and stopped at the edge of the two-lane road. The morning rush had already gone, but a trickle of cars sped by, sending dirt clouds into the already cloudy air. Those must be the important people, she thought. Those who were so accomplished, so successful that they could get to work when they pleased. She wanted to know those people.

When there was a big enough gap in traffic, she dashed across the road, her overnight bag bouncing against her side. This was the exact spot at which she would die, but of course she did not know that. Nobody knows the exact spot, or moment, at which they will cease to exist. No one wants to know, and even if they did want to know, they shouldn't.

She didn't really want to see Catherine. The last time she'd seen her, just a week before, all Catherine talked about was the parties she'd been to, as if life was nothing more than a parade of smartly dressed people pretending to care about one another for an hour, two tops, then retreating home to rest up so they could pretend all over again the next night.

To Myrtle, it seemed like Catherine had all the freedom in the world. She worked the cosmetics counter at Gimbels department store, which provided her with just enough of an income to share a room with another girl in a downtown hotel and to keep herself outfitted in whatever New York City women who went to those sorts of parties were supposed to wear.

Myrtle rarely bought new dresses. The money George allowed her barely covered groceries, but she'd gladly buy expiring meat if it meant she could pocket a few cents. She'd save whatever was left and then make a trip out to the city and to Gimbels when Catherine was working. She'd pick out a bright lipstick and pay full price for it, and Catherine would drop another and maybe some eye shadow into the bag. She wanted her big sister to always be beautiful and have nice things. Myrtle pretended not to notice.

It wasn't much of a station, across the road from Myrtle's home, and she only saw one or two men outside the train. They stared at her as she walked toward the passenger car, as confidently and comfortably as if they were watching their own dog trot along the platform.

She hated taking the train. She'd much prefer driving herself to the city, but George would never let her drive one of the old cars he fixed up at the garage. She knew how to drive too; her dad had taught her back on Long Island. Just before he died and she married George.

She took out her book, as much for the material itself—a romance—as for an effective defense against the eyes turned her direction.

She liked being looked at because she knew what it represented. Desire. Wanting. It was the only power she felt she had left. Of course, the harsh reality—which she, too, knew—was that the power didn't last. Not over the men, who'd direct their short-winded elations onto the next moving target as soon as they'd hit the first, nor in the nature of the power itself. The body decays, the face withers. It's what they must do.

Her face was that of her mother's. Not in the sense that many daughters look markedly similar to their mothers, but in an uncanny, even unsettling, way. It seemed the creator was feeling lazy the day Myrtle was born, and instead of giving Myrtle her own twist on those predetermined genetic features, he simply stuck her mother's face—which he'd already spent much time and energy creating—onto that newborn baby's soft little head. The face had done well enough the first time around, so why not give it another go? That's how Myrtle began life—with a shortcut, identical face.

One day, when Myrtle was just old enough to wade into the Sound by herself because she'd learned to swim the previous summer and Catherine still couldn't, she'd drifted a little way down from where the rest of her young family sat atop the gravelly sand. Because the sun had been burning especially violently, many other families had also elected to visit the Sound that day. The water was cool, although it seemed to Myrtle that it heated up slightly with each new body that entered it. She made a game of counting each one that came in, each set of legs that gingerly disappeared below the surface, in the case of the larger bodies, or eagerly thrashed in, the protocol for the legs that were about her size.

The top half of a larger body was coming her way. In fact, many bodies, big and small, were moving her direction, but it was this one's movements that sparked an instinct in young Myrtle to grab at the too-distant sand with her eyes, scanning for her family. Unable to find them amid all the umbrellas and uniform human shapes, she looked back at the man approaching her in the water. She definitely did not know him, and he was definitely coming for her. His chest was covered with matted-down dark, straight hair and his eyes were locked on her own. That's all that she remembered of him—the wet, black mass cloaking his chest and the questioning eyes, so focused on her.

She stood in the water, awaiting him. It was her first taste of the erotic, even though she didn't yet recognize it as erotic. The dark, shiny hair, the dark, shiny eyes.

"Josephine," he said. Her mother's name.

Myrtle didn't answer. She was filled with jealousy, maybe even anger, over not being Josephine. She shook her head, breaking the man's spell.

"I . . . I'm sorry," he stammered. "I thought you were someone else. But that would have been impossible."

As he walked away, more dark hair retreating on his back, she both loved and resented her mother more than she ever had.

Usually, having her mother's face served her well. It got her easy friends in childhood and easy dates when she got older. It got her George, who showed her such a true, loyal love that she married him. It got her to exactly where she was today.

One of the things Myrtle often wondered about was how that face of theirs would age. She never saw her mother get old. She never saw her not young and beautiful.

She fretted often about getting older and losing the only currency she thought she had. Clearly life hadn't yet revealed its true beauty to her, which had nothing to do with hers.

The train raced toward the city, an increasing number of buildings blurring past the windows. Green, a color Myrtle didn't see much of at home, began popping into view, as trees were regenerating the leaves they'd lost during winter.

She, too, started to feel alive again. Being alone in a place not her own did that to her. The very same day, with the very same potential, felt like crushing despair to her at home. But here, whizzing toward the unknown, she only felt optimism about what could possibly be.

She'd change over to the subway and take that to Herald Square, where Gimbels and Catherine would be. She'd look around at the things she couldn't afford to buy, with the detachment of someone well aware that she couldn't afford to buy them. She'd have lunch, alone, on the sidewalk somewhere, watching people go by and occasionally dreaming up a narrative for them, maybe involving a secret lover or illicit business dealings. This was all of great interest to her. This was, at this point in her life, all that she wanted. To escape from her own life and imagine that of others.

The lurch of the braking train brought Myrtle out of her romance novel and back into her day. She looked up to find a pair of eyes looking down at her legs. This reassured her. Those legs had thickened in recent years. As her mind and emotions had grown increasingly lethargic, so followed her body. So much so that she almost didn't recognize it as her own. She silently thanked the man for appreciating a part of her that she did not appreciate.

As the train wheezed its way to a full stop, Myrtle stared at the rush of humanity outside. Men balancing cigars on solid lower lips, women holding onto one another with the bravest of familiarity, little boys whose eyes looked like they'd seen one too many disappointing adults. She knew that she didn't belong there, but that made it all the more thrilling.

It was a quick walk to the subway, one that became more and more clogged with people the closer she got. Her overnight bag rubbed against one person after another, and she apologized in vain, her words falling into the air as the bodies rushed past. No one cared about her or her bag, a thought that both distressed and freed her.

She filled in an empty space on the platform, like a missing piece in a jigsaw puzzle, bringing the scene to completion. So many people, knitted so tightly together. Myrtle sucked in her breath, involuntarily trying to shrink herself and get some space in a spaceless place. The subway train squeaked its way through the mass of people on either side and opened its doors to them.

Myrtle rushed in and secured a seat, her overnight bag set on the floor between her legs. The car filled up, brimming with people yet strangely devoid of sound.

Surveying her fellow passengers, her attention clung to a young man seated across from her. Even sitting down, she could tell that his body was long and broad. He was handsome in the way that money made some men handsome, which is to say that he would not have been considered so had he not had that confident air and expensive suit wrapped around him.

With so many bodies between them, and depending on the directional sway of the train, at times she could only see his shoes. Black patent leather, without a single smudge. How could there not be a single smudge? she wondered.

As the train delivered passengers to their destinations, the space between Myrtle and the man cleared, giving her a less and less obstructed view. He caught her watching him.

Over the course of a day, a month, a year, we look into the eyes of countless people, casual interactions that are so easily forgotten that they shouldn't even be considered forgotten because they were never really noted or remembered in the first place. So many black pupils, surrounded by banded rings of muted colors, as unique as visible fingerprints, go completely unnoticed. Eyes meet, lips move, and we move on, completely missing the humanity of those we encounter, subconsciously dismissing those eyes as ordinary, expected things that we routinely experience. Eye contact as just another overlooked action in a sea of daily overlooked actions.

When Myrtle Wilson's eyes met those of the man across from her on the subway, this was not one of those overlooked actions.

He looked back with such an intensity that her entire body took note. She glanced up to the cigarette advertisement above his head, embarrassed that he'd caught her staring. But she had to know if he was still looking. Down went her eyes, back to his.

There was no time to process the feeling that flooded her body. It was now just another part of her—as suddenly there as sprinkles of rain let loose by a fleeting cloud on an otherwise sunny day. One moment she felt one way, which wasn't much of anything, really, and the next a whole other, new way.

Tom and Myrtle looked at each other and there was a knowing that shouldn't have existed between two strangers on a subway train. A connection forged across seven feet at twenty-five miles per hour.

She looked away again and again, memorizing the juicy red of the cigarette ad and its thick black lettering. And she looked back again and again, nearly always finding his eyes burning into hers.

Myrtle didn't think about what could have happened. She only kept looking, to the red sign above his head and back down to his eyes. She lost the embarrassment she felt when he first saw her looking—now it was a game. How much of herself could she show him with a glance? Could she show him everything?

There were now only a handful of people left on the train, and those seated near Myrtle and Tom noticed their attraction. The two were now freely giving looks not usually cast about public spaces. The voyeurs pretended not to see, but their bodies also were awakened by this happenchance meeting. Their eyes dipped to the floor in shame but turned back to the two to watch what happened next.

If Myrtle could have seen herself, she would have been shocked by her public flirtation. But she wasn't one of the voyeurs on the train, she was the star, too caught up in the performance to care who might be watching, judging. After years of slowly losing the passion that used to vibrate through her body, it was back in an instant, and its return exhilarated her.

When the train reached her stop—the one that would take her to Gimbels, to Catherine, to the life she well knew—it didn't even occur to her to get off. She was riding the high of feeling something again, and she didn't want it to end. George owed her that much, she thought. A few minutes of feeling alive again.

Don't get off, don't get off, she'd hope at each stop. And she'd stare right back at him, even licking her lips. Who is this person, salivating over a stranger? she thought about herself. But she kept going, and he didn't get off.

He smiled and got up. His gray jacket stretched tight across his broad shoulders. Those black, smudgeless, patent leather shoes taking steps toward Myrtle. He sat down in the empty seat beside her, pressing his heavy body into hers.

"I'm going to have to call a policeman," she told him.

"Call him," he answered, those intense eyes now just inches from hers.

"Do you always go around like this on the subway? Looking for women to harass?"

"Only on Tuesdays," he said. "What's your name?"

"I don't know that I should be giving you my name. What's yours?"

"Tom Buchanan. What's your name?"

"Myrtle Wilson."

He held out his hand. "I'm very pleased it's a Tuesday—my day to harass pretty girls on the subway—Myrtle Wilson."

She smiled and pressed her thigh closer to his. She'd never done anything like this before. She hid her left hand beneath her purse, as if by hiding her wedding band she could undo twelve years of marriage.

Thinking about George, about where they were now and where they could have been, she only felt betrayal. He's taken so much from me, she thought. He owes me. He owes me this.

Tom was a stranger, which almost by definition made him one-dimensional and ripe for the imagining. Myrtle didn't really much care who he was, anyway. No, it was who he could make *her* be that piqued her interest.

"Where are you headed?" he asked. "Off to get your hair done? Meet friends for lunch?"

"I'm going to see my sister," she answered.

"Do you think your sister might be able to wait a little while?" he asked. "I'd sure like to get to know you better, Myrtle.

Get off the train with me." It was a command, from someone used to commanding.

From casual looks to mere words to a proposal that would undoubtedly lead to culpable actions. Or would it? she thought. Simply talking to another man wasn't a crime.

"I can't do that," she said. "My sister's expecting me. And I'm not the sort of woman who gets off a train with strange men."

"I'm not a stranger. I'm Tom Buchanan, I live in West Egg, and you're Myrtle Wilson. We're practically old friends," he said.

"And where is it you're going, old friend?"

"Wherever you are, Myrtle. Let's have lunch. I'm sure your sister won't mind."

She smiled a giddy smile, because that's exactly how she felt—giddy. Nothing could have excited her more—not if a check fell from the sky, not if she finally convinced George to move them out west to California, like she'd been trying to do for years—than this interaction with the stranger on the train. But *stranger* isn't the right word for someone whose eye contact produced such a spark. This was *someone*, Myrtle thought, as much because of his nice suit and smudgeless shoes as for their spontaneous connection.

The train began filling up again. One of the groups that boarded was a trio of young, very pretty women. They sat across from Myrtle, the prettiest, a short-haired blonde with a precariously short dress, in the seat Tom had owned just minutes before. The girls laughed and talked, clearly not worried about the inches of fabric their dresses lacked and their exposed canvases of skin. Myrtle didn't like them one bit.

"I can't go to lunch with you, Tom. I have a prior engagement, and it would be so rude of me to cancel," Myrtle said, without conviction.

It was at this point, as she spoke these hollow words, that she first let the possibility of going off with Tom enter her mind. Couldn't she revisit that long-lost feeling, just for today? She wouldn't do anything she'd regret, she reasoned.

"You got sick. It came on suddenly—while you were riding the subway to see her. Oh, it was awful! A headache. You thought your head might just split wide open, it hurt so bad. You don't know what it was, but rest, you needed rest. There was no way you could meet her feeling like that, like your head was going to split wide open," he said, thrilling her more with each word of his lie. "'You poor dear,'" he said in a high-pitched voice, encouraged by her smile. "'Of course I understand why you had to cancel. Take care of yourself, Myrtle!'"

"It's true that I am starting to feel a little lightheaded. There's some pain here," she said, touching her head lightly. "I'd hate for it to get any worse."

"It would be positively irresponsible of you to meet your sister," he said.

"We'd just have lunch, you and I? Just a friendly lunch and then we'd head off, me one way, and you back to wherever it is you're headed?"

"Of course," he answered. "If that's what you want."

It's important to note here that there are always two ways of thinking about things. The first is how we think about things before they happen to us. The second is the very different, often opposite way we think about these very same things after they've happened to us. So, before you pass judgment on poor Myrtle Wilson, remember that you're stuck in that first way of thinking—before they've happened to you. If you're not, if you've made the leap or fallen over to the other side, well, you know the journey. You know the moments that led up to this. You know all isn't as it seems. You know that right and wrong are meaningless outside of context, and that context is dubious and subjective.

Myrtle was about to make that leap herself, or that fall. It happens quickly, although not usually painlessly. Whether it's the head or the heart's fault is irrelevant. The heart typically takes the blame for these sorts of things, while the brain knows better yet conspires anyway. The brain, in collusion with the body, gives us permission to make the mistake by rationalizing it away. It's the mistake's most powerful ally.

But all of that is behind the scenes—the lights switching on over here to take your attention away from what's happening over there; the complicated inner workings that make the outward work so effortlessly. Myrtle wasn't aware of any decision-making process at all. In fact, if you were to ask her, at a later date, what happened during this subway ride, what she was thinking, she wouldn't be able to tell you much.

Only this: you can't live forever, you can't live forever.

Those were the words pounding through her head, as heavy as her heartbeat, right before she said, "Let's get off this train then."

Tom smiled, not a smile of surprise, but a self-assured smile that let on that he was more than a little familiar with getting his way. This was lost on Myrtle, too shocked by what she'd freely consented to do, and too naive to believe that something like this—something so disruptive to her own life—could ever be commonplace in someone else's.

"That's exactly what I wanted to hear, Myrtle Wilson," Tom said, standing up as the train slowed.

He looked down at her with eyes so full of lust that she almost didn't recognize them as human eyes. That was her chance to turn back, to recognize those eyes as the animalistic, inhuman orbs that they were and retreat to the expressionless pair she knew at home.

Instead she stood up, bumping against his body as the train came to a quick halt. The doors opened. He led; she followed.

George owed her. Nothing would happen. You can't live forever, you can't live forever.

CHAPTER 2

THE SUN BURST OVER the open subway stairwell, illuminating the concrete, the people crowding the sidewalk, and pretty much everything else in its path. No longer in the dark tunnel of what now seemed like an alternate reality, Myrtle watched the large, gray-suited body in front of her indifferently. She felt like she just woke from one of those half-naps, where the unconscious taps a toe into the waters of the conscious mind, but then turns back to its more comfortable home.

She was fully awake, fully aware, that she, Myrtle Wilson, wife of George Wilson, was following another man who she knew nothing about except that he was most definitely not her husband.

She followed him up the stairs, into that bright sunlight, and when he turned around to make sure she was still behind him, she looked into his eyes and continued to follow him, over to a quiet street corner, where they stopped.

"I want to show you something, Myrtle," Tom said. "I have to make a stop before lunch. I hope you won't mind. It'll just be for a minute, and I think you'll like seeing it."

"Where?" she asked, looking around.

"I have an apartment, not too far from here, and I left something there that I need for a meeting this afternoon. Would you mind stopping in with me to grab it? It's a nice apartment with a nice view of the university. I think you'll really like it."

Whatever happened next, she felt, she'd already committed to on the train. The decision had been made and now it was her obligation to experience it. It seemed like she was watching herself on a conveyor belt, being carried along to an unknown destination, but as she'd already consented to take this ride, she oddly felt no fear or shame. She was merely executing the plans already laid.

"Sure, I don't mind," she said.

"Great, I'll get us a cab."

When he lifted his arm to hail the taxi, the initial passion she'd felt on the train returned. The jacket fabric pleated over his broad back, and Myrtle thrilled at the thought that this man, who clearly must be well-to-do and important, was getting a cab for her. That right now, she was a part of his world, the world she'd instinctively expected to be a part of, but never was. And when the car pulled up—as if fished out of the street by that pleated jacket, that large white hand—she jumped in as quickly as she could, unsure if her eagerness was due to a fear of her changing her mind, or him changing his.

Sitting so closely with what felt like all the privacy in the world offered by the cab's leather seats, Myrtle felt shy, but still excited by Tom's company. She was still innocent at that moment, and she watched it carefully, because she knew she may not be much longer. She didn't want to be. She was ready to collect her payment from George for the years of drinking and lying, neglect and abuse. She'd endured years, she thought. Of course she could have this moment. She wasn't under any spells as she turned her head toward Tom's, knowing what she'd find.

He grabbed the back of her head and pulled it toward his, kissing her with the kind of desperation that she didn't think she'd ever receive again. She pulled back.

"Maybe we shouldn't do this," she said.

"Do you not want to do this?"

She answered by grabbing him right back, kissing him so hard their teeth clanged against each other and their noses collided.

His hands spread across her back, down to her waist, circled to the front, and worked their way up. She wanted him to grab her breasts, and when he did, she let out a moan that made the cab driver stare into the rearview mirror. She didn't care. As long as Tom didn't stop kissing her, touching her, nothing else mattered.

Soon his hands worked their way back down, down to her knees, where her dress ended and skin began. Then up, up over her thighs, slowing down inside, then rushing under the only fabric she had left for him to penetrate.

He opened his eyes to hers, to make sure it was all right. Why was she allowing this to happen? she wondered. She should stop him. She should close her legs, stop the cab, and run back home to the garage. Instead, she spread her legs wider.

She leaned her head back against the seat, allowing his fingers to slide in and out. She tried not to make a sound, to breathe normally, but the look of desire on Tom's face intensified everything she was feeling.

She writhed with his movements, pulling herself closer to him. Outside the city kept going. A woman pushed a baby in a bright blue carriage, a policeman crouched over a weathered homeless man lying in an alley, suited men bought newspapers and hurried on—all oblivious to Myrtle in the cab, squeezing Tom's thigh tighter and tighter, his hands moving faster and faster.

An angry driver repeatedly honked his horn—the stoplight had turned green and Tom and Myrtle's cab wasn't moving. As their driver finally hit the gas, lurching the car forward, Myrtle came, quietly and intensely.

When she opened her eyes, their cab had caught up to the blue carriage. The baby's mother looked over at Myrtle through the window and smiled. Then she looked back at her baby, tucking the blanket around his neck, and disappeared into a door.

"Good girl," Tom whispered. "Good girl."

He kissed her again. His desire peaking while hers collapsed.

"We're almost there," he said.

Myrtle didn't want to be anywhere. She wanted to extend the surreal minutes in the cab, to live in a drawn-out state of excitement for as long as she could. Where her heart was beating so fast and her breath was coming so quick that she couldn't possibly think, couldn't possibly be held responsible for this other man touching her.

It had been so long, she thought. She knew that she'd felt this way with George at the beginning, but even when she tried, alone in bed at night, him passed out somewhere downstairs, she couldn't recapture the passion she felt for him before they loved each other. She'd found that pre-love attraction again today, and it felt better than anything else she could imagine. It seemed impossible that she was supposed to live the rest of her years without ever feeling this again, when it felt so good.

A few leaves drifted past the window as the cab rolled by the stately brick buildings of Columbia University. It pulled up to the curb of an equally stately apartment building across the street.

"Thank you, sir. Appreciate it," Tom said, stuffing a five-dollar bill into the cab driver's hand. The meter read eighty-five cents.

Myrtle avoided looking in the driver's direction, a little embarrassed by what had transpired, but also proud to be the sort of woman traveling with the sort of man who gave large tips. Looking up, the redbrick apartment tower stretched toward the cerulean sky. It looked like a postcard, Myrtle thought. Just wait until Catherine hears about this.

"Let's head up," Tom said. "It's not anything much, just a little spot that I get away to once in a while. When Dai—when I need a break. It looks right over the campus, though, and I've got a nice record collection, if you like that sort of thing."

"What sort of person wouldn't like music? Of course I like 'that sort of thing,'" Myrtle said.

"You'd be surprised. There are all sorts of people in the world. All sorts of people."

A doorman swept open the large, brass-capped doors as Tom and Myrtle approached. He nodded at Tom, but didn't speak a word. The lobby was full of textures and colors that pulled Myrtle's attention every which way. She wanted to memorize every detail: the emerald velvet curtains, the peacock-blue silk pillows, the damask wallpaper peeking out above the shiny wood paneling. She wanted to know this hall, to be the sort of woman who could return to it.

The loud clapping of her five-and-dime heels on the glossy marble floors made her feel self-conscious. Bloomingdale's shoes wouldn't make this much noise, she thought.

"This is beautiful," she told Tom.

He wrapped his arm around her waist and grabbed her overnight bag. This intimate move in his public domain surprised her. It added to her feeling that she was performing a role in a play. Everything seemed so unreal and far away from her everyday life.

"I can't wait to get you to the apartment," he said, the animal look returning to his eyes.

Once the elevator had been called and the doors came together, sealing them into the mirrored chamber, he pushed her up against the wall, pressing his heavy body into hers.

As they rose above the city, floor after floor dropping beneath them in seconds, they wrapped themselves more tightly together. By the time they reached the fourteenth level, Myrtle was again thinking, "You can't live forever, you can't live forever."

They bumped their way down the hallway, Tom reaching into his pocket for keys with his left hand while he pulled her head to his with his right. Once more she felt that she was back on that conveyor belt, fulfilling whatever destiny had been decided for her on the subway. No fear. No shame. Just the excited anticipation of a woman getting a stolen glimpse at something cherished she'd thought she'd lost.

Beneath that surface-level excitement lurked the obligatory feeling that all women know. Tit for tat; I scratch your back, so you scratch mine. Myrtle got hers in the cab, so of course Tom needed his now. She knew what he expected, and now instead of feeling owed, she was the one who owed another. Her role as a woman was to be seen, and then to serve. It was now her turn to serve.

Tom opened the door and led her inside. The living area was cramped with too-big, too-luxurious furniture for the space. Myrtle felt like the walls, sofa, and tables were closing in on her.

"Let me give you the tour," Tom said. "First, here's the couch."

He set her down upon it, not forcibly, but directly enough for her to know that the next act in this play was set right there on the sofa, and her role required her to be a large part of this scene.

Myrtle complied, becoming a more eager participant with the feel of his warm breath on her face. Like many things, what began as an obligation became a welcome event.

She kissed him aggressively, and when he went to pull her onto his lap, she was already climbing on. His hands wrapped around her back, and they spun their way forward, moving up across her stomach and then breasts. When he reached under her dress, she instinctively moved his hand away.

"No, no," she said. "It's your turn."

"It's both of our turns," he said, reaching back.

Even though she'd come this far, Myrtle knew she wouldn't have sex with Tom. There's a difference, she thought. She would not cross that line. Clearly the method of penetration affected her respect for herself and her ability to look her husband in the eye when she inevitably returned home. By preserving that act for man and wife, the betrayal wouldn't be as severe. This is how Myrtle thought about things as they were happening to her.

She cut him off by grabbing for his trouser button and zipper. She felt unsure of what to do with it once she reached it—having been monogamous for so long and having defaulted to quick and efficient sex, it had been years since Myrtle had used a man for genuine enjoyment. She tried to remember what it had been like when she first tasted the joys of giving a young man pleasure, how he liked to be gripped and rubbed.

Tom didn't seem to mind that she used her hand instead of what he'd originally intended. He unbuttoned the front of her dress and pulled her bra over her head, staring, open-mouthed, as her bare breasts bounced and danced inches from his face.

With her spare hand, Myrtle cradled them, rubbing their fullness and tight nipples. Never before had she realized the full power of her body; she'd been too young to understand the first time around. Now she saw it reflected in the desire beaming out of Tom's eyes. What she didn't want to understand was how fleeting and transferrable the body's power was.

With jerky movements, Tom's face contorted, and a steady flood covered Myrtle's hand. She felt grateful. That it was over? That he chose her body at that moment? That she got to experience all-consuming lust again?

He kissed her; he wasn't sure what else to do. But he liked her, and he assumed that women always wanted to be kissed by men and so that's what he did.

"I'm so glad I got on that subway train," he said. "You know, I almost didn't. I thought I'd drive into the office today, but then I thought about how bad traffic has gotten lately and I decided against it. Didn't want to deal with it. And then I got on that train and saw this beautiful woman sitting across from me. As soon as I saw you, I knew there was something special there."

Myrtle smiled and willed herself to believe every word he spoke.

"I still can't believe I'm here," she said. "I mean, I'm glad, but this isn't something I've ever done before."

Neither of them had mentioned marriage or their spouses, even though it was evident, by the gold halos around their ring fingers, that they were each legally bound to another. Myrtle had known Tom was married back on the subway—his thick, flashy ring wasn't exactly inconspicuous. Because she's a human being, she did what most humans do, which is to assume that he was just like her. So Myrtle believed, at least in the very small amount of mental space that she'd given to thinking about this in the past half hour, that Tom, too, must be stuck in a disappointing marriage to a disappointing woman.

"I'm married," she started. "You are too. So why are we here?"

Her question caught him off guard. He was used to barreling forward, chasing the next high without ever questioning why. He enjoyed that someone took interest in him enough to wonder why he did something.

"We're attracted to each other. We have a connection. Maybe we shouldn't have done anything about that, but we did. Everything isn't always black and white. Things are more complicated than that," he said.

"What's your complication?" she asked.

"My complication? Now that's a big question, Myrtle. I don't know. Things change over the years. People change." This sentiment of Tom's is true for most, but, ironically, he'd barely budged from spoiled boy to spoiled man. Maybe it was the people changing around him that caused his complications.

"Yes, they certainly do," she said.

"What's your complication?" he asked.

"I never expected to be in this situation. I guess that's probably what everyone says who gets in this situation," she laughed. "I love my husband, but I don't love what he's become. I thought our lives would be . . . just different from what they are. Isn't it the scariest thing in the world that love changes?"

"Everything changes. People, feelings. How long have you been married?"

"Twelve years," she said. "You?"

"Just four. Do you have kids?"

"No," Myrtle said. "No, that doesn't seem to be happening for us. For me." For most of her life, having children seemed to be a given for Myrtle. A birthright. But the baby had never come. She could not create the life she wanted. Neither her own, nor a child's.

"I'm sorry to hear that. You seem like you'd be a good mother," Tom said, seeing the shift in her manner. "I've got a two-year-old daughter."

"She must be precious," Myrtle said.

"She is, she is. Daisy—that's my wife—she dresses her up in these white lace dresses. Don't ask why she's dressing a two-year-old all in white, but she does, and she looks just like an angel."

"What's her name?"

"Pamela. We call her Pammy."

"Did it change things? Having your daughter?" Myrtle asked.

"Between me and Daisy? Sure, a little. Daisy's focus shifted, but, you know, not as much as I'd expected. She's not as . . . I don't know the right way to say it, and I certainly don't want to say anything negative about her, but she's not as attentive as a mother as I'd assumed she'd be. That's not really fair, though, because she's young and she's just doing what her mother did with her. Sometimes, though, I forget that both of us are parents. That probably sounds especially terrible to you," Tom said.

"Because I can't have kids?"

"No, well—"

"It's all right. It was really hard for me to come to terms with at first. It never occurred to me—or to George—that we wouldn't be able to have children. And he really wanted to be a dad. But now we've accepted it, and it just is. His baby is his garage now, anyway," she said.

"He's a mechanic?" Tom asked.

Like her marital status, George's working-class occupation was a fact of life that Myrtle would rather have Tom not know. Now he'd know for sure, if he hadn't already, that she wasn't a part of his social set, the kind who can buy spare apartments, hire nannies, and wear smudgeless patent leather shoes.

"Yes," she said. "When we met, he was an artist. Or he wanted to be an artist. He was very talented—probably still is, but I wouldn't know because he stopped painting years ago. When his dad got sick, he took over the garage. I thought it was temporary, just until his dad was well enough to work again. But he never got well, and when he died George took over. We've never left."

For the first time in years, Myrtle thought of one of George's paintings. It was a landscape of Manhasset Bay, all puffy green trees, the ocean rippling like a sheet hung up to dry in the wind. Where was it now? Was it packed away somewhere, its beauty hidden within the flaps of a cardboard box?

"You don't want to live in New York?" Tom asked.

"I've been here my whole life, and I love it in a way, but I wanted a change. We used to say that we'd move to California. I love the beach and the sun. It was probably crazy, but we had this idea that we'd move to Hollywood and George could paint sets for the movies. That was a long time ago." Those painted ripples, just like a sheet in the wind.

"California, eh?" he said. "I'm not that big on New York myself. I'm from Chicago and Daisy moved from Kentucky. It was her idea for us to leave. We had some problems in Chicago, and it seemed like a good time to try something else. Daisy couldn't get us out of there fast enough."

"So why New York? Was that where Daisy wanted to go?"

"No, I think she would have gone anywhere that wasn't Chicago. My father fixed me up with a job out here and we found a nice place out on the water. Life just sort of dropped us in New York and left us here." That's how it was for people like Tom and Daisy. There weren't choices made so much as circumstances that happened. Happy accidents that ushered them through their lives.

"What do you do?" Myrtle asked.

"I work at an investment company. My father's best friend owns it, and I pretty much just show up once in a while for meetings or client lunches and try to schmooze them. It's not that interesting," he said.

"Well it's got to be more interesting than sitting above a garage all day, staring at billboards and listening to motors turn over."

"That doesn't seem like the right sort of situation for a woman like you, Myrtle."

"It could be worse," she said. Myrtle just now noticed that the couch fabric was printed with several ladies swinging in a garden. Their colorful dresses floated over arching greenery, their faces painted and carefree. "This is an interesting couch you have here, Tom."

"You like my ladies? This was my grandmother's. When she died, my father insisted I take it. Daisy wouldn't have it in the house, though. Not to her taste, she said. I sort of got this apartment just so I'd have somewhere to put it!" She'd been the first one to tell Tom no, his grandmother. No, he could not jump on her couch, that monkey of a little boy. It was curious, being told he couldn't do something he wanted to do. It drew him to her.

"I like it," Myrtle said.

"I think it grows on you," he said, tracing the outline of an especially elated woman with his finger, carefully contouring the silhouette of her body. "The rest of this stuff"—Tom gestured at the furniture packed into the tight space—"it sort of just appeared. I asked my secretary to decorate the apartment, and this is what I got."

Myrtle looked enviously at the bookshelf, tables, lounge, and chairs that filled up the room. She'd always wanted to select her own furniture, but George wouldn't have it. His father left them everything they needed. You could sit in his chair, sleep in his bed, and eat from his table—why on earth would they need a different one? he railed.

All of a sudden, she felt very out of place. The ride on the conveyor belt was over. That predetermined destiny had been fulfilled and free will returned to her. She took another look at the swinging garden ladies, wishing that she could somehow leap into their scene, put on a fancy dress, and swing gleefully in the sun right along with them.

"I should probably go now, Tom," she said, rising up above the ladies. "It was a real pleasure to meet you, but my sister must be wondering where I am."

"Oh, yes, of course," Tom said, a look of disappointment crossing his face. Myrtle noticed.

"I really did enjoy our morning together," Myrtle said.

"I did, too, Myrtle. I didn't expect this to happen, but I'm glad it did. I hope I didn't bore you with talk of my job and life."

"Not at all! It was really nice to talk to someone. Especially a stranger. Not that you're a stranger now, but sometimes I think it's easier to talk with someone you don't have a history with, who doesn't already have all these preconceived notions about you. Like you said, people change. Sometimes the people in your life, though, don't seem to let you change."

"A clean slate," he said. "No one tethering you to the past."

"Right," Myrtle said, picking up her overnight bag. "Well, I think I'll head down now. It was nice meeting you, Tom. I'm glad it was your day to harass women on the subway."

"Let me get you a cab. I'll go down with you."

This time when the elevator doors closed them in, Tom was reserved, standing a good distance from Myrtle. Myrtle incorrectly interpreted his aloofness as disinterest in her, and, for the first time that day, began to feel shame. Shame that she'd betrayed her husband. Shame that she'd made a fool of herself on the subway. But most of all, shame that she was being cast off by Tom for not being beautiful enough or rich enough or simply enough for him to want to see again.

The sound of her shoes tottering across the lobby floor echoed even louder upon her departure. She walked quicker, willing away the tears threatening her eyes. Everything seemed unfamiliar. The passion, which had consumed her so fully and suddenly, had gone, leaving her vision skewed by vicious apathy tinged with humiliation.

Outside Tom caught up to her, grabbed her arm, and signaled for a cab.

"Thank you, Myrtle." Right there on a New York City sidewalk, with the cab waiting and students rushing off to class and that blue baby carriage rolling once again along, Tom kissed her. After several seconds he let her go, turned, and walked away.

Myrtle, half in love with him and terribly sorry, nearly fell into the cab.

They never did have lunch.

CHAPTER 3

Myrtle was in a daze. A cloudy, disbelieving daze. The weight of what she'd done was beginning to force its way through that daze, but for now she was living out those last few minutes before knowing herself as an adulteress, a cheater, a woman who couldn't—least of all by herself—be trusted. She could still see her former self in these minutes, the woman she had always been before that morning on the train. Those minutes were almost a goodbye. A beautiful, reluctant shedding of the part of her that had believed in her and George's love for too long.

She couldn't see George during those minutes in the cab. She couldn't see Tom, either. She only saw herself, in the way that she wanted to see herself, but not how she really was. This was a shame, because Myrtle in those moments was probably lovelier than she'd ever been. Her cheeks were flushed, her eyes sparkled; Myrtle was more vibrant than she ever thought she could be. But she couldn't see that and she didn't know it was possible, and so she instead looked out the window and onto the city and watched a ghost of herself superimposed over blurry buildings and steam-oozing manholes.

It was both a relief and an annoyance when the driver spoke to her.

"So going to do some shopping today, ma'am?" he asked, his strong Long Island accent very familiar to Myrtle.

"Yes," she replied with a smile, even though she had no intention whatsoever to shop. She did, however, want to be agreeable to this person she'd never again see. It seemed like the most important thing in the world right then. "Gimbels is one of my very favorite stores."

"It's a good one," the driver said. "My wife likes to look around in there. A little more than I'd like, if you know what I mean. She goes on and on about the coats and the dresses. And the cosmetics counter. She'll come home smelling like she took a bath in perfume. It's awful, just awful, but she thinks she smells just like the Queen of Sheba."

"My sister works at one of the cosmetics counters. Maybe she's to blame for dousing your wife in perfume." Nothing else mattered to Myrtle outside of having a perfectly pleasant conversation with her cab driver. Just smile and converse. It was so important.

"Oh yeah? That must be an interesting job. Telling ladies how to make themselves look better. I don't think I could get away with that."

"I don't think I'd trust you picking out my lipstick," Myrtle said. Smile. Focus. Do anything but let on that that man she'd been with was not her husband.

The driver laughed. Myrtle felt an outsized amount of pride in this. She was succeeding in being that perfectly pleasant person it felt imperative to be during that drive. The longest, never-ending ride from the woman she'd been to the woman she was about to be. It was a bridge she didn't quite want to cross, and so she stayed in that conversation as if it was the most crucial she'd ever have. I will keep smiling, she thought. I will keep smiling.

"Neither would I!" he laughed. "Red. How many different shades of red can there be anyway? According to my wife, there must be about sixty."

"I'll bet she's beautiful in all her reds," she said. "It's all about finding just the right shade. We have to go through sixty to find that magic one."

"I can't tell the difference. She always looks great to me," he said.

With those words—words that Myrtle took to mean that the cab driver was a loving, faithful husband—the disbelieving daze fell away. She was hit with the reality of what she'd done, and it filled her stomach with what felt like a tangle of flapping bats, trying to escape. She couldn't remember ever feeling that physically uncomfortable. Certain she'd throw up in the cab, she rolled down the window, breathing in the air in big, stifled gasps.

"Hey, are you all right?" the driver asked. "You don't look so great. Are you feeling okay?"

"I'm fine," Myrtle said. "I just needed some air." Now her immediate need wasn't to keep up the agreeable conversation, but to end it.

She'd been with another man. She hadn't had sex with him, but she'd wanted it. George owed her. How could she have done that? It wasn't that bad, really. It could have been worse. It had been years. George didn't need to know. Who did need to know? Please stop thinking about it. She wanted to see him again.

The cab pulled in front of Gimbels. The bats flap, flap, flapping in her stomach, beating their wings inside of her. Opening the door felt like an escape, made worse by the realization that outside of the cab was the beginning of her reckoning. She looked at the car and the driver and wanted to jump back in, to drive backward down the avenue, to fall back into the pleasant conversation that had nothing to do with the great treachery she'd committed, back before the bats began to flap. She wanted to reverse it all, to erase everything so she could stop feeling this way. Just make this bad feeling go away.

"You sure you're okay?" the driver asked again.

"Yes, yes, I'll be fine," Myrtle said. "Thank you."

Dizziness swirled in her head while the thrashing continued in her stomach. Caving to the physical ailments striking her meant confronting what she'd done, and she couldn't do that. She couldn't let her mind go back to Tom's apartment. When it did the bats flapped harder, more violently.

She had to tell Catherine. Even if she didn't understand, even if she'd never again look at her with reverence in her eyes, Myrtle had to speak aloud what had happened, if only to allow the bats to fly out of her open mouth. Desperate for relief, she spun through the revolving glass doors and into the department store's men's section. She noted each and every black patent leather loafer that she passed. The lights reflecting off them illuminating and distorting her strained face.

Catherine leaned against her counter, opaque pastel bottles obscuring her chest and the piles of bracelets strangling her wrists. The sisters saw each other at the same moment and they both smiled. Catherine's was happy and genuine; Myrtle's was manic and forced.

"How much longer do you have?" Myrtle asked, trying not to sound as anxious as she felt. Divulging everything to Catherine would make the feeling go away, Myrtle thought. She could return to her normal self, to her normal life.

"I can probably get off a little early," Catherine said, thick red hair dropping into her eyes. "Something's wrong."

"I had a morning," Myrtle said simply.

"George?" Catherine asked.

"No, not George." Even as the tears filled her eyes, even as her body shook, an involuntary, rabid smile commandeered Myrtle's mouth. Worried, Catherine called up her supervisor, saying there was a family emergency she had to tend to and that the store was dead anyway so could she please leave a bit early to take care of matters. When she hung up the phone her thin, pale wrist looked like it would snap in half from the weight of the bracelets.

"What's going on? You've got me all worried now," Catherine said as they moved through the aisles, silks and tweeds and georgette closing in on them.

"You don't need to worry," Myrtle said. "But something happened this morning. Something different."

"What? What happened?"

"I don't know how to say it," Myrtle started. She realized that she truly didn't know how to verbalize the soul-upheaving experience she'd had. What words could she use to explain the feeling of seeing Tom on the train? How could letters, strung together to make sounds that we recognize and identify as things, ever express the inexpressible? The contents of her head, already so jumbled, could not be readily accessed and shared.

Catherine waited. She had a lifetime, almost thirty years, of waiting on Myrtle. Myrtle always had the answers, and all Catherine had to do was wait for them to be spoken to her, and so there was no discomfort for Catherine in this pause. She didn't feel a drop of the agony that flooded her sister.

"I think I made a mistake," Myrtle started. "This morning, coming to see you, I took the train to the subway, and, well, there was a man on the subway. And I can't believe I'm saying this and I don't know how to describe it, but, Catherine, you have to believe me that *something happened*. It was like . . . like I had known him from before. But we'd never met. I'd never seen him. But he was looking at me from his seat across the train and it was—it was intense. I've never had a feeling like that before, from just a look. I swear it was just a look, Catherine, but that look." She stopped to shake her head, staring beyond Catherine and into the mirage of Tom's eyes. "It felt good. There's been nothing but bad with George for so long and it just felt good, and I wanted to feel good again and so I went. My God, I followed that man off the train, Catherine. I can't believe I did it. I can't believe that was me. You know I've never done anything like that before. But the way he looked at me, it was like we knew each other. It was like we had something special, from right there, out of nowhere. I don't know if it was me or if it was him, but we just went off together. He called a cab and I went with him to his apartment. Don't look at me like that! You have to understand, Catherine, you just have to. I don't know what happened. It didn't feel like me. It's like I was watching a movie, but I was in the movie, but I was also just watching at the same time. I didn't have sex with him. I didn't do that. But I cheated on George and now I feel terrible, and I don't know what I'm supposed to do. What am I supposed to do?"

"Jesus Christ, Myrtle. I was not expecting that."

"I know, I know. It sounds so awful. Hearing myself telling you this, I see what you must think of me. But please, please don't think that of me. I'm still the same person—I'm not one of those women. I just—I made a mistake. And now I don't know what to do. What am I supposed to do?"

"Are you going to tell George?"

"He'd kill me, Catherine," Myrtle said. Catherine knew that her sister may have been exaggerating, but maybe not by much.

"Well, then you just forget it ever happened," Catherine said. "A moment of insanity, that's all. Do you know who the man is? You aren't going to see him again, are you?"

"No, no, of course not. I won't see him again. I know his name, but that's about it. No, I can't ever see him again."

"Is he married too?" Catherine asked, unable to resist satisfying her penchant for gossip.

"Yes," Myrtle answered. "And he has a daughter."

"Myrtle!"

"I know. I didn't know about his daughter until after, though," Myrtle said.

"After . . . what?"

"We just fooled around a little. I told you, I didn't have sex with him."

"It's not that bad, Myrtle. George will never find out, you'll never see this guy again, and everything will be fine," Catherine said.

Hearing her sister say that she'd never see Tom again didn't provide Myrtle with any comfort, but rather filled her with disappointment. While the rational part of her brain overloaded her body with negative emotions in an effort to prevent this sort of thing from ever happening again, it couldn't sway the animal part of her body away from the pleasure it had received from Tom. She wanted—quite badly—to see him again, and part of the sadness she felt and part of the damn flapping bats in her stomach was out of fear that she never again would.

"It doesn't feel like everything will be fine," Myrtle said. "But Catherine, the thing is, it felt really good. I know I should feel awful—and believe me, I do—but I think I'm glad that it happened. Isn't that horrible? I'm happy that I cheated on my husband."

"It's not like things have been great with George; you don't exactly have the happiest marriage. I understand why you did it, and I don't think you did a bad thing. You're not a bad person. You're not a bad person because of this one thing, Myrtle." Catherine sensed that Myrtle needed her approval, and since she was the sort of woman who forgets to ask herself what she thinks about things and instead defers to everyone else's opinions, she said what Myrtle wanted to hear.

"With everything that's happened with George, I felt like . . . almost like he owed me this," Myrtle said. "Maybe that's all it was. Maybe this was just my way of getting back at him for everything."

"That makes sense."

"And I can't see him again," Myrtle said. "Obviously I can't see him again. He probably wouldn't even want to."

Myrtle mentally added up the total amount of time that she'd known or at least had been aware of Tom. Maybe twenty minutes on the train, another ten getting the cab and getting to the apartment. Probably no longer than a half hour inside and then a few minutes leaving the apartment and getting kissed before he disappeared. Altogether, she had spent just over an hour in his presence. Yet in that hour she felt that they understood each other fully. That even though she didn't know his age or birth order or whether he drank coffee in the morning, she believed she knew what would make him laugh and worry and fall in love with her. There's probably no need to comment on just how wrong she was; let's allow poor Myrtle to feel that she had something right.

"What do you know about him, besides that he has a wife and a daughter?" Catherine asked.

"I know that he's from Chicago and works at an investment company and that he loved his grandmother. He has money. Enough to have a nice apartment separate from his house. And he's sad, sad in the way that, the older I get, the more I see everyone is sad in this same way."

"Not everyone is sad, Myrtle," Catherine interjected.

"You are," Myrtle said. "I am. George is, and Mom and Dad were. Do you remember when we were kids and we couldn't wait to be grown-ups because it meant wearing makeup and buying whatever we wanted? That was all getting older was to us—makeup and shopping. And I wonder why everyone is so miserable. What a disappointment!"

"To be fair, a good chunk of my life is devoted to makeup and shopping," Catherine said.

"And going to parties with random men. I guess maybe you are living the life we thought we'd have."

"And I'm still miserable! At least sometimes."

"I wonder why we didn't see the sadness then," Myrtle said. "Maybe kids can't see it. If they did, they'd never want to grow up."

Myrtle noticed that her body had relaxed and the bats had calmed down. It seemed to her that by speaking what had happened, that it made it less true. That one act of forgiveness was all she'd needed to mend the chasm between mind and body.

"It was amazing, Catherine. Being with someone new, someone who doesn't drink and swear at me all day. Someone with motivation and ambition. It felt so good. I hate that it felt that good because I don't think I'll ever feel it again."

Catherine, unfamiliar with feeling good herself, wanted nothing more in life than to keep up the facade that Myrtle had it all figured out. Because if Myrtle was on the right track, then surely Catherine was right behind. And then she'd get to, well, where exactly she didn't know. But she had to be going somewhere, didn't she?

"You deserve to be happy," Catherine said. "Find him!"

"Find him?"

"Yes. You know his name and a little about him. There are ways. You could find him."

"What if he doesn't want me to find him?" Myrtle asked. "I can't. It's bad enough that I did this once—that's a mistake, a slipup. To continue it, knowing how wrong it is, that's something else altogether. I couldn't live with myself."

"So you're going to go back to George and live above a garage for the rest of your life? I love you and I know what you're capable of. I want you to have the best possible life. Maybe this wasn't just a fling. You said you had a connection—maybe this is the guy you're supposed to be with."

"He has his own life. A wife and daughter and job and, well, money. I highly doubt I fit into all that. He already has it all."

"And he was still with you," Catherine said. "So clearly he doesn't have it all. Happily married men don't pick up women on subway trains. Maybe you're meant to be happy with him."

"Until I'm not," Myrtle said. "Isn't that how it works? I'm not a kid anymore; I understand how these things go. I was happy with George, too, at first. I loved him, couldn't get enough of him. Falling in love with George was the greatest experience of my life, and I miss it. I miss it so much. But I know better now. I know that it changes and that time takes all those good feelings and the butterflies and the excitement and it leaves you with nothing when it's through. I need to remember that. It wouldn't last with Tom, either. We had a great morning. I shouldn't ruin that by pressing for more."

"But what if it could last?" Catherine asked.

"It can't. It doesn't."

"I think it does for some people. Maybe you just didn't pick the right person to try with."

It was unusual for Myrtle to hear Catherine say that anything she'd done had been wrong, but since she was looking to rationalize seeing Tom again anyway, she welcomed the criticism as permission.

"I would seem crazy if I tracked him down," Myrtle said. "That would ruin it right there."

"If you've suddenly gained that kind of self-control, then I'm impressed. But my sister goes after what she wants, so I wouldn't be surprised if the next time I see you, you've got another good story to tell."

"It's a one-time thing," Myrtle said. "That's all it can be. I'm going back home to George, and I'm going to use this as motivation to try harder. Maybe if I do better, he'll try harder too. Maybe this can turn into something positive for us."

"Whatever you decide." Catherine's bracelets, which had been bouncing and clanging while the sisters walked toward the hotel where she lived, scraped against her dry skin, leaving a dull red mark. It didn't matter to her, the scraping. The bracelets were so pretty.

"Are you wanting me to start an affair?" Myrtle asked. "Do you know what that would mean? What kind of person that would make me?"

"The kind of person you are is not defined by a single action."

"If it's an affair, it's not a single action. Today was a single action. If I do it again—and again and again—that's different. I'd just be . . . surrendering."

"Surrendering?" Catherine asked. "So instead you're surrendering to the life I know you hate?"

"I don't have options," Myrtle said. "What are these options you think I have? You think that this rich guy with a wife and kid is going to drop everything for me? For a married woman without a penny? It doesn't work that way. This morning was probably nothing to him. The best thing I can do right now is forget that it ever happened."

"You're not sounding to me like you want to forget this happened. You want it to happen again, and who can blame you? Heck, if a rich, handsome guy wants to put the moves on me, I'm ready to go."

"I'm not going to look for him. I can forgive myself for this, I think. I don't think I could if I went any further. I love my husband. I do. We're not perfect, and things have been especially unperfect lately, but we've been together for so long. I wouldn't know me without him."

"Listen, I know you love George," Catherine said. "But you were on a subway train this morning, coming to see me, and something happened. Something was said by a man you'd never even seen before. Something that made you forget that you loved George. That doesn't just happen."

"You're romanticizing this," Myrtle said. "You're making it out to be love at first sight or soulmates or some crap like that.

That's not what it was. It was . . . an attraction. It was just lust; two married, lonely people attracted to one another. And we were both stupid enough to act on it."

"I've always hoped that marriage would end the loneliness," Catherine said.

"Marriage just gives you another person to be lonely with."

The sisters entered the run-down hotel where Catherine rented a suite with a seamstress named Charlene. As they crossed the lobby, Myrtle thrilled at the thought of her earlier trip across a lobby, with Tom's arm around her waist, his hands about to be all over her. The way he took control, pushing her against the mirrored wall in the elevator and kissing her with passion she'd forgotten existed. Just hold on to the feeling, she thought. Forget the man, but hold on to that feeling of being wanted and awake again.

They didn't talk about it for the rest of the night. Charlene came home and told them about a party she'd attended the night before. She went on and on about the house, the band, the drinks. She'd met a man there, and he'd sworn he'd call her today, but there were no messages and no sign of him and why did he even bother to say that if he had no intention of following through?

Hours later, when Myrtle got into bed next to Catherine, the silence brought Tom back, the memories intensified by the distance of the day. The look in his eyes on the train. Her legs spreading wider in the cab when she should have snapped them shut. Climbing onto his lap and his mouth grabbing for and sucking her nipples like he'd never experienced a woman's breasts before. His kiss, right there on the city sidewalk. His broad back, walking away.

In the midst of her excitement, she felt them again. Flap, flap, flapping in her stomach. She lied there for hours, the titillation and the flapping vying for her attention.

CHAPTER 4

Tom wasn't on Myrtle's subway train home the next morning. Logically she hadn't expected him to be, but still she'd hoped. She'd looked for him on the sidewalk outside the station, searched for him squeezing through the turnstiles, scanned every tall male body on the platform, and glanced around the car more than was socially acceptable.

When, at the second stop, she'd been looking down and caught shiny, black patent leather shoes stepping onto the train out of the corner of her eye, the blood froze in her veins. But the body and face didn't match the shoes. Her heart pounded at the speed of the racing subway, thumping incessantly along the track.

Outside the third stop, a large crowd waited, the collective murmur of quiet conversation humming, almost buzzing. The sound, along with her mounting anxiety, made her recall another buzzing.

Shortly after her father had died, Myrtle took a walk through the empty fields just beyond her childhood home. Not because she liked taking walks, but because she thought that walking outside in nature was what she was supposed to be doing at a time like that, and so she'd walked.

She didn't cry—hadn't cried for a few days at that point—but still she couldn't appreciate the glowing blue sky and iridescent green leaves reaching for it. She'd set out to get lost in that natural beauty, but again, she wasn't much for walking or pausing, and so the experience was more focused upon setting one foot down in front of the other, which is a sort of religious experience in and of itself, if you think about it.

So intent on continuing those footsteps, Myrtle didn't notice the low, black cloud approaching. She didn't see it, in fact, until she'd heard it. A swarm of bees hummed straight toward her, and by the time she realized that hundreds of hard-bodied little bees shared what was supposed to be a therapeutic walk with her, she couldn't escape their path.

She could still feel the breeze on her face, a breeze created by the force of beating wings, skimming her skin. She instinctively swatted them away, making contact with their freakishly sturdy little abdomens, thoraxes, and a stinger or two. Still they swarmed, diving into her hair, landing on her flailing body, pricking her skin.

Her panic eclipsed her grief, which was the first time that anything had eclipsed her grief. She tried to outrun her tiny tormentors, but her two legs were no match for the hundreds of pairs of beating wings. It took a gardener shouting, running, and waving his hoe at them to convince the swarm to fly elsewhere.

"Are you all right?" he'd asked her once the bees had departed.

She looked at her hero, a sweaty man about her father's age, memorizing the creases framing his face. "I think so," Myrtle said.

The man climbed back up the hill he'd descended. Myrtle never thanked him, but she thought about him often after that day. She'd feel the wind on her face and be jolted back to the attacking bees and remember him. Soon she'd think of him alone, at home, without any breeze at all. She'd only seen him for maybe thirty seconds—and in her state of panic, it was a wonder she'd processed his face at all—but he kept appearing in her dreams as clear as her father's face had been.

She thought about the man so much that she assigned him a personality, quirks, and, most dangerously, a desire for her. That was the first time that Myrtle used a man to escape what her life had become.

It was excellent practice in the art of distraction, which was absolutely necessary to any woman unable to choose her own path. But she took it, perhaps, too far, sharpening her fantasies and imagination to such a fine point that reality never could compete.

Getting off the subway, she looked around again for Tom, even though she thought it was impossible that a man like him would be anywhere near the train that rumbled through the Valley of the Ashes. There were no patent leather shoes to be seen there, just scuffed work boots and cheap kitten heels. She felt, simultaneously, a sense of belonging and revulsion.

Myrtle pictured George, his trusting blue eyes drilling into her untrustworthy own, and willed herself into a calm, steady state. She would never tell him, she resolved. She couldn't let on that anything out of the ordinary had happened while she was gone. She must convince him that she was exactly as she'd been when she'd left the previous morning, faithful and untouched.

By the time the eyes of Dr. T. J. Eckleburg came into sight, their bright blue casting judgment on the darkness beneath them, Myrtle was anxious to return to her regular life, which she believed would be a little less regular following her encounter with Tom. But what can an hour do, when life and death aren't involved? Myrtle's hour, so far from her home in both distance and scope, didn't have the power she'd assigned it. This hour, and the next and the one after that, held equal potential for altering her course, but she couldn't see that, and so she got off the train, still believing that yesterday was all that mattered.

The garage doors were rolled open, giving her not just a glimpse into George's life, but the entire view, as played out in scenes of broken-down Fords and greasy parts. She'd shared her own life with these machines for more than a decade without ever stopping to wonder why. How had these scraps of metal muscled their way in? Why hadn't she demanded softness and beauty? Was it all just too late?

George sat at his desk in the corner, nearly hidden by, well, nothing. His presence had become so diminished that he was often hidden in plain sight.

"I'm back," Myrtle called.

He turned around, his hair the color of dust, his skin even lighter, and Myrtle reconsidered telling him everything. Not out of guilt or respect for her husband, but out of the disdain that his pale skin and hair activated in her. Merely being around him, even just seeing him, made her want to cause him misery. That was the guilt she carried just then, for wanting to make her husband miserable, while still loving him. The juxtaposition of both wanting to hurt him and protect him disarmed her.

"Did you have a good time? How's Catherine?" George did not get up from the corner.

All Myrtle had to do was answer George's questions. Some polite banter, easy answers—that's all she needed to provide before heading up to her living quarters, where she could then fall apart or laugh at George's new role as the cuckolded husband, or whatever she needed to do in private, away from his eyes. But she couldn't answer him, couldn't bring herself to speak the lies she'd rehearsed.

"Myrtle? Did you hear me? I asked you a question," he said, forcibly and irritated.

This was the man she was bound to, the one she'd willingly—eagerly!—tied herself to on that sinking ship of matrimony. Together they were going down, down into the watery depths. Either of them could have untied the ropes at any time, saving themselves and the other, but they'd already resolved their fates to the bottom of that ocean, and so she pulled the knot a little tighter.

"Catherine is fine," Myrtle answered. "The same as always. Everything is the same as always."

"Sammy came by yesterday with some parts for the HAL Touring. Told me Mary had a heart attack. Forty-five. Forty-five and she had a heart attack."

"Is she going to be all right?" Myrtle asked.

"She's dead."

Before Mary's dark, always sparkling eyes flashed through Myrtle's mind, or her tight, dark blond curls, she did the math. How many years did Mary live that Myrtle hadn't? Eleven. And how much life could be lived in that span? Thinking of George, too much. Thinking of Tom, not enough.

"That's terrible. I can't believe it. How is Sammy doing? When did it happen?"

"A few weeks ago, I reckon," George said. "He seemed not too bad. Told me about it pretty straight. Didn't seem too shaken or anything. He's probably used to it by now. Used to talkin' about it and telling people."

"That's his wife. He couldn't just get 'used to it.'"

"I said used to talking about it. He lost his wife of twenty-some years, I'm sure it ripped him up. And now he has to go around telling everyone he meets about it, because he can't just not tell them that his wife is dead out of the blue," George said. "Dropped dead of a heart attack. Forty-five years old. And he has to go around making everyone else feel all right about it."

"Poor Sammy. We should do something for him," Myrtle said.

"We should."

George's face showed genuine concern and empathy, and Myrtle remembered, at least at that moment, how much she valued having the potential to be his object of concern and empathy. If he wouldn't have been enraged by her story—of feeling alone and hopeless and undesired and then meeting a man on a subway who, with a look, made it all go away—she knew that George would have had the capacity to understand. If it wasn't her, his wife, he could cut through the sharp judgment people were supposed to feel toward people like her and instead see the wounded being who needed healing. But this was her, this was his wife, and because of that legal title, he couldn't see her the way he saw everyone else. Couldn't allow her to have flaws and stains and pitfalls. Couldn't see that her wounds—certainly some of them—came from him, and so Myrtle didn't have access to George's concern and empathy the way the rest of the human race did.

Saved by a dead wife, Myrtle headed up the dark, squeaky wooden staircase to the upper rooms that sheltered and caged her. One would expect those rooms and their contents to look the same as they had the previous morning when Myrtle had last seen them, but that was not the case. Everything looked sparser, emptier, and Myrtle wondered how she'd ever lived without a painting on that wall or a chair in that corner.

Now that she'd made the journey home, she set out on her daily business of passing the hours. There were the morning hours post coffee and breakfast where she waited until lunch. Then the long hours between lunch and dinner. Then, finally, the waning hours of night when she'd count down until she could shut her eyes and let her subconscious fully flourish. Basically, Myrtle spent her days waiting for meals and sleep.

In the purgatory between breakfast and lunch, Myrtle unpacked her overnight belongings and ruminated on the impossible things she'd done. She thought about Tom, and where he must be right now and what he must be doing. She assigned him thoughts, and of course they were about her.

In her mind, he wondered what she must be doing too. He felt unstable in that he needed to know more about her. Wanted desperately to see her again—not to touch her or to orgasm (although that would be fine), but to hear what she thought about the absolutely ridiculous hat that the man selling newspapers outside was wearing (it looked like his head got lost inside a bell), or if she hated that Marion Harris song as much as he did (she did). He slipped into needing her opinions on his experiences, if only to bear witness to those experiences, and he realized, suddenly, as if he'd just felt the first drop of rain, that he was falling for the woman on the subway who he'd only known for an hour.

These were Myrtle's purgatorial thoughts before the task of making lunch took her attention away from the fantastical. Without them she'd have to focus on her own life in these upstairs rooms that needed a painting on the wall and a chair in the corner. Myrtle most definitely did not want to lose herself to reality the way she lost herself in her romanticized thoughts. Nobody does.

The kitchen was small. There was no other way it could possibly be. It, along with an attached sitting area, bedroom, and bathroom, all had to fit in the space over George's shop, Wilson's Garage, which wasn't all that large. It fit a few vehicles at a time, spaced out and often laid bare, their innards littering the cold asphalt floor.

The kitchen had a small window, but it did not face the eyes of Dr. T. J. Eckleburg the way the bedroom window did. It looked out upon, well, nothing. In spite of the home's proximity to the biggest city in the country, Myrtle's surroundings were bare. For thousands of feet, nothing grew or erupted from the ground. She could look outside her kitchen window and be without a single sight, like staring into the visual equivalent of white noise.

However, today there was something out there.

A small, charcoal-colored dog ran in circles, figure-eighting its way through the dust and ash. It jumped. It rolled around. Its mouth opened and shut, and even though Myrtle couldn't actually hear it through the glass and over the noise from the train on the other side, she assumed it was yelping happily at someone or something.

It was. Slowly creeping into Myrtle's kitchen window range of sight was the dog's companion, an older man who moved as unhurriedly as the dog moved excitedly. Like everyone else around there, the dog's man was not well dressed, and he could be forgiven—although he wouldn't be—for not bounding through the world with enthusiasm.

Myrtle compared the two mammals' movements, as it was impossible not to with such a glaring dichotomy. The dog springing forward, spinning around, capturing every inch of the dirt and the air with its ceaseless energy. The man toddling along, confident in his value relative to the dog, so much so that he could take his time and the dog would always, always wait.

The relationship was, Myrtle thought, quite pleasing. One pulled the other forward, while one held the other back from danger. She could have seen it another way—the man holding the dog back from its full potential and desires; the dog an unnecessary burden on an already burdened man—but she did not.

Now the dog exited the frame, and Myrtle watched the man slowly pass through. He looked forward—at what exactly?—inching along. She wondered who he was, where he was going, how his life had deposited him, alone minus the dog, in an empty, ashy field of nothing. But at least he had that magnificent little dog.

She knew all too well how she arrived and remained in that field of nothing, and it's only natural, really, that her mind began scheming and dreaming of Tom as her way out. A man had gotten her in, and it would take a man to get her out.

Myrtle was quite aware that anything she thought of regarding Tom was fictitious, but she consciously, willingly surrendered to the fantasy. Some people had jobs, passions, partners, families—Myrtle had fantasies. This was her employment. Sure, it made it hard to feel what was real when she spent the majority of her time and mental space in the unreal, but it was the only way she knew how to spend those monotonous, relentless hours, and wasn't living life in the happy, alternate reality of her daydreams a close second to actually living life?

She prepared lunch mechanically and reflexively. Another item checked off the list. These were her daily accomplishments—

the casseroles and plates of roasts and potatoes. Her achievements were devoured and forgotten in ten minutes' time, and she'd start again anew a few hours later.

George creaked up the stairs, and they ate, as they had for years, side by side at the table George had grown up taking meals at. If George had made a wrong turn in his life, it was this: he had fallen into the rhythm of an easy, predictable life. He'd been gifted with something extra, but he'd traded the difficult potential for success for the comfort of never having to put in the effort and feel the pang of rejection. He had natural talent. He'd been an excellent painter. But who can support a family creating art?

There wasn't a family, though, not the size that George had anticipated. The children he'd wanted never materialized, but their ghosts certainly did. They showed up in summer at the park, in the form of other people's children screeching and playing. In winter, bundled in giant jackets that made them look like little marshmallows floating down the street. He saw them in the morning, on their way to school, and in the evening, piling into Michaelis's restaurant next door for supper. The ghost of his little boy sat beside him while he worked on Fords, studying his moves and admiring his expertise.

The little ghosts of the children he'd never have followed him everywhere, reminding him that he would never be the man he'd expected to be—a father. This was not something George could understand. How something so eternal and seemingly simple as procreating could have escaped him. His life didn't look like what he'd thought it would, but no one's does.

So instead of a tableful, it was just him and Myrtle. He'd thought that taking over his father's business was the right thing to do. And maybe it was at the time. George wasn't the most intelligent man, but he knew enough by now to know that somewhere along the way, something went wrong. It wasn't just the lack of kids that haunted him, it was a feeling that he had been so close to happiness, but he lost it somewhere back, and it had moved on without him.

His loyalty to his own family and to Myrtle was strong. The work he did in the garage on the cars was for both of them. Continuing the family business, providing for Myrtle—it all required him to hustle and toil in grease, all day, every day. He thought her idea of moving west to California was ridiculous. Starting over wasn't something he could do; continuing was.

Continue they did. They continued to sit in the same seats, and they continued to chew in the same way and talk in the same tone. They'd both come to rely upon each other so hard that it was silly for either one to realistically think about life without the other. Never mind that neither knew the other at all anymore.

"Someone's dropping off a car this afternoon," George said.

"That's good," Myrtle replied. "More work."

She thought she was being supportive, in spite of being jealous that he had something to occupy his time. He thought she was spoiled, relishing that she had the freedom to choose how she spent her time while his was dictated by bill collectors and rents due.

"Michaelis is doing something," George said in between chews.

"Doing what?"

"I don't know. He's had a bunch of deliveries. Not the usual stuff."

"Deliveries of what?" Myrtle asked.

"Strange things, even for him. Fabrics, and furniture that don't look like it goes in a restaurant."

"He told me he wanted women customers. Tea and cigarettes."

"Huh," he said.

"Probably just one of his things. Ways of making money."

"Why would women come down here?" George asked, oblivious to seeing that he made a woman come down—and stay—here.

"Got me," Myrtle said. "He thinks for tea and cigarettes."

"He also got some sort of insects."

"What?" she asked.

"I don't know. Some sort of insect delivery. He's a strange one. You never know."

"Yep."

"I've gotta get back to work," he said.

Myrtle took their used dishes to the sink. Once again there was nothing outside the window. She'd already forgotten the man and his dog.

The absence of feeling between her and George, a vacancy that had been aggressively present for at least the past several years, suddenly overwhelmed Myrtle. An absence of anything isn't typically felt—what's there to feel when nothing is there?—but this absence was strong and forceful. Her husband, the person closest to her in the world, aroused no passion nor interest. She wanted to feel something—anger, lust, contentment, anything—but when she thought of George, all she could conjure was that total lack of feeling. Like he was the field outside her kitchen window.

Tom—Tom inspired things. Tom was still a guest star in her imagination, not a regular in her life, which left it up to her to write his character. He would be affectionate and stubborn. He could be a great dancer or a terrible liar. He could be one thing now and an entirely other thing an hour later when her mind's scenario shifted. Everything was, at this point, when she'd only had an hour to experience him, entirely up to her.

Oh, the power! The power of controlling a powerful man. Anyone who says they have no interest in that is lying. To control power is to receive validation on the loftiest scale. It fulfills the primary narcissism that rules us all, no exceptions. To say you have no interest in that sort of power is to deny you are human, somehow exempt to birth and death and everything that comes in between.

Myrtle was not exempt, and she enjoyed the massive illusion she'd created of holding power over this powerful man. To her, because Tom had those shiny, patent leather shoes and an apartment in addition to the home he shared with his wife and daughter, Tom represented the rich, ruling class she wanted to access. By conquering him, she rose to the top of it all, a total knockout of everyone who'd ever stopped her, simply by having more than her.

But this was all relegated to her head. She thought it was safer there than acted upon. She didn't realize that the drawn-out, heightened echo of her imagination was far more dangerous than any real-life encounter.

By keeping Tom trapped in the confines of her fantasies, she could still feel virtuous. Or as virtuous as a woman of average moral integrity could feel after following a man home off the subway.

She would not see him again. How could she? It was an obvious decision, but it carried with it a weighted blanket of depression. If only she could reexperience the previous morning again, just once. She'd be a more active participant that time, not passively letting it happen to her, but reveling in every look and touch, memorizing those feelings so she could call them up when she needed them, which was too often.

Just one more time, she thought. Once more when she was ready for it. Plus, if she saw him again, she'd most likely find that he wasn't what she thought. That he wasn't so great after all, and, who knows, the attraction may not even be there. If she could just see him again, she thought, it could all go away. She could go back to her everyday life with George and not have to wonder about and idealize this would-be relationship with another man.

George would never find out. She knew that. He'd never know the difference between their lives before she'd met Tom and after. And if it didn't negatively impact her husband's life, what was the harm?

Our brains have several incredible skills, and one of the most incredible is the ability to rationalize anything. Absolutely anything. It's how Myrtle journeyed from point A—condemning adultery of any kind; what sort of woman do you think her?—to point B, eager to start an affair, and believing that it wouldn't hurt her husband, in just over a day's time. Our brains are splendid, deceptive, manipulative little creations.

Facing down the solitary hours between lunch and dinner with nowhere to go and nothing at all calling upon her time, Myrtle picked up the romance novel that she'd last read on the train into the city yesterday morning. But after her own romantic encounter, each page felt distant, fake, and it couldn't compare with her own stories running through her head.

After a few hours of picking it up and putting it down, George called up to her from the garage.

"Myrtle, Myrtle! Get down here! You won a prize! There's a man on the telephone asking for you. He said you entered a drawing, and you won the prize!"

"I didn't enter any drawings," she called back. "It must be a scam."

"He said you won, and he needs to give you instructions to collect the prize. Just come down and talk to him. See what it is. Maybe you forgot you entered."

Being the type of woman who always believes she has a chance, Myrtle may very well have entered a drawing, or several. She hurried down the stairs and grabbed the phone receiver off George's desk.

"Hello? This is Myrtle."

"Myrtle, this is Tom Buchanan. From yesterday."

The tops of her hands, where the forks of veins rise with blood coursing through them, fluttered.

"Oh hello," she said, shocked, but still cognizant that George stood a few feet away and was listening.

"I told the man on the phone"—Tom didn't call him her husband—"that you'd entered a drawing and won a prize, so play along."

"Oh yes, I remember now," she said. "Yes, that must have been a month or two back."

"I want to see you again. I think we should see each other again. Say yes."

"I am not sure I can collect the prize," she said slowly. George's face fell.

"I can't stop thinking about you," Tom said. "Meet me Tuesday morning at the apartment. Please. I just want to talk to you. It was nice just talking with you. I have to see you again, Myrtle. Say yes."

She'd imagined a lot of scenarios with Tom today, but none of them involved him calling up her husband's garage and begging her to see him. She was thrown by the fact that reality was eclipsing her fantasies. This seemed more unreal to her than her imagination.

"Yes, I can come and get it," she said. "Tuesday, you say?"

"Beautiful! I can't wait to see you. The address is—are you ready for it?"

"Yes, what's the address?"

"It's the Diver Building on 116th and Amsterdam. Apartment 1422. I'll be there early, maybe nine. I'll wait for you."

"Thank you. I'll collect it Tuesday morning."

She hung up the phone. George was grinning from ear to ear.

CHAPTER 5

TUESDAY MORNING PULLED MYRTLE toward it as soon as she'd hung up the phone. Her anticipation dominated every hour leading up to it, and when Tuesday morning finally arrived, Myrtle was a wreck.

For one, it was the first time she'd be seeing a man in a beyond-friendly sort of way in more than a decade. Their previous encounter had happened so quickly and impulsively that she hadn't had time to worry about all the things she was anxious about now, like how to even kiss. And by meeting at his apartment, after their first highly charged encounter, she felt pressure to finish what they'd started. As it was the starting she so often dreamed of and more rarely the finishing, she felt particularly inept.

There was also the fact that this was a premeditated act of disloyalty. She wasn't swept up in a moment. This was no simple, dishonest mistake—no longer a one-time aberration. She knew what was about to happen, and any self-delusion of naivete was gone.

It's a sad, terrible thing, adultery, or cheating, or stepping out, or whatever you want to call it, but there's also something beautiful beneath the ugly. For most men, it may just be ugly, but for the women, there's often a rediscovering of the younger women they once were. Of finding a kernel of themselves they'd lost, who resurfaces in the arms of men who are not their husbands. It's vile and subversive to think this way, isn't it? That women committing betrayals against men can still be so beautiful?

Myrtle may not have been aware of her beauty while riding the subway through Manhattan's underground core—quite the opposite; she'd forgotten how uneasy such levels of self-consciousness felt—but she felt the giddiness of expectancy. She felt the world widening with potential as she got closer and closer to where Tom waited. Whatever would happen in the next few hours, she determined, she would enjoy. She wished she could open up every pore across her skin to fully receive her own passionate treachery. She'd made the decision to see him again, and she may as well allow every possible version of herself—those she knew and those she'd never know—to experience this together.

Before she saw him again, she still hoped that this meeting would be the cure. That if she spent more time with Tom, she'd see that this wasn't really something she wanted, and she could end it. She believed that seeing him again would put the fire out in her imagination, which, to her credit, does happen on occasion. Increased familiarity, though, can also ignite new fires—ones she didn't know existed and didn't know how to fight. Myrtle didn't know how these things went. This was only her first time.

She didn't know which stop to get off at. There was a young man, maybe twenty, who carried a book bag filled with so many pages that all the answers to every question must have sat there in that bag. All you'd need to do is flip a page and there you go—an answer to something. So much knowledge, so readily accessible. But the young man didn't open a book, didn't look as if he had the answers to everything in such close proximity. His expression was vacant and unaware of the power he carried around with him stuffed into a buttery, tan knapsack. Still, Myrtle looked to him for her exit. Where he got off, so would she. And those pages of answers would lead her to—what? Not her own answers. Probably just more questions.

She knew of the streets at which Tom waited, and she assumed that this boy with all of the books was a student attending school across the street at Columbia University. All of that youth and thinking, just across from Myrtle's site of knowing better and contradicting better judgment.

He exited the subway at what she approximated to be the correct stop. She didn't recognize the green wrought iron gate barricading her from ancient-looking brick buildings, but she walked on alongside it anyway, warmed by the sun and thoughts of what could come.

This was not her time to think of George, and yet she did, in an odd way. Myrtle became aware that her heart had been breaking every day for years. And that realization gave her courage and hope that she could endure more inevitable heartbreak and accept the punishment and pain that were surely headed her way. She was right; they were. But she wouldn't have much longer to feel them, nor anything else.

George was with her then, but only as the man chipping away at her, diminishing all that she ever thought she could be. She would lie to him, she'd have to. About the raffle, about where she was, about anything that could get in the way of her seeing Tom. Myrtle was now complicit in the deceit, and this decision brought her a condemned sense of calm.

And so along the green wrought iron gate that she didn't recognize, Myrtle walked toward Tom, who she truly believed had the capability to restore her. There, she pretended to be exactly who she was. Yes, pretended.

His building rose above its surroundings, because it's not like a man such as Tom—with all of his arrogance and insecurities—would choose a squat building to house his affairs. Its height made sure it was visible, beaconing to Myrtle, or to other arrogant, insecure men and their defeated mistresses.

She didn't pause at the corner or take a deep breath at the door. She didn't avoid the concierge's eye contact or slow her step on the way to the elevator. All of Myrtle's signs of apprehension or misgivings were invisible, hidden by layers of foundation and perhaps too bright of a lip color. She went right in, right up to his floor, without any external hesitation.

Then she reached the door. His door, which made it so important to her that it knocked whatever confidence she'd mustered right out of her. That's where she paused and finally took the deep breath. That's where she wondered what she was doing there, what it would lead to, and what all those years with George represented. She let them, the years, slip away as she pressed her knuckle to the wood.

The man who answered was the same broad, dark-haired, well-dressed man who'd led her there the week before, but still she barely recognized him. He'd grown more handsome in the tunnel of her imagination, his eyes softer, his smile warmer. This Tom, the real one standing before her, was a stranger. He had the look of an eager suitor, but without any of the understanding.

How must she look to him? she wondered. She assumed a letdown, which made her want to hop out of her clothes right then, to compensate for being the woman she was.

"Hello," he said.

"Hello."

They both sort of stood there, knowing what was supposed to happen next, but still not moving. Tom, the more seasoned of the two, was the first to act.

"Here, come in. Thanks for coming—it's good to see you again."

Myrtle found the familiar swinging ladies on the sofa and felt that, maybe, she was among friends.

"Did you have any trouble finding it?" Tom asked. He was surprised that his movements and words were so cliché. He hadn't expected to be nervous. This wasn't the first woman he'd greeted at this door.

"No, not really. I've been here before, you know," she said.

"I think I remember."

"I was surprised you called."

"I was surprised you said yes," Tom said.

"So was I."

"It didn't take long to find you," he said. "The garage."

"And the raffle. How long did it take you to come up with that?"

"Not as long as you probably think."

"I don't usually do this, you know," Myrtle said.

"I think you mentioned that last time."

"I don't."

"I know. I appreciate that you came, Myrtle."

She was relieved. The attraction that pulled so strongly the last time wasn't there. She'd been right to see him again, she thought. She'd done the best thing for her marriage, for George.

"I enjoyed our last conversation," Tom said, coming down upon the swinging ladies. "I thought it would be nice to talk with you again."

"Yes, I liked talking with you as well."

"Is there anything new with you? How is your sister?"

"You remembered—" she started.

"Of course I remembered."

"She's doing fine. She's always much of the same. Always on the lookout for something or someone different, but still the same."

"And you? Are you looking for something, or someone, different?" Tom asked.

"I think you know the answer to that. I think me being here is the answer to that."

"That's a good answer."

"You must be looking for something different too," she said.

"I guess I am."

He was not. What Tom was actually looking for—searching desperately for—was more of the same as that he'd always known, which is total, dominating privilege. Growing up as the son of one of the richest men in Chicago, Tom inherited a superior standing from birth. He knew nothing of struggle or of proving himself because the proof was in his address, his private education, his assured future.

He'd never been challenged and had always been doted upon, and he'd never questioned why this was. He just assumed that this is how it should be for people like him.

Anything that deviated from this confident ease of life scared him. No, he did not want something different. He wanted to recapture his glory days, when passing a touchdown only confirmed his greatness. But there were no more football games. No more opportunities to offer up anything to a cheering crowd. His only remaining identity was as David Buchanan's son. He couldn't think of a single thing he had to offer outside of being born the only son to a rich family. The older he grew, the more aware he became that he did not merit his elevated station in life. Luckily, he found that he could quash this awareness by conducting multiple affairs, to quell his deficient feelings by instead making everyone around him feel inadequate.

"It's hard to know whether we're looking for something else because the original was wrong in the first place, or because the 'else' is more right," Myrtle said.

"I don't know that any two people having an affair have ever spoken about their spouses so much."

"Are we having an affair?"

"I don't like the word," Tom said. "We don't have to use certain words. Really, you're controlling the situation, Myrtle.

I saw you on the subway and I knew that you were something special. That I wanted to get to know you better. Nothing else really mattered. Then I did get to know you better, and I liked you even more. I wanted to see you again. Now whatever happens from here, that's up to you. I liked you, I like being with you, and I find you very, very sexy. I'd like to see where this goes, but really, it's up to you."

Judging by Myrtle's reaction—pulling his face to hers and initiating the kiss—it was the illusion of power that was a turn-on. It wasn't Tom she wanted—at least not the thoughts and actions that made him him—but what he represented. If she could make him desire her, then surely she'd have that which she thought she desired. The feelings of having importance, material wealth, and unending passion.

Then she stopped.

"I'd like to know more about you," she said.

"What would you like to know?"

"Your favorite season, how you like your job, your politics, the books you like to read. I want to know everything."

"Let's see, my favorite season is summer, my job is just all right, politically I like a new party called the Anglo-Saxon Clubs of America, and I'm currently reading a book about race. If we don't look out, whites will be submerged by lesser races," Tom said. Talking about what he perceived to be lesser races also calmed his own feelings of inadequacy.

Myrtle, made entirely agreeable by her newfound power, wasn't about to question or contradict anything coming from its source.

"It's really disconcerting actually," he continued. "All this race mixing. The other races, they're trying to get into ours to bring us down. I read that if things continue the way they're going now, that the white race will be wiped out entirely within two generations."

"I didn't know that," she said. To both her credit and discredit, Myrtle wasn't concerned about race mixing. She was a woman who lived above her husband's garage and who mixed with all manner of races.

"Most people don't," Tom continued. "The newspapers, they're not writing about this stuff. They're controlled by the Jews anyway. You'd be amazed by how much of the wealth in this country is controlled by the Jews. It's shocking, and if we don't do something about it, it's only going to get worse."

Tom was getting worked up by something other than her, which made Myrtle regret her attempt to engage him in conversation. These opinions of his were not attractive to her, and she thought, once again, about how meeting him today was a good idea. One that would save her, would save George too.

"That would be a shame," she said. "I don't think you and I can do much about that right now, though. What about other books? Do you read any novels?"

"Not since school. I read mainly nonfiction these days. I try to stay informed. What do you like to read?"

"It's kind of embarrassing. I read those cheap, drugstore romance novels. Not all the time, of course, but probably too many."

"I've never read one," he said. "What goes on in those sorts of books?"

"You know—there's the ordinary girl, maybe a widow or a poor man's daughter—and then the strapping stranger who marches into town and falls madly in love with her. That sort of thing."

"That's what women want? Strapping strangers?"

"It's not the stranger part, or even the strapping," she said. "It's that they fall in love with the unassuming girl. The heroines are usually pretty ordinary, pretty relatable. The men fall in love with that ordinariness. I guess we want to believe that that's possible."

"Seems strange that would appeal to you," Tom said. "You're not at all ordinary."

"I'm as ordinary as they come! I have a normal, very uneventful life, grew up in your basic family. I think I'm their exact target audience."

"I don't see that. You're too genuine to be ordinary. Having your own opinions and speaking them—which you seem to do—asking real questions, those are the most abnormal things I can think of these days. And you get excited about things! No one I know gets excited about anything."

This was true. In Tom's world of money, the pursuit of money, and the fantasy of money, the thing to be was blasé. It was almost a competition of who could care the least. Everything was based on pretense, so what was there to care for anyway?

"Do I?" she asked.

"I see it in the way you look at things and react. You have a different energy than the people I know. I've said things—like talking about your energy!—that I would never, ever say around anyone else. You go deeper. It both embarrasses me and excites me. Just saying all of this embarrasses me."

"Sorry."

"Don't be," he said.

"I'll embarrass myself too. I don't usually talk like this with other people, either. George and I barely talk at all. Whatever my energy is, you must have it too."

She had thought that this—spending more time with him, learning about him—would break any attachment she may have created. If absence makes the heart grow fonder, then surely the contrary must be true—presence makes it grow colder. And when he opened the door and she saw the actual, physical Tom instead of her mind's conjured Tom, she truly felt relief that the world she'd imagined up would not come to be. She had not wanted him then. But she was beginning to want him now.

"I'm glad I'm the one you're talking to," Tom said.

He stopped talking. They both stopped talking. It was one of those moments that never happens, when you look at someone else and somehow your thoughts are perfectly aligned and perfectly known. If magic exists, it's in these statistically improbable moments of wanting the same intangible thing at the same absolute moment as another human being.

Had Tom shown her any vulnerability with his words, he took it all back with his actions. While she wanted to control perceived power, he wanted to control the version of himself he felt slipping away. The young man to whom everything had come so easily. Success, self-worth, women.

To maintain his control, he needed to take her firmly, aggressively. She let him pin her down, eye to eye with those friendly, swinging ladies. She let him pick up her hips and push into her. It was not at all romantic, nothing like she'd imagined it. The only thing the act itself had in common with Myrtle's fantasies was the urgency.

Now that she'd fully completed the physical part of her betrayal, she expected to feel flooded with guilt. Instead, she felt grief. A deep sadness and longing for all the things she'd never have. She knew that she could neither possess Tom nor achieve this level of passion with George. She wanted to cry, wanted to mourn the sex that would not change anything at all. After doing what had previously been unthinkable, she was the same woman who would return to the very same life.

She didn't show this, though, because that's not what was expected of her.

Tom quickly got himself dressed and threw Myrtle's dress onto her. He was satisfied and ready to move on to the next part of his day. She was self-loathing and needing his validation more than ever.

"Myrtle, that was fantastic. I'm really happy I got to see you today."

She looked at him quizzically. She hadn't expected such an abrupt ending.

"I've got a meeting. Just came up this morning. I'm sorry to rush out on you like this, but it's important. Feel free to stay here awhile if you like."

The kind of woman that Tom wanted would have no problem with this, she thought. Since she needed to be what he desired, she pretended that had been all she wanted with him too. Even though she really wanted everything, for him to surrender his very sense of self to her and anything else he could muster.

"I have to leave soon anyway," Myrtle said. "When I'm in the city, there are always things to do."

"Great," he said. "I've got to jet, but you can let yourself out?"

"Yes, of course."

"Can we do this again?" he asked. "I'd love to do this again."

"Yes, of course."

He kissed her, more tenderly than he'd been minutes ago. She wondered how the same man who had just taken her so roughly and carelessly on the couch could kiss her like that.

"I'll call you," Tom said, shutting the door behind him and leaving Myrtle alone and half-dressed in his unfamiliar apartment.

She wanted to escape immediately. She wanted to never see him again. She wanted to climb into George's arms and sob and feel the security and reliability that he represented. And yet she knew that she'd be back here. She would do it again and again. Anything to be in Tom's orbit. The alternative—returning to what she saw as her hopeless life where nothing ever changed, and to George, who would never look at her like Tom looked at her—it was even more despairing.

She buttoned her dress like clergymen fastening their collars, slowly, solemnly, ritualistically. The swinging couch ladies didn't look so cheerful anymore. They looked like what they were—performers lifted from whatever lives they had led and placed in a man's garden to swing for him, as he thought they should do, for eternity.

Myrtle wondered what else Tom stored in his apartment. What other curious objects lie beyond this room.

The kitchen was smaller than even hers, but much more modern. It even had an electric refrigerator. The counters weren't cluttered with loaves of bread and spices, evidence that it wasn't much, if ever, used. Two doors stood shut just off the kitchen. One opened to a bathroom, again, strikingly bare against the crowded, overstuffed living room.

The other door led to the bedroom, which was, like Tom's choice of sofa, more feminine than she expected. Crushed velvet pastel shell chairs butted up against a matte wood dresser and nightstand. The four-poster bed was covered in a floral bedspread that clashed with the floral-print wallpaper.

Myrtle wondered if Tom ever slept in the bed. She didn't want to acknowledge what she knew he actually used it for, so instead she speculated that he and Daisy led separate lives. Maybe they'd fight, and he'd come into the city and crawl his big body into this rickety bed and imagine a different life for himself. Maybe he thought about her here. Basically, Myrtle assigned to Tom the exact same traits and actions that she possessed and performed. Curious, that she thought of him as a woman.

She left the bedroom, careful to close the door behind her so he didn't think she'd cared enough to explore his surroundings. She wouldn't want him to think that she was interested enough to open that closed door. Myrtle would have opened much more, had Tom been considerate enough to leave personal traces for his mistresses.

The sun pierced through the window now at a blinding angle, making even the imprisoned swinging ladies hard to see. Feeling that there was nothing left for her then, but knowing she'd return as often as beckoned for, she left.

Floating its way back to earth, the elevator slumped down, down until it could not descend any farther. As it floated, Myrtle willed the guilt to come. She wanted to feel enraged, to condemn herself, but the self-inflicted attacks would not surface. She did not feel much at all. Her brain only wondered what she would do now, where she would go next. As if she'd gone to a movie where the projector broke and the audience was let out early. What to do instead?

That "instead" bothered her. It implied what should have been but was not. She'd risked everything, and for what? A quick encounter that did not even come close to living up to her expectations of it. Instead of filling her emptiness, it amplified it. And on top of it all, she couldn't even make herself feel guilty like any decent, self-respecting woman should feel.

Outside, a chubby young girl dressed in a bright yellow tulle skirt to rival the sun stood with her mother on the sidewalk.

Myrtle noticed her because the skirt was so unexpected, so out of place. The little girl, with a too-puckered face, looked up at Myrtle, stunned.

"Wow, you're beautiful," she said, with wide eyes and a voice like thick honey.

Myrtle looked around, assuming the girl was speaking to someone else. But there was no one around; it was her.

"Thank you," she said, surprised.

An unbeautiful little girl telling her she was beautiful. The tears poured from her eyes.

CHAPTER 6

THE HEAT CAME EARLY THIS YEAR. Spring had peeked out from behind winter's clouds but, not having liked what it saw from the humans below, retreated to wherever dormant seasons rest, letting summer emerge early to scorch the earth.

Myrtle and George Wilson's upstairs apartment was already unbearably hot. The humidity blew in through the windows as a reminder that even their comfort level was beyond their control.

Myrtle sat outside the gaping garage doors, breathing in heavy, gasoline-scented air while watching the streaming sun rise higher and higher. In its wake, the blue sky bled into the blinding white. Up and down the sun would arc, reliably bleaching the sky and then returning it to its own dazzling blue.

Beads of sweat dripped down the back of George's neck, disappearing into his damp collar. He pounded away on an engine or a carburetor or maybe even a wheel for all Myrtle knew. For having lived in such close proximity to so many car parts for so long, she knew surprisingly little about what they were and how they functioned. "You'll never need to know that," George had once said to her, many years ago, when she'd asked how the engine operated.

The blue eyes of Dr. T. J. Eckleburg cast their judgment upon the couple, but only Myrtle noticed.

A tow truck slowly cruised up the road, clouds of burnt dust rising behind the red Fiat 505 it pulled. Myrtle watched it approach, knowing it would stop here, outside of her home. This is where the damaged came to be restored. Too bad it worked the opposite for people, she thought.

The man who jumped out of the tow's passenger side looked like George. Not physically—the stranger's dark brown hair and skin and bigger build couldn't have been further from George's light and lanky body—but in the half-desperate, half-hopeless way he carried himself. It was an odd juxtaposition, the intensity of the desperation being tempered by the apathy of the despondency, but both elements came through. Or maybe Myrtle was just too experienced at reading them to let them go unnoticed.

Hearing the door slam, George set down his wrench and went over to see what else was broken, what else would take his attention and hours.

"What can I help you with?" George asked.

"My car broke down," the man said, the despair in this voice rising above the hopelessness. "I was on my way to a job interview, and it just clunked out. Wouldn't you know it? Wouldn't that just be my luck right now? I don't know what's wrong with it—it's always worked fine. I only bought it a couple years ago. And I've got to get to this interview, and the engine just won't turn."

"Let's get it unhitched and I'll take a look. Maybe it's a quick fix."

"My interview is supposed to start in twenty minutes," the man said. "I'm not going to make it. Say, do you have a telephone I could use to call them up and tell them I can't make it?"

George looked at the man in his cheap suit with his hair slicked back and his panicked eyes. He recognized the anguish, the feeling of losing a last hope as it slid through your sweaty fingers.

"I'll take you," George said. "Where do you need to go?"

"It's on the outskirts of the city at the Merchants Paper factory. Are you sure it won't be too much trouble? I'd really appreciate it. I could pay you—you can add it to the bill for the car."

"It's no problem at all," George said.

Myrtle could still recognize the kindness in her husband. George was a good man, the knowledge of which only made her recent behavior that much more confusing. She didn't know why he could not be enough for her. The same could be said of her life in general.

She watched the two men—one, the man she knew best, and the other a man she didn't know at all, yet so familiar in the way he carried himself that she felt she could accurately surmise his personality. A strange thought occurred to her. If there were men who could be incapable of murder, then these two would be them. Those meek hands couldn't clutch a weapon in rage. Couldn't pull the trigger. But of course most men were capable of murder. They're the gender that hastens death.

Tom could kill a man, Myrtle thought. Tom was a typical man, which, to Myrtle, meant he possessed the ability to lose himself to anger and jealousy and vengeance. All three can spring up out of nowhere, and then destroy everything. How can nothingness become so strong, so fast? Myrtle questioned why she found that lack of control attractive. She didn't find an answer, but at least she asked herself the question.

She thought about Tom a lot. Sometimes she'd replay their two encounters, either for confirmation that yes, their relationship had potential, or no, it was already over. Sometimes she'd imagine a future with him, full of intensity and desire and money and other things she wanted but did not have. Sometimes she wondered why he hadn't called, creating emergencies and excuses for his lack of communication.

Yesterday she'd looked up the number for the Thomas Buchanan residence. She had it written down on the back of an old grocery receipt, folded up and slipped into a pair of stockings in her bureau drawer. It had taken much self-distraction and fortitude to leave it in the stockings, to not memorize it, call it.

In a situation such as theirs—the relationship between Myrtle and Tom—control belongs to the one who needs it least. Control runs from the one showing weakness, scurrying off to the other for no reason outside of the fact that they lack the desire or ability to care. Control loves the inability to care.

So Tom had it, all of it, which left Myrtle frantically chasing it in the form of a phone number printed on the back of a grocery receipt. Would calling him herself represent her power, in that she, too, could dictate when and how they would see each other? Or would it reveal that she craved him more than he craved her?

Each time the phone rang, her heart leapt with hope. And each time it was one of George's customers, it sank into the pool of doubt that flooded her body. She hated that her future seemed dependent on the whim of a dark-haired, shiny-shoed man to make a phone call. She cursed the drama of the ringing phone, but she was powerless against the rise and fall of optimism that it propelled.

It had been so long since Myrtle's feelings were invested in a man, or in anyone outside of her sister, who was the only consistent person, outside of George, in her life. But there she was, tied up in the mirage of wished-for love. Had it been this hard when she was younger? She tried to remember. Had she felt this crazed?

There were men—or rather, boys—before George. Most of them were matters of mutual affection, typical young love that begins in a naive crush, crescendos into a brief spurt of life-or-death feelings, and then quietly exits both parties. One boy hadn't fit this life cycle.

Peter was a few years older than seventeen-year-old Myrtle. He was everything an older boy should be to a seventeen-year-old girl—tempestuous, handsome, and mysterious. He also wasn't interested in her at all. Myrtle either didn't notice, or didn't care.

Inspired by her strong feelings upon initially seeing him, Myrtle started believing, if she hadn't already before, in love at first sight. There was no other explanation—it simply had to be. The spark she felt looking at him had to mean something. It couldn't be that this was one of those cruel jokes played upon humanity—that we could feel so strongly for another destined to feel nothing. To Myrtle it meant that he would return her feelings if she could just get into his proximity enough. She just needed to get around him as much as possible so he, too, would feel that kindling of emotion and realize that of course they should be together.

Myrtle learned everything she could about Peter. Where and when he worked, who his friends were, where he liked to go. Then she'd insert herself into these places and situations. This all seemed very logical to her, and it was so important that she utilize logic in this very irrational, mystical sort of situation. She needed to believe that her strategy made sense, because if it did, then it would surely take her in a neat, straight line from where she was to where she wanted to be.

Peter noticed the younger girl who suddenly appeared everywhere he was. At first, he dismissed her, but it got difficult for a young man to dismiss such easy prey. To his credit, he did try for a while. His attentions were fixed on Mary Filtbon after all. Myrtle didn't interest him, but there she was, always around.

He knew he shouldn't have gone off alone with her. He knew that she had a crush on him, and he wasn't out to hurt anyone's feelings. But Mary Filtbon wasn't paying him any attention, and there Myrtle was, so eager to make him like her.

She would get over it, he thought, and eventually she did. It took months of tears, sobs that attempted to shake what was wrong with her out of her body. Because that's all Myrtle learned from her time obsessing over Peter—that something was wrong with her. Why else wouldn't this boy choose to be with such an adoring, loyal girl? She must be deeply flawed, she believed, if her love couldn't inspire someone to requite it.

Seventeen-year-old Myrtle didn't want to be herself. She only wanted to be who Peter wanted. And through her efforts to bend her natural tendencies, strengths, and weaknesses, to mold herself into what she thought might please him, she lost her most valuable currency. To be the rare person not trying to be somebody else.

After Peter, Myrtle was different with other suitors and lovers. She fell in line with the expected, joining the ranks of the typical, becoming the girl we're subconsciously taught to either want, or want to be. It served her fine. Her relationships became more successful, each lasting longer than the last until she met George and achieved the victory we call marriage.

Over the years, though, her patience with pretense eroded. Or maybe she learned, through her own disappointing experience with that commonplace matrimonial victory, that she was just too exhausted to costume herself in other people's expectations.

Which is how Myrtle got to where she was now—consumed with long-buried, Peter-esque thoughts for Tom, a scribbled-upon grocery receipt in hand. To physically interject herself into Tom's world, she couldn't just show up at the mansions and fancy parties. She'd have to wedge herself into his proximity a different way.

If Myrtle had a usual sense of equilibrium, it had been blown apart since meeting Tom. She couldn't remember how it was that she'd spent her days for the past twelve years. They felt foreign and wasted in her new climate of heightened anxiety and reckless confidence. If her marriage had been terrain, everything that came before had been the plains, and now she was scaling mountains. Her emotions, and, maybe, good sense, followed this topography. Rising and falling, leaving her breathless to catch up, too oxygen deprived to think clearly.

She had to call him. She had to know if her tumultuous emotional journey had a destination. No one should have an interior monologue as long and uninterrupted as Myrtle's, where anything can be rationalized by a filibuster of thoughts. It was this incessant, endlessly needy voice that convinced her to call his number.

Her main worry was that he wouldn't want to see her again. That, like to Peter, she'd been more of a convenience than a necessity. This would be difficult, but at least she'd know before further embarrassing herself. She was also concerned that Daisy would answer the phone. Hearing her voice would be Myrtle's first proof that she was real. Everything had been suspended so high above her normal existence, a voice on the other end, no matter how poor of a connection, could be the clarity Myrtle feared. While she needed Daisy to exist in order to feel optimal power over Tom, she wasn't so callous that she enjoyed what that power meant to this other woman.

There's no doubt that Myrtle viewed Daisy as her foe, but she was also a sort of accomplice. She, too, vied for control over Tom, and it took both of them to engage Tom in a struggle, to weaken him for the ultimate conqueror. Because of this, Myrtle felt herself part of a sisterhood with the unseen Daisy. This was another way that Myrtle made herself feel that she was a part of Tom's life.

George hadn't yet returned from driving the man to his interview, but Myrtle knew she didn't have long before he'd be back, and her solitary opportunity would be gone. She tried to think about it once more. Tried to weigh the pros and cons of calling his home and revealing her interest. Her pulse raced much too quickly, though, to think about anything other than hearing his voice on the other end.

The receipt wasn't going to last much longer if she continued to hold it so tightly. The fragile paper was a poor choice of receptacle to hold her prospects. She read off the inky numbers and letters, some smearing like marble over the receipt's fibrous body. She picked up the telephone, trying to force her breathing and heartbeat into a normal state of calm as she waited for the switchboard operator. With a quivering voice that sounded much higher than her own, she recited the smearing digits.

It rang twice, the longest, clearest rings Myrtle had ever heard, before a male voice answered.

"Buchanan residence," it said.

"Hello, may I please speak to Tom?"

"May I inform him who's calling?"

In all of her thoughts surrounding this call, Myrtle had never considered anyone other than Tom or Daisy answering the phone. Had it been Tom, she would have proceeded with the conversation she'd silently rehearsed. Had it been Daisy, she would have hung up immediately. Either that or given her a line about Tom being needed for an emergency at work, claiming to be a secretary. She'd become comfortable allowing herself to make that decision only upon hearing Daisy's voice. But this was neither Daisy nor Tom, and the decision whether or not to confess something so simple as her name panicked her.

"This is Myrtle. I'm a secretary at his office." A truth and a lie struck her primal brain as safest.

"One moment, please."

He was there, which meant that her answers were coming. She'd become so agitated over the past couple days as a result of not knowing where they stood or how he felt or even if they'd see each other again, that any answer would be a relief. She steeled herself for the worst, but still she hoped for what she considered to be the best outcome—that they'd arrange a time to meet.

"Hello, Myrtle?" Tom sounded annoyed.

"Tom, hello," Myrtle started. "I hope you don't mind I looked up your number."

"I don't know if it's a good idea, you calling my house."

"Oh, well, yes, I suppose you're right. I certainly don't want to get you into any trouble." He hadn't minded risking her relationship when he called the garage, she thought.

"It's all right," he said. "I was thinking of calling you myself. We just need to be careful, you know."

"I know. I'll make it quick. I was wondering if we could meet again." She said that as a statement, not a question. A question would have betrayed her insecurity, and she wanted him to think her rather apathetic to this whole situation. It was reciting this offer as a statement rather than a question that she'd been most determined to do.

"Yes. Give me a time, and I'll make it happen," Tom said.

"Monday? I can be free all day."

"Then so can I. Meet at the apartment in the morning?"

"Yes, I can do that."

"Great, I will see you then. And Myrtle, try to be more careful in the future. Calling my house is pretty risky. People are here, you know."

"I will. I'm sorry."

"I'll see you Monday." He hung up the phone.

Myrtle got what she'd wanted—more time with Tom—but she felt more shame than success. Her boldness had irritated him. She concerned herself quite a bit with how she may potentially negatively impact Tom, but not at all with how he actually negatively affected her.

She couldn't regret calling, though. It had netted her a day with him. At this point, she'd dropped the delusion that spending more time with him would make her want him less. She was no longer looking for a cure for the affair. No, she wanted more of it. If there was something she could do to infect herself further, she'd do it.

A few minutes later, George rolled up with the man he'd taken to the interview. Myrtle settled back into her seat in the sun, pretending that she had not just flung herself deeper into a highly sexual and emotional affair with another man. It was just the heat that troubled her. It was just so damn hot.

"Your husband is a great man. A real gentleman."

Myrtle looked up at the man, noting how the desperate could also be the most excessively grateful.

"He's a nice guy," she said.

"No. No. He got me a job! He didn't know me from Adam—I could have been any bum off the street looking for a free ride. Obviously, I ain't got no money. And he didn't just take me to my job interview, but he said he'd fix my car for free—just charging for the parts—so I could drive to work and support my family again. He's not just a nice guy. He gave me my life back. My self-respect."

The stranger looked at Myrtle and said all of this as if he was trying to convince her of her own husband's merits. As if he'd actually arrived back at the garage ten minutes earlier and knew of her plans. Examining him and his ardor, she had to convince herself that this stranger wasn't some sort of clairvoyant and that, in spite of how he looked at her, she was innocent in his eyes. In all eyes, except her own.

"I'm glad he could help you," she said.

"He's a saint. You're married to a saint."

Myrtle wanted to tell him about the empty vodka and whiskey bottles the saint left hidden around the house. How many she found, nearly daily. How sometimes the saint hit her late at night if business wasn't good or she'd spent too much money at the hairdresser, or if a male customer had looked at her the wrong way. How the saint had promised her a life full of love and adventure and instead pent her up in this sickly valley that no one ever left. How this kind, saintly gentleman wouldn't so much as listen to her anymore, but could lie so, so easily. How lonely she was with this ghost of a drunken man, who had digested her youth and spit back the woman she barely recognized.

"Yes, I'm married to a saint."

While George repaired his admirer's car, Myrtle retreated to the kitchen, its steamy air more comfortable to her than the man's fables. She envied George's ability to help. That's what he did, day in and out, help people solve the problem of their vehicles, thus getting all of their thanks and accolades. Myrtle couldn't help anyone. Her skills were not employed and her gifts were too far buried to be of any service.

Myrtle's contributions were limited to these two rooms—the kitchen and the bedroom—and the recipient of her contributions, at least up until recently, had been only George. She started on dinner, thinking about what she could make ahead for George's lunch on Monday while she would be with Tom. She didn't want him to have to make his own lunch while she had sex with another man.

"What's for dinner?" George asked, lumbering up the stairs in the way that indicated he'd been drinking.

"Spaghetti and meatballs."

"That's fine," he said.

"Doesn't matter if it's fine. It's what we're having."

"What's with the attitude?"

"Why aren't you charging that man for your work fixing his car?" she demanded. "We can't afford that—for you to be doing stuff like that for free."

"Don't you go telling me what we can and can't afford."

"I can when you tell me we can't afford anything at all. That I'm spending too much on groceries to cook up your meals. Then you go and do volunteer work."

"That man doesn't have any money to spare," George said. "It's a quick fix." He felt fine taking money from the owners of the roadsters and the Rolls-Royces. But the ordinary people, as he thought of everyone else, they needed a break. He needed a break.

"Then it shouldn't cost him too much, but he still needs to pay," she said.

"This ain't your business, Myrtle."

"If it was maybe we'd actually make some money."

"You watch your mouth!" George shouted. "You don't know the first thing about running a business or working or anything other than sitting up in your room lounging around doing as you please. A real tough life you've got here. Just spending the money without ever having to make it."

Myrtle set his plate down in front of him. She didn't want to fight with George, didn't care enough to put in the effort.

"You're so spoiled," he said. "Do you know that? How spoiled you are?"

Myrtle continued to eat in silence. It didn't matter what he thought about her anymore. It hadn't for years. The girl who would cry if he looked at her wrong couldn't feel any sadness at all over his current state of disrespect toward her. If anyone ever wonders what a decade can do, that's it.

The food filled his body and soaked up his liquor. He didn't want to yell at his wife. She was still the best thing he had. George had always felt inferior to Myrtle—her face more attractive and her intellect sharper than his. A chasm that only grew wider the older they both became. He'd known what people had thought back then and still think now. Why'd she marry him? All these years and he still couldn't come up with a good answer. He gave up more and more of himself to her—why couldn't she see that?—all in an effort to try to be worthy, to try to be his own answer. He resented her, not for forcing that attrition of his former self, because she hadn't asked for that, but for not recognizing his crumbling, and not putting him back together. He'd so willingly fallen apart at her feet, but she'd left the pieces there on the ground.

"John invited us over to their house tomorrow night for dinner," he said.

"Who's John?"

"The man from today. With the broken 505. He and his wife want to have us over for dinner."

"As a thank-you?" Myrtle asked.

"I guess."

George didn't drink any more that night. Or at least Myrtle didn't think that he did, but she knew that she couldn't ever really tell for sure. He did it secretly, shamefully, and they rarely spoke of it. It had become like the children she never bore—constant, invisible companions, tripping them up, holding them down. Equally intoxicating, the lack of children and abundance of drinking were the two topics that they should have examined together, but neither had the will.

Myrtle washed up before bed, carefully removing the makeup she wore only for herself. When she climbed into bed, she saw that George lay there naked, his penis erect and expectant. The sight didn't arouse any emotion outside of slight annoyance, and no one said a word. He pulled off the long, thick nightgown that she wore and climbed on top of her, fingering her for an instant before entering so he could feel that she welcomed this. He didn't kiss her but looked down into her eyes while fondling her breasts. Her nipples hardened, not because of his touches, which actually made her slightly nauseous with their false shows of affection, but because she thought of Tom. The only way she could ever get wet for George was by thinking of another man or situation. It had been this way for as long as Myrtle could remember.

Not a mind reader and too oblivious to the female mind to ever suspect this was the case, George assumed that Myrtle's orgasms—always steady and reliable—were set off by his movements.

Sex with George had become a form of masturbation to her. She was alone in her thoughts, completely reliant upon her own imagination, and he was the deeply known instrument—so familiar to her after all these years that he may as well have been an extension of her own body—that brought her to her solitary climax.

It took George longer. He still thought of sex as an act between two people, specifically he and his wife, and he refused to replace her face or body with that of a schoolgirl he'd watched pass by earlier in the day. George remained faithful to Myrtle in these moments, always ensuring it was her physical presence below him that got him off.

Their mouths never had contact. Not via touch nor sound. Their sexual communication was limited to skin and fingers, jolts and breath. It was an act of infinite optimism and complete resignation. It was functional and unnecessary. It was how it had been for years, and then it was over.

CHAPTER 7

"THERE'S ABSOLUTELY NO REASON for these things. None at all."

Catherine tore the extra pillows off her borrowed hotel bed, exaggerating the effort it took to do so.

"And yet there they are," Myrtle said.

"There they are. Forty-five tiny, useless pillows. Who could use these anyway? Whose head is that small?"

"A toddler's."

"Just in case forty-five toddlers sleep in my bed," Catherine said.

"You never know."

"They think they look nice. All those pillows on the bed. And it's not really my bed, so I can't even tell them that no, I'm not having a toddler sleepover and I have no need for all of these tiny pillows."

"Couldn't you ask them?" Myrtle said. "To take them off."

"I can't just ask them. It's their bed."

"Why not? Save them the trouble."

"It's not a big enough deal for me to ask them."

"Seems like a pretty big deal."

"It just doesn't make any sense to have this many pillows on a bed. It's too many."

It was Sunday night, the night before Myrtle would go to Tom again, and she'd made Catherine her accomplice. This had Catherine feeling like they were kids again, when they'd team up to devise elaborate stories so one or the other or both could stay out later than their parents would ever allow if they actually knew what one or the other or both were up to. A friend's dead dog, a last-minute group project for history class, a tryout for a play that didn't exist. They were always united, Myrtle and Catherine, an unstoppable microcosm of two, or that's what it felt like to two teenage girls who didn't yet know that you could be married and dreaming of another, or live in a hotel and sleep in someone else's bed with forty-five tiny pillows on it.

They got into bed next to one another, and Catherine, unused to feeling another body during her sleeping hours, scooted closer to Myrtle, to physically press lightly against her, to feel her body's realness.

"What do you think you'll say to him?" Catherine asked.

"To who?"

"To who. To Tom. Tomorrow. What do you say to each other? Is it like a normal date? A date for married people who aren't married to each other?"

"I don't know," Myrtle said. "I don't plan what I'm going to say."

"But it happens in the morning, which is not like a normal date. The whole daylight thing. I can't say anything I want to say with all that brightness. I just don't think the sun should be out while two people get to know each other. Certainly not if you're having sex."

"I don't know if we're going to have sex."

"What's the point of having an affair if you're not having sex? That's like going to a restaurant and ordering dinner and not eating it. That's what you're there for."

"It's not just about sex," Myrtle said. "There's more to it than that. Do you think I'd be doing this if it was just sex?"

"So you've had sex with him."

"That's not what I said."

"But you have."

"Maybe."

Catherine laughed. "Translation: you've had sex and it was phenomenal and that's why you pressed so hard to see him again."

"I didn't press that hard. I just called. He called me the last time."

"You're both calling each other because neither of you wants to be sleeping with who you're married to," Catherine said. "Makes sense."

"George and I do still have sex." The act of consummating their marriage made it more valid to Myrtle, that that act, which meant nothing to her, legitimized the concept of their marriage.

"And how's that?" Catherine asked.

"How's your sex life?" Myrtle asked right back.

"That's an easy answer: nonexistent. That's why we need to talk about yours."

"I don't know what is going to happen tomorrow," Myrtle said, knowing very well what was going to happen tomorrow.

"Is it better because you know it's wrong?" Catherine asked.

"I hope not! I don't want to be the kind of person who takes pleasure out of doing bad things."

"You're so worried about being a certain kind of person," Catherine said. "I don't think people are that easy to catalogue. Like sex is so black or white or something."

"In this case, it seems to be. Sex with anyone who isn't my husband is wrong. That seems to be the accepted narrative."

"It's a piece of paper," Catherine said. One that she wanted, but she didn't know why. Morality confined to and defined by a piece of paper.

"I want to be married," Myrtle said. She did; this was true. As a woman born in the late 1800s, there was nothing else for her to be but married. As a child she knew she'd someday get hips, grow gray hair, and be married.

"Do you?" Catherine asked.

"There are good things about it, yes."

"Just not to George."

"I thought I did," Myrtle said. "Up until a week or two ago, I thought I did. This is probably just a phase. I'm acting out because I'm angry at him, but we've lived together for so long and we really do love each other. I'm just so unhappy with our life right now, and I'm frustrated with him for being so content with it. How can he be content with this? Tom is probably just my escape. Honestly, I don't know what the hell I'm doing with Tom. What am I doing with him?"

"You're doing exactly what you just said you're doing," Catherine said. "You're escaping."

"So does that mean I'm only using him? That I don't really have feelings for him?"

"Not necessarily," Catherine said. She didn't really believe that a woman could use a man. Even as, at least outwardly, an independent woman, free from relying upon men for finances or support or whatever else it is that nearly every other woman her age relied upon men for, Catherine couldn't believe that a man could have anything but the upper hand. Even though she didn't need them, she always felt beneath them.

"Do you know anything about his wife?" she asked, curious about the woman on the other side of her sister's affair.

Daisy Buchanan. Myrtle associated the name with class and money and beauty and suffering. Her generalizations were remarkably close to the truth. She was also ruthlessly jealous of her, but that's to be expected when that beautiful, rich, suffering woman is married to the man you want to be with.

Myrtle wanted to know everything about Daisy, and the thing is, she already did. But try telling her that her guessed-upon presumptions were entirely accurate, that learning more would only mean knowing less.

"Just her name," Myrtle said. "And that she comes from Kentucky and moved to Chicago but wanted to move away. Oh, and that she likes to dress the baby in little white dresses."

"I'd probably put my baby in little white dresses too."

"That's impractical."

"It's an imaginary baby. I can put it in whatever I want," Catherine said.

"I wonder what Mom and Dad would think about not having any grandchildren."

"Just another way we would have disappointed them."

"I think they would have wanted them," Myrtle said. "I guess that's one good thing about dying young—you get to skip out on all of life's mounting disappointments. The older we get, the more disappointed we get."

"I think about Mom whenever I see those little marzipan candies," Catherine said. "Do you remember the ones? The little fruits? They just put out a display at the store the other day and it took me right back to Mom and how Dad would bring those home for her and she'd get so excited. Did she ever eat them? I don't think I ever saw her eat them. She just loved to look at them."

"You should buy some," Myrtle said.

"And not eat them. Just look at them."

"I always wanted to squish them."

"That's mean!" Catherine said.

"That's not mean! They were so cute and compact—especially the squat little pumpkins. It would have given me so much satisfaction to squish one between my fingers, but I never did because I knew how much Mom liked to look at them. That's love—when you really, really want to squish something, but you do not."

"Well now you can," Catherine said. "Now you can squish one without breaking Mom's heart."

"Maybe I will. I'll go to your store tomorrow and buy a pack and squish every one."

"Myrtle's Monday to-do list: fuck a rich married man and squish marzipan fruit. Sounds like a banner day to me."

"Oh my God. I'm seeing him tomorrow," Myrtle said.

"You are."

"I'm having an affair. I'm actually having an affair."

"Full blown," Catherine said. "How does it feel? To be in it."

"It feels awful, but in a good way," Myrtle said. "I want to be doing this. I'm making the choice to do this, even though it feels like a terrible choice. I don't even know if it's about him, or if it's more about me. If we are just using each other to escape our own lives, then what do we really mean to each other anyway? I'm risking all of this to get away from all of this."

"It's your way of ending your marriage without having to end your marriage yourself. You want George to find out," Catherine said.

"No!" Myrtle said. "No, I definitely don't want him to find out. For both of our sakes. It would destroy him."

"I think that you're so used to being married to George that you can't see yourself without him anymore," Catherine said. "I get that. But from the outside—from me and other people who know you—you're not just George's wife. You exist independently of him. Everything that you are comes from just you and has nothing to do with him. You would be fine without him. You'd still be you."

"I wouldn't even know how to be alone."

"You're always alone."

For some reason, when Catherine said that in the dark, the eyes of Dr. T. J. Eckleburg surfaced in Myrtle's mind, materializing into hazy, round, blue orbs. It was the word *alone* that summoned them. They were always watching her, accompanying her, keeping her from ever being truly alone. They were just paint on a wooden billboard.

"I'm not ready to do anything, to end anything. I don't see that as an option," Myrtle said.

"Because it's not your option. You can't end the marriage, not practically. Only George can do that. Which is why you're making it easy for him."

"I feel like I'm in a clinic right now."

"Just practicing my analytical skills, that's all," Catherine said.

"Do you ever turn them on yourself? Or is it just me?" Myrtle asked.

"Oh, I'm an open book. Insecure, emotionally unavailable, probably because I lost Dad at a highly formative time."

"As opposed to a lowly formative time, when it would have been fine for him to have died."

The breeze of a thousand beating wings on her face. The sweaty older man, the hoe waving in the air. Was she all right? He climbed back up the hill, but he stayed with her. Her father was dead, so she had to keep that man alive. She never saw either of them again. Not her father, not the man.

"It makes a difference," Catherine said. "Our experiences shape us. I think you're resistant to that, maybe because you want ultimate control, but these things that happen to us, they matter."

"So everything that's happened up until now has led me to having an affair. I can't tell if that makes me powerful or powerless."

"Neither. It just makes you a human being like the rest of us. Only your life is a whole lot more interesting than ours right now."

"Because of the affair," Myrtle said.

"Of course because of the affair. We're wired for passion and rivalry. The entire history of the world is nothing but passion and rivalry played out over and over. You'd think we'd be bored of it, or maybe learned from it by now, but alas, here we are, still talking about your affair."

"We don't have to."

"Well we're not talking about your marriage. Stable marriages don't make for interesting history. We want lust and betrayal and violence. Give us a show, Myrtle."

"Thanks, you're rooting for a tragedy for me," Myrtle said. "I think you need to find another hobby outside of all these psychology books."

"I love them. They make for great party games. Whenever I'm bored, I find someone in the crowd, maybe a man wearing an especially flashy suit. Why is he wearing such a suit? Does he want everyone to notice him? Or does he want the opposite—to disappear into the suit? To hide whoever he really is, maybe a rage-filled psycho killer for all I know, beneath that suit. So instead of being the crazy murdering guy, he's just the crazy guy in the flashy suit," Catherine said.

"This is what you do at parties?"

"Sure, it passes the time. Most of the parties I've been going to lately have been so boring. I need to get invited to one of Gatsby's parties."

"To whose?" Myrtle asked.

"Gatsby. You haven't heard of him? Of course you haven't heard of him. You haven't heard of anyone. He's this millionaire, fairly new in town, and he has this huge house in West Egg. His parties are becoming legendary. A girl at another counter went to one last weekend. She said it was bananas. There were four different bands set up all over the house, and more alcohol than she'd ever seen in one place—and this is a girl who can drink. She said everyone was so zozzled. She said there were swans in the pool! People just crowd into this house, driving from the city at all hours. Everyone goes."

"Then it doesn't sound like you need to wait on an invitation."

"I need to find his house," Catherine said. "And then I need to find the man, this Gatsby, and make him fall in love with me so I can live in a giant house with a pool full of swans."

"You don't ask for much," Myrtle said.

"Just a pool and some swans. We'd be so happy together."

"Can you imagine having that kind of money?" Myrtle asked. "So much that you don't even care if swans ruin your pool?"

"Gatsby money. I wonder why he does it. Lets all these people—strangers—come ruin his house every weekend and drink all his booze. When I'm Mrs. Gatsby, I'll put a stop to that," Catherine said.

"Tom has money. I doubt he has Gatsby, swans-in-the-pool money," Myrtle said. She had no idea that Tom did have that kind of money, just a different sort. His older money didn't buy lavish parties and swans for swimming pools, but it was still there. Quieter, if money can ever be quiet. "I wish I could see his house."

"Tom's?" Catherine asked.

"Yeah. It's strange to have a relationship—if that's what you can call this—where you can't really know anything about the person's real life. I can't see where he lives, meet his friends, or see how he spends his days. I only get such a small slice of it. And he only gets a small slice of mine."

"Do you think that makes it harder to get to know each other? Having to have a clandestine relationship and all."

"Of course," Myrtle said. "We can't really be a part of each other's lives."

"I think it makes it easier," Catherine said.

"Oh no. More of your psychology crap. Let's hear it."

"Most people's everyday lives are superficial. They're filled with obligations and false pleasantries and all of the fake stuff we feel like we have to do to fit in with society. I mean, do you feel like your days with George are the most pure expression of you?"

"Of course not," Myrtle said.

"Maybe you can be more yourself with a stranger who doesn't have any preconceived notions about you," Catherine said. "When we have deeply entrenched relationships, we tend to fall into established roles. Like you and me. With someone new, you can be whoever you want to be."

"Well that's not exactly genuine then," Myrtle said, thinking of who she'd be tomorrow and hoping that that future self would have the answers she did not. But alas, time doesn't always equal progression.

"It could be," Catherine said. "I'd argue that getting pigeonholed as the people we were ten, twenty years ago is even less genuine."

"What are our roles?"

"You and me? You're the big sister, so it's natural that you're a little, you know, bossy, and you like to control things. You expect me to submit because that's what I've always done."

"That's not very nice. I'm not bossy."

"It's not a bad thing. I admire you and always have. I've always been happy to follow you. You go a good direction. Usually," Catherine said.

"I don't want to just lead you, you know."

"I know."

Myrtle hadn't ever consciously considered the control she had over Catherine. This was the first time in her life that this power didn't give her pleasure.

"Maybe we should rethink our roles a bit," Myrtle said.

"Maybe."

This was the love that Myrtle needed. The effortless, native love that cannot be erased over time. It was everything that romantic love was not, and that's probably why Myrtle overlooked this innate sisterly love. It was always there, which made it so much less interesting.

"Good night," Myrtle said. "You know I love you."

"I do know that," Catherine said. "You know I love you too."

CHAPTER 8

Somewhere along the way, over the course of humanity's long, twisted path of evolution, we chose monogamy. It was, truly, a choice. Like most of our choices, it was likely motivated by that dangerous cocktail of ego and fear. We needed someone to experience our lives with us if only to authenticate them and provide meaning. We needed someone to stand by us during the days and sleep next to us during the nights to keep us from feeling afraid. So our egos and our fears decided to turn everything we'd previously known upside down. They decided we should mate for life.

Maybe it was done in an instant, one collective decision to shift to this new set of monogamous morals. If so, what a moment that must have been. More likely, though, the change occurred over time, starting with a single couple, with other pairs falling in line, generation after generation, until the sexual tides had turned. The community became a group that became a partnership. And then there were two.

Whenever great changes are made, mistakes are also made. No one gets it entirely right on their first go. Monogamy must have presented difficult challenges to those first adopters. A sexual revolution of the restrictive kind, really. Tightening up our worlds into the fragile bodies of a single, other, faltering human being.

Clearly, they tried. They prevailed, even. Monogamy won out, because the benefits—security, better health, emotional balance—are so calculated and evident. True, this is a sterile way of thinking about love, but it's doubtful those first monogamists were romantics. They had no notion of souls, let alone soulmates. Our ancestors, hunting and gathering to survive, were not overly concerned with destiny and feelings.

It's possible that monogamy never had anything to do with love at all. It still doesn't, in many parts of our world. But here today, in Myrtle's America, *love* is the buzzword. Love is the question, the answer, and the reason for living. It's what she, and the rest of her human seekers, prize above all else. Love is the current justification for monogamy.

If we take one away from the other, what are we left with? A common joke is that marriage kills the love, or at least love's predecessor, lust. Lust is the lightning that teases out the thunder. You see the flash, and then count the seconds in between, to see how close love is creeping behind. Until the lightning is gone.

Take away the monogamy, and love loses its structure. This was fine for the humans way back when, but so was rubbing sticks together for warmth and chasing down bison with sharpened rocks. We're not quite the same species anymore. We're softer, yet more rigid in our sexual demands. What worked for them will no longer work for us.

This is where Myrtle lives. Where the fusion of love and monogamy must be protected at all costs. (Unless you're a man, which she is not. They have a little more leeway in matters of the heart and penis.) Where does that leave her? She is no longer monogamous in her love. Her love is not monogamous. She is, while walking the streets of Manhattan toward Tom's apartment, feeling her way through uncharted territory. She has broken with her contemporaries, but she's too far removed to sympathize with her ancestors. She doesn't deserve sympathy anyway, this cheating woman. Does she?

The long, twisted path of evolution that led to here, to this. But this is only a pit stop, a coordinate on the line that will continue along without us, and we'll never know where we're headed. We won't be along for that ride, just as the Neanderthals aren't along for this one. How strange and foreign we'll seem to those future descendants. Maybe as strange and foreign as those who came before feel to us.

The path doesn't end. It may halt, become faint, circle back around to its starting point, trudge up, and plummet down, but it's infinite in its ever-coursing route. It's evolution; by definition, it cannot end.

Whether Myrtle was pushing the path forward or backward can't be known to us. She simply *was*, and now she was pulling open the giant doors—where was the smiling doorman?—to enter the marbled hall of fantasies that led to her captor, or maybe her liberator.

She was starting to recognize the lobby fabrics and furniture as part of her own borrowed world rather than the coveted property of someone else's. That made her feel like she belonged there even less. It was hers in as much as an elaborate set belonged to the stage actors in a play. Everyone knew it would be torn down when the run was over.

There's anxiety, and then there's the anxiety of a married woman walking so premeditatively—Myrtle had never before walked so deliberately—to her new lover's door. A walk that carried impossibly high expectations and desperate excitement with every step. If you didn't hate her, you envied her, and even if you hated her, you envied her.

She felt pathetic because she was putting too much out there, giving Tom the power to return her to her station, but there was something electric in that surrender too. She didn't need anyone else to pity her because she already did enough of that herself, and she volunteered for any humiliation that would come her way. Myrtle exposed and steeled herself. She knocked on the door.

The Tom who answered this time, the second time that she'd come to him, matched the image that starred in her thoughts. The flesh and blood Tom looked at her the way her imagined version did.

She didn't know what to say, and hello seemed too superficial, so she said nothing.

"It's really good to see you," he said, kissing her lightly, then softly, then harder, then pushing her up against the door with the pressure of his mouth.

It was easier to do this, to receive him, then to force a conversation that wasn't there and that she didn't want anyway, so she encouraged his aggression by sliding her leg up and around his hip. He grabbed her upper thigh with one hand and began unbuttoning her dress with the other, still pressing her head and body hard against the door. She liked the feeling that there was nowhere for her to go but here, trapped between two firm, unyielding objects.

Myrtle broke her face away from his kisses and looked him in the eyes when she unfastened his belt buckle. She wanted him to know that even though it was she who was cornered, she still had control, and this was exactly what she wanted. The kind of sex that she'd said goodbye to years ago. The kind of sex whose loss she'd mourned, but now here it was, back from the grave.

Her dress, fully unbuttoned now, parted to reveal the little she had on underneath. Tom pulled down her cotton knickers—which weren't nearly as pretty as the silky underthings she saw in Catherine's store—lowering himself along with the fabric, until he was on his knees in front of her. He pulled her leg around his shoulder, nestling his head into her. Myrtle sunk back farther against the wall, taking extra pleasure in watching the top of his head bumping against her.

It felt good, of course, but it also felt uneasy, like the rush you get winning an award that you're afraid to collect in front of a large group of people—it's wonderful, but also uncomfortable. She tried to focus on the wonderful part, to divorce her body's gratification from her mind's concerns, but the two, the enjoyment and the worry, were too intertwined, battling it out for full attention. She closed her eyes, dropping lower and gripping the doorframe with both hands. She kept her eyes shut, because maybe if she didn't watch what happened, Myrtle could trick herself back into her own bed, into her own fantasy where something exactly like this had happened, only without the other body to complicate the sensation.

She stayed that way, hands and muscles cramping, eyes squeezed shut, willing herself to come, more for Tom's benefit than for her own. Even this act was about him. After a few minutes—filled with guilt alternating with bliss alternating with agony alternating with indulgence alternating with restraint—Tom's efforts settled the battle between her body and mind. The body, per usual, won.

He stood up, and Myrtle felt grateful that she had the ability, simply by being a woman and by possessing a woman's natural parts, to please him so easily. All she had to do was endure the rhythmic banging against the door, and not for long, either. She rotated between eyeing Tom and eyeing the familiar swinging ladies on the couch.

After, he led her into the bedroom, where he removed the clothes he'd left on for the act, and removed hers as well. Now they were naked, now that the sex was over.

He held her in the bed, over the covers because it just kept getting hotter as time marched on, pounding the pavement of the year. Their bodies still searching each other's in the open air and light.

"I think I missed you last week," he said.

"You think?" Myrtle asked.

"I can't be sure, but it felt like missing."

"Hmm."

"Hmm? Didn't you miss me?" Tom asked.

"Maybe," she said. "It might have felt a little like missing."

"Did you think of me?" he asked.

"Think of you how?"

"Like what we just did. I want to think about you thinking about me like that."

"I'll be thinking about that for a long time," Myrtle said.

"Good girl."

A siren blared as it raced down the street, a reminder that all was not well. That people were getting hurt, dying even, all over the world.

"What did you really do this week?" she asked.

"Besides missing you?"

"Oh, did you full-fledge miss me now? I thought you just might have missed me but weren't sure."

"You're right," Tom said. "I can't say with one hundred percent certainty that I missed you. But I might have. Maybe. Probably."

"No really," she probed. "What did you do? What is a week like for you? I want to know more about you and your life."

"I go to work. I go home. I meet friends for dinner, for lunch. The usual, basic things," he said. It was true that Tom did all of those things, but he also did more. He avoided calls from his family, and he avoided his wife. Seeing Daisy made him feel empty. The mere presence of her full mouth and dark, bouncing hair depleted him. And so, while he in so many ways revered her, he also avoided her. Better to dodge the depletion than to refuel.

"What are your friends like?" Myrtle asked, trying to edge closer to the center of who Tom was, or who she wanted him to be. "Who's the bad one and who's the good one? There's always a bad and a good one."

"The bad one's easy," Tom said. "Frank Miller. A compulsive gambler, drinker, and womanizer. If Frank's around, you'd better watch your money, your booze, and your women. A hell of a lot of fun, though. At my bachelor party he stole some poor man's roadster. I don't know if he ever gave it back."

"He stole a car?"

"In front of the Palmer House hotel," he said. "Drove it around all night."

"All right, and the good one? Don't say it's you."

"The good one's a little harder."

"Nice crowd you've got," Myrtle said.

"There's a guy, Daisy's cousin. Nick is his name. He's . . . innocent. He's from Minnesota and we went to Yale together. He just moved here, to the city. He hangs back, keeps quiet, but in a way that suggests he's thinking about things, almost trying to get into your skin. He seems like he's trying to figure you out, in a sympathetic sort of way, though. You want Nick on your side, I think, and Nick wants to be on your side," Tom said. "Even when he doesn't."

"Nick wouldn't steal a car."

"That might be the best description of him. Nick wouldn't steal a car."

"He's Daisy's cousin, you said? Is she like him?" Myrtle asked.

"Don't talk about her." He said it hard, like the words were heavy clubs coming down on Myrtle, squashing any sense of equality she may have felt. His tone stung her. She felt every inch of her nakedness.

It was quiet inside the room while each thought of Daisy, her ghostly presence too much for those four walls. Outside, people shouted and horns honked in the distance. Daisy was out there, somewhere, too.

Tom wasn't one to draw many lines, especially where his own morals were concerned, but he did have one rule: the women were not to speak of Daisy. It was a simple rule, he thought, easy to follow. They—the women—got him, which included what he believed to be some pretty desirable perks. But they needed to respect the authority of his marriage. Traditions must be upheld. He could protect Daisy in this one perverse way and protect his views of society and hierarchy right along with her.

Myrtle laid there in silence, afraid that any sound she made would reveal how much she hurt. The saliva welled up in her mouth, but she wouldn't swallow, wouldn't risk Tom learning how much she cared about him via her normal digestive functions.

Tom had been there before, admonishing a woman laid out before him. He didn't feel the discomfort Myrtle felt, but rather felt perfectly at ease enforcing his expectations of her. Because of this, he spoke again first.

"And you?" he asked. "What was your week like?"

She hesitated. Not only because she was reticent to say anything then, but because her mind could not leave the shame it had fallen into. Verbalizing the things she did, the people she associated with, the subjects that aroused her curiosity, this was all unreachable to her. All Myrtle could access was her embarrassment of being naked next to a man with a wife she could not speak of.

"My week? There's not much to say about my week."

"I don't believe that for a second. Fascinating women have fascinating weeks." It was so easy for Tom to move from reprimands to compliments. Clearly, he had practice.

"My life isn't fascinating," she said. "Not at all. I don't go to work. I watch my husband work. I visited Catherine yesterday and stayed with her last night. We talked about little marzipan fruit. How's that for fascinating? Little marzipan fruit as conversation fodder."

"What are marzipan fruits?" Tom asked.

"Never mind. You really don't know?"

"No, never heard of them. Are they something you eat?"

"One would think," she said. "Never mind. It's just one of those childhood things. A memory that doesn't even make sense why it's a memory. Something so mundane, but somehow it registered for both me and my sister. A really simple thing that earned itself memory status. Meanwhile, I can't remember Christmas morning or a single birthday party."

"Because it's the little things," Tom said.

"That's what they say. It's the little things that matter, that become big things. It doesn't make sense, though. If they become big things, then they're big things, not little. Maybe it's the Christmas mornings that are really the little things. Maybe everything is absolutely equal in importance, but we want certain things to matter more, and so we assign more significance to them."

"What are the biggest things that have happened in your life?" he asked. "Wait, can I guess?"

"Sure, although if we're going with all the things being equal in size, you're bound to be wrong. And right."

"Getting married is a big thing," he said. "You were probably very excited about that. An eager bride. Let's see, there's got to be some big childhood disappointment. There's always something that divides that carefree part of our lives from the rest, when we realize that the world isn't just crying for our mommies. Or maybe our mommy stops responding. Oh Christ. Did you lose your mother?"

"No, no," she started. "Well, yes, but I wasn't a child. I lost both of my parents, actually."

"I'm so sorry. I shouldn't have said that." He thought of his own mother, who was never really there for him to lose. He knew so little about her that she felt like a character in a movie. Like she was an actress, playing the role of his mother.

"No, you're fine," she said. "You didn't know. And I like this guessing game. What are my other big things?"

"Now I'm afraid to guess!"

"Big happy things," Myrtle said.

"Big happy things. Okay. You're very smart. You must have won some big award in school. Some sort of smart kid award."

"I can't remember winning a smart kid award, but I did do well in school, yes. I don't know if that's a big thing or just a thing, though."

"I can only think of more sad things," Tom said. "There are so many more big sad things than big happy things."

"So just the marriage I guess, then. And here we are . . ."

Tom laughed. "Yes, and here we are."

She wanted to ask him about when he first got married, how he knew Daisy was the one and how on earth those feelings—the strongest he must have ever felt—could have changed so much. The last part is what she needed the answer to. It's what she'd ask God if she ever got the chance. It was the source of all her agony, the suffering-rich focus of her mind's meditations. How do our seemingly unconquerable loving feelings fade away? When we want to defeat them, they rear ahead, galloping out of our control, expanding exponentially in spite of our best efforts to tame them. Then, when we have all we need, when we acquire those who we love—and they love us back!—why don't the feelings grow then? Why does a twenty-year love look and feel so different from new love? Why were she and Tom escaping into each other?

She couldn't ask him these questions, though. His marriage was everything to her, but he'd give her nothing. It would remain the missing variable in the algebraic equation of their relationship that she was trying to solve. Myrtle hated not knowing the answers.

"What are your big happy things?" Myrtle asked.

"Getting married, I suppose. The birth of my daughter. Winning championships in prep school and in college. I was lucky enough to go on a lot of nice trips growing up, but I don't know that I'd count those. Meeting you on the train."

"Oh come on," she interrupted.

"Really. It's embarrassing, but you're making me believe in love at first sight."

"You're way too sensible for that," she said. "You know that doesn't exist." She spoke the words solely so he would counter them.

"I told you it was embarrassing! I don't know how else to describe it. I've never felt this way so fast about someone, and it happened as soon as I laid eyes on you on that train. Don't make fun of me." Tom may have been exaggerating about the timing—he hadn't fallen for her at first sight. But it was true that he felt strongly about her. While Daisy made him feel empty, thinking of Myrtle made him feel full. He liked feeling excited about something again.

"I'm not making fun of you," Myrtle said. "That's probably the sweetest thing I've ever heard."

For someone looking to control another person's feelings, which was exactly what Myrtle was doing here, no better words could have been spoken. She made a mental note to remember the high of this moment. Tom, expecting her to swoon over his words more, made a mental note to remain more guarded going forward.

"Are you hungry?" he asked. "Should we get some lunch?"

"Starving."

"Let's go out. Lantham's?" Tom suggested.

Lantham's represented all that Myrtle believed her life lacked. It served fancy, expensive food to important people who got written about in the paper. It was where Charlie Chaplin choked on a chicken bone, for Chrissake.

"Really?" Myrtle asked. "Won't you know someone who might be there?"

"I always know someone there," Tom said.

"You're not worried about them seeing us together?"

Tom paused, careful in his answer.

"I'm happy to be seen with you, Myrtle. The men we might see, they understand."

What Myrtle understood was that she probably wasn't the first woman who wasn't Daisy that Tom brought to Lantham's. What she also understood—or at least would come to understand soon, probably when alone in her thoughts—was that Tom's professed feelings for her weren't real. Rather, they were clever defense mechanisms conjured to give him the hope and endorphins he needed to keep going. The same as hers.

The two got dressed separately, semi-hidden from each other, as if covering up their bodies revealed more than the original shedding of the clothes.

On the elevator ride down, it stopped a couple floors below to let on a man and a woman. The woman wore a loud, floral-print dress, the kind that advertised that its wearer, too, had a loud personality and wanted to make sure you knew that about her. Her male companion faded into the background of her dress, and he appeared overly happy to do so.

"Oh Chester, would you just look at her? Look at those classic cheekbones. You must photograph her."

"Yes, very classic," the man said. "You're a classic beauty."

"Chester's a photographer," said the woman in the loud dress.

"I photograph dogs."

"But also women," she continued. "Classically beautiful women like yourself."

"Yes, I also do people. Events. But mostly dogs," the man said.

"Do you live in the building? Chester would love to take your photograph sometime."

"You could come to the apartment to sit for a photograph," the man offered. "I have a studio set up in the front room. The dogs come there, but people as well."

The couple stopped talking and stared at Myrtle, the subject of their interest.

"I, well, no, I don't live here," she said. "That's very kind of you to say, though."

"Just visiting, then?" the woman asked. "Visit again! Come and see us! We love visitors. We live on the twelfth floor. Lucille and Chester McKee. It's lovely to meet you."

Lucille McKee extended her hand to Myrtle just as the elevator doors opened to the lobby. At the same time, Chester made a delicate attempt to shake Tom's hand, who pretended not to notice.

"It's nice to meet you both," Myrtle said. "I'm Myrtle."

"Myrtle, we're apartment 1212," Lucille said. "It's easy to remember. Two twelves! Come over anytime; we're almost always home. This one doesn't like to leave very often. Except right now because he has an appointment with a girl to cut his hair, but that's not very often and we are usually home. He takes lovely photographs, and I just know that yours would be especially lovely."

"Thank you. I will remember that."

"Lovely to meet you," Lucille said, pressing ahead. "1212! Don't forget!"

"I'm changing apartment buildings," Tom said as soon as they were out of earshot. Maybe even before.

"What? They seemed nice!" Myrtle said.

"I'm sure they're nice. But that dress and that man." Tom could handle boldness and even crassness in women, so long as they were still young and beautiful. Those same traits were unforgiveable in older women.

"Not your typical society folk?" Myrtle asked.

"It's not about society. It's about common decency, and they don't have it."

"I think I'll have my photograph taken."

"You do that."

Tom didn't think twice about hailing a cab, even though the subway could have taken them withing a couple blocks. George would never, she thought.

Myrtle wasn't concerned about seeing anyone she knew at Lantham's. Although it was, of course, a real place, prior to today it had been as real to her as the Eiffel Tower, so far away and out of reach. One of those ostensibly glitzy, illusory spots that she'd never experience for herself. Her set, if she could claim to have a set, didn't go to places like that.

Tom put his hand on the small of her back and led her through the restaurant's doors and up to the podium, where an overdressed man surveyed the room with the intensity of a child in a toy store. Waking up this morning, with the outlandish expectations and jitters that come with seeing your affair partner, Myrtle could not have created this scenario. She'd dreamed up a lot of wonderful, intimate conversations and moments with Tom, but she'd never allowed herself to take their relationship out into public. Not even in the confines of her mind did she open herself up to the possibility of existing with Tom outside of his apartment. Being out in the world with him, and in a place like this, knocked her off her perceived course, which hadn't been that steady to begin with. Myrtle was almost sleepwalking—sleep-flailing, really—through Lantham's, with Tom's hand on the small of her back and silk-clad people with slicked back hair and diamonds in their earlobes laughing and talking all around her.

"It's always good to see you, Mr. Buchanan," the toy store man said as he seated them at a small table in the corner.

"Have you been here before?" Tom asked. He knew her answer, but he wanted to hear her say it.

"No, this is my first time."

"The Waldorf salad is good. And the chicken."

"The Waldorf salad sounds great," Myrtle said.

"Good. That's what you'll have," he said. "Do you see the heavy man in the glasses over there? With the bald man in the gray jacket? That's Harry Wilson. He's the guy that got Harding elected. Paid off all the mistresses and made deals to get Mellon in his corner."

"The president has mistresses?" Myrtle asked.

"Of course the president has mistresses, and he's got Wilson to keep it quiet. Over on the other side of the room—no over there, with the yellow tie and the mustache—that's Henry

Lodge of Massachusetts. He's the Senate majority leader. When he comes to town, the town runs out of whiskey. And that table of men over in that corner—there's five of them, you see?—those are classmates of mine from Yale. The big guy there in the middle, that's John Benning, one of my best friends."

Tom caught his eye and waved him over. John Benning, along with the man seated next to him, headed over to Tom and Myrtle's table.

"Tom! You weren't at the Hamms' dinner party last night," John said. Eyeing Myrtle, he continued, "You must have had more pressing issues to attend to."

"Myrtle, this is John Benning and Teddy Beveridge. Good friends of mine from college. Boys, this is Myrtle Wilson. Be gentlemen, now." Last month, Tom had helped John arrange for a procedure. He'd gotten himself into trouble. Or rather, the young secretary in his office had gotten herself into trouble, and, seeing as Tom knew about these things, he helped get them out. He didn't think twice about introducing Myrtle to John.

"Very pleased to meet you, Myrtle. Our condolences for getting stuck with this guy as your luncheon companion," John said, unmoved by the fact that Myrtle was not Daisy. The other man remained silent. Myrtle, not knowing how to interact with someone in Tom's circle, also stayed quiet.

"I'll see you over at Randolph's?" Tom asked.

"Always," John responded.

"Enjoy your lunch," Teddy said, in a tone that said the opposite.

This should have been one of those big happy moments in Myrtle's life. Having lunch in an exclusive restaurant with a wealthy man who'd just told her that he'd loved her the moment he'd seen her. He'd just introduced her to his friends, assigning her exactly the kind of importance she sought. Instead, she felt nauseous, sick, and dizzy with displacement. She was an impostor, and everyone in the room knew it. The weight of their titles and jewels tilted Myrtle's equilibrium, revealing the huge chasm between what she thought she wanted and what she actually did.

Tom sat across from her, talking on. The presence of the other diners didn't jar him, as it did her. The exposed nature of their interaction didn't faze him. He spoke on, oblivious to the rebellion occurring in her body and mind. He could allow himself the pleasure of an open dalliance. She could not.

The next day, Myrtle would not remember that lunch. She knew that it occurred and vaguely recalled what it was she ate, but she didn't know what Tom had said or if anything significant had happened between them. So uncomfortable in that setting, Myrtle's mind had flown away from the cage of her body, distancing itself from the very situation it had longed for.

Since Myrtle wasn't present enough to recount the details, here they are: Tom enjoys very much to talk about himself, especially if the subject is the superiority of the white race. Lantham's puts dried cranberries in its Waldorf salads, for zing. Henry Lodge overserved himself, and as a result he crashed into a waiter bringing a bottle of champagne to Harry Wilson's table. Tom gave a long speech on why women should not have the right to vote, and Myrtle absentmindedly agreed. Josephine Baker may have been seated two tables away, but one can't be sure.

Outside the restaurant, saying goodbye, Myrtle's consciousness returned. She was there for his kiss on her cheek, for his promise to see her again soon. She was fully aware of him walking away, presumably to an office or a wife or some other mythically real part of his life. And she was all too present as she started on that long, twisted path back to the Valley of the Ashes. Back to George. Back to monogamy.

CHAPTER 9

MYRTLE WOKE UP THE NEXT MORNING feeling that all things were possible. Yesterday she'd had lunch at Lantham's, something so preposterous that it felt like it didn't really happen. Much like the entirety of the affair. Feeling invincible in this storied haze, Myrtle decided to exaggerate further, drawing heavy eyeliner and red lipstick on her face, in an almost dehumanizing way. All to spend the day in a greasy garage. She thought she looked lovely.

There were times when Myrtle put on makeup to make herself feel better, and times when she did so because she felt she needed to because the day's or night's events required it, but that morning she put on more makeup than she normally would simply because her spirits soared so high that only the brightest red lipstick could adequately match their exuberance.

She appreciated her hair and face, and even the extra inches around her body, more than she had in who knows how long, and isn't it funny how our appreciation of ourselves is so tied to other people's opinions of us, even if we disbelieve their opinions on everything else? We can disagree on ninety-nine issues, but if the hundredth is that they think we're pretty or handsome or have the most lustrous hair, well, we cling to it like the gospel. They're certainly right about that.

So Myrtle, buoyed by Tom's desire for her the previous day, felt that she in her red lipstick and eyeliner looked positively beautiful. Even better that she had nowhere to go; the dichotomy of the gray ash and her crimson lips would only be more pronounced there in George's garage.

George noticed that his wife had put more effort than usual into her appearance that day, but he'd stopped questioning her minor, quotidian decisions years ago, and so she did not register as anything more than a passing thought to him. There were carburetors and invoices to tend to. The things that defined his life and occupied his hours.

Myrtle dragged her chair into the sunlight, setting it up directly across the open garage doors from the gas pumps out front. It was another hot day, the sun burning the land below through the cloudless sky. Myrtle thought, for a second, about other parts of the world where it was cold or dark at that very same moment and how impossible it seemed that the same sun could be so different depending on where it landed on the globe.

She worried that it was too hot already, but only because of the sun's power to inspire sweat and melt off her makeup. Otherwise, she liked the heat, enjoying the feel of an invisible blanket warming her skin. Again she thought that elsewhere it was night or it was snowing, and how could that possibly be when the cloudless day was just beginning? The world is so much bigger than we make it, she thought, but only for a second.

George was under the hood again, solving a problem that Myrtle didn't care enough about to understand. She only knew that the solving of those problems funded her life, and that was knowledge enough for her to be thankful that such problems existed. The loud clanging, the heavy tools, the grease that sometimes poured out like maple syrup tapped from a tree, those were the things she counted on to keep the cogs of her and George's life turning. Things that were loud and heavy and dark and viscous.

From her perch, Myrtle could see the train unloading, black smoke exploding from its phallic upper appendage. She could also watch cars speed by, emanating a mist of dust in their wake. But mainly she just stared at the black letters on the skin-colored pages of her book, breathing in the escape that fiction offered her.

One of those speeding cars swung off the road and pulled up to the gas pump that George had set up a couple years earlier to supplement his mechanic's income. It was an aqua Bour-Davis, long and bug-eyed with four young faces looking out over each door.

"Morning," George said, approaching the bright blue vehicle. "Need a fill-up?"

He was surprised to see such a nice new car being driven by teenagers. He instantly resented them and the easy, lazy lives he assumed they led.

"Yes, sir. As much as you can get in there," said the driver, a boy with sandy hair and eyes.

All four doors opened at once, as if the move had been choreographed, and the four kids—three boys and a girl—stepped out.

The passenger seat had belonged to the girl, a very tall, tan blonde who Myrtle thought was too attractive to be romantically involved with any of the boys, who she found rather homely, or maybe they were all just stuck at the peak of teenage awkwardness.

The foursome headed over to the curb, where one of the boys took out a pack of cigarettes and a matchbook from his pocket. He flipped open the top and held the box out to the girl.

"Yuck, no way. Those things are gross," she said.

"I'll take one," the driver said. "She just hasn't developed the taste for 'em yet."

"Your mother will kill you if she smells those on you, you know," she said.

"My mother won't get anywhere near enough to me to smell anything today. She's off in a parlor or a department store somewhere. Smelling lovely bouquets, I'm sure."

The three boys all lit cigarettes, sucking and puffing a little too theatrically, and glancing over at Myrtle in her chair from time to time. Looking up from the page, she was pleased to see the young men looking her way. But why not? she thought. She was twice their age but knew she didn't look it. At their age, a woman—meaning someone older, someone experienced, someone like herself—was probably highly appealing. She met and held their stares, very much enjoying the attention from boys so much younger than herself.

George admired the vehicle. It was one that always caught his eye when it sped by or stopped in for gas. If he ever bought a new car, and he knew, painfully, that he never would, a Bour-Davis would be near the top of his list. He took in its lines, angles, and curves, caressing its contours and shiny metal plating with his envious eyes.

"Hey, are you guys seeing this?" one of the boys asked.

"Seeing what?"

"This dame over here. In the chair."

"She really thinks she's something," the sandy-haired boy said.

"Who is she? The wife of a guy who runs a gas station in this run-down, godforsaken stretch of highway? And she's all done up like she's going off to Broadway or somethin'. At ten in the mornin'."

They all laughed and looked back at Myrtle. The girl uncomfortably, but still laughing.

"She looks ridiculous," one of them said.

"Her mouth looks like a clown's."

"At ten in the mornin'."

"She thinks she's real swell stuff, sitting out here in the middle of nowhere all dressed up for nothing."

"I admire the effort," the girl said.

"What for? What's the point? She's trying way too hard."

"Her mouth looks like a clown's!"

"Lay off her, you guys," the girl said. "You're all a bunch of jerks."

"Oh come on. We're just messin'. When a broad paints herself up like that in a place like this, she's askin' for it. She looks ridiculous."

"It's sad. A woman her age trying so hard."

"She's not that old."

"She's like our moms' age. Imagine one of our mothers strutting around like that, with that tacky lipstick, and to just sit in front of a gas station."

"She really does look ridiculous."

"Just stop it, all right?" the girl commanded. "You've said enough."

George heard the whole exchange. He didn't give much, or any, mental space to the issue of women's cosmetics and grooming trends, so listening to this group of kids ridicule his wife so readily was both a surprise and an indignity. He didn't understand how a lipstick choice could inspire any commentary at all, let alone mockery.

If he had resented them before, for the mere reason that they were young and driving a car that would always remain beyond his reach, then he loathed them now. He gripped the pump tighter, the gas flowing through the smooth pipe, splashing into the tank to fuel these children's further endeavors. He thought he should say something to them. Thought he should confront and shame them. But what would that do, he figured, besides degrade himself, Myrtle, and their life further. So he said nothing, did nothing, pretended not to notice. He clung to the gas pump, listening to its purr.

From then on, after that day, whenever George saw a Bour-Davis drive by, an anguished feeling, sudden and sharp, would override the nothing he typically felt.

Myrtle hadn't heard everything. She didn't make out their words or that they were talking about her until the greasy-haired kid said something about a clown's mouth. Then she tuned in, reddening as she realized that they were making fun of her. Ridiculing the appearance she'd been so proud of before their words expelled that pride and brought on humiliation. Instead of feeling that all things were possible, she felt the same nausea and dizziness she'd felt at the restaurant the day before. Once again, she was found out as being an impostor.

She tried looking up, an old trick she'd learned years ago to stop the tears from coming. If you look up, they will stop, either from gravity or a good old-fashioned placebo effect. She couldn't let teenagers cause her to cry. That would just prove them right. That she was so desperately pathetic that passing kids and their careless words had the power to devastate her. Allowing anyone the power to devastate her was something Myrtle thought should be avoided.

She didn't look to George to notice if he, too, had heard them. His ears were the same as her ears, and there would be no additional embarrassment incurred had he heard.

The trick didn't work. She felt the wetness creeping over her eyes, filling the space between the two black lines she'd so painstakingly drawn. When she could no longer resist the urge to blink, the salt water surged over, trickling down her cheeks, one drop slipping between her red lips, the thought of which now made her cringe.

What could she do but run inside? She wasn't tough enough or bold enough to remain steadfast in her chair, allowing them to know that she'd heard their opinions but didn't care. She did care; cared too much about the words coming out of kids who were only first learning of love and time and who couldn't even yet conceive of time's effect on love. So she ran into the garage, up the steps, and fell onto the most uncomfortable chair in the house in tears.

"Now see what you've done," the girl said. "A bunch of jerks."

"She didn't hear us."

"Of course she heard you."

"She's way over there. I didn't think she could hear."

"She's the one who put on that lipstick."

"Just shut up," she said. "I wish I'd never come along with you guys. Smoking and being jerks to some poor woman for no reason at all. How would you feel?"

"I wouldn't wear bright red lipstick." No one laughed. The boys weren't quite as excited about the cigarettes in their hands anymore. Two stomped them out.

The driver shuffled back to the car and to George to pay for the gas.

"How much?" he asked, looking at the gas tank instead of at George.

"Dollar fifty."

The boy gave him a five-dollar bill and quickly got into the car. He motioned for the others to get in. Anxious to speed away from the scene of their careless insults, they left in a cloud of guilty dust.

A moment later, George was by Myrtle's side. Silently, because he didn't want to make her feel worse by acknowledging what had happened with words, he got down on his knees and put his arms around her. He held her shaking body, feeling the wetness of her tears against his ear. They stayed like that for a while.

When the initial emotion left Myrtle's body, she pulled away from George. She saw the black streaks of her eye makeup on the side of his face and smiled. She wet her finger with her tongue and rubbed the marks.

"You've got my makeup on you."

"That's all right," George said.

"I feel so bad."

"You don't have anything to feel bad about."

Myrtle remembered that she did, in fact, have something to feel bad about, and she came very close to telling George everything about Tom, right then, as she rubbed her blurred mascara off his face. But she couldn't clean up that mess as easily, and she was thinking as much about breaking her own heart as his when she told herself to keep quiet.

He gave her one more squeeze before his discomfort led him back down to the garage. When he was gone, she recognized how much she still needed him. She realized that the narrative in her head—that she lived alone, without the love and attention she wanted—was not as true as she'd thought. She understood that he loved her, and that they were enduringly woven together via the years they'd spent and the words they'd both spoken and never said.

George would always be there, Myrtle believed. He was that sun in the sky that could always be counted on to come out and warm the spinning earth. No matter how much Myrtle spun, whether it was light or dark, George was in the garage, working, toiling. And yet.

There's no thrill to certainty. No emotional high to relearning the same thing day after day. At some point the steadiness we think we desire becomes more monotonous than our tumultuous human natures can tolerate. Then comes the acting out, the addictions, the desertions, the escapes, the affairs. There will always be trade-offs.

Myrtle realized that she'd taken George's loyalty and reliability for granted. She truly did not want to think about Tom or need to see him again. She was desperate to be content enough with George that she didn't require outside fulfillment. And she was furious with her own psyche for letting her down. For this deficiency of what? Of attention? Of self-worth? Of significance? The self-contained deficiency that kept her seeking the feelings she'd never find. The deficiency that would keep her going back to him, because fleeting feelings were better than none.

Even there, in that place of great appreciation for George and the security he provided, Myrtle craved the newness of Tom and that intoxicating state of being desired by him. Only the knowledge that she was of sexual value to this important man could neutralize the damage done by the reckless kids. It was not enough to possess the certainty of George; she needed to raze another to gain the unknown.

She told herself it was only temporary. Because no one ever tells themselves that their self-sabotage is a permanent situation. When the idea surfaced in her mind to call Tom and ensure a time to see him again so she could get another hit of the good feelings associated with being wanted, she didn't have the strength to fight back with common sense. Also, the word *surfaced* is probably incorrect when describing how the idea to call Tom came to fruition. It did not pop up out of nowhere, free of aforethought and manipulation. It was sabotage, plain and simple. It was weeks, probably years, in the making. The accumulation of neglected needs, dormant insecurity, and dusty marital desire.

When she looked in the mirror, she didn't see what she'd seen just an hour earlier. Her appearance disgusted her. How could she have ever thought that she'd looked good? The kids were right. She looked ridiculous. Garish and overdone. She saw her age in the creases rippling around her mouth and eyes. The bloodred cracks in her lips. The beauty had gone out of the reflection, and now all she saw was stark ugliness, attempting to be covered up by paint and crayons.

Myrtle washed it all off, scrubbing hard, punishing herself. When she looked again at the glass, she stared into her own eyes, stormy blue and sorrowful. She thought she must have been wrong for perceiving that sorrow as rather beautiful. Still, she thought, they were. Unrimmed and unlined, full of emotion and unutterable sadness. She thought they were beautiful eyes.

Tom would not want her to call; he'd told her to be more discreet. She didn't want to do anything to upset him, but her ability to make decisions based upon being on the losing end of a power imbalance was significantly impaired at the present, and so she picked up the phone. She asked the switchboard operator to connect her to the number she'd memorized, even though she'd also memorized Tom's warning tone as a reminder to not ever again use it, and felt her heartbeat quicken in the silences between rings.

"Buchanan residence." It was the same male voice that had answered the last time. A butler, Myrtle assumed, because her version of the rich included butlers and thick diamond necklaces and other things that seemed expensive, and really were.

"Hello, is Tom there?" she asked.

"I'm afraid he's unavailable right now. May I take down a message for him?"

"No, no, that's all right."

"I can inform him that you called and have him call you back at his convenience," the voice offered.

"No, that's not necessary," she said. "Thank you." Myrtle felt she'd gotten away with something important. She was relieved he wasn't home, but she tried not to think about where he might have been.

Myrtle spent the rest of the day barefaced and meek, avoiding George and diving instead into the passionate lies of her romance novel. When George came up that night, later than usual because he wanted to give her time alone to heal, or maybe simply because he didn't know what there was to say after the teenagers had said it all, he did not even notice that she'd removed her makeup. Her features looked the same to him, her face equally attractive or unattractive. Attempts at change were lost on him.

Unlike her, he didn't remember what it felt like to fall in love. As it wasn't something he ever tried to recall, he could not miss it. This absence put him in a whole other space-time continuum from Myrtle. All that she wanted was all that he'd already lost. It's really no wonder that they lived such disparate lives.

He could still feel her pain, though. With her, for her. He silently sent her mercy, and then went back to his own nothingness. Compassion, like getting a $3.50 tip, was rare for him.

CHAPTER 10

When living a double life, each foot is planted on either side of a widening chasm. The problem escalates with the widening. At some point, you have to choose a side, planting both feet firmly together, but still watching as part of your soul drifts away. Until, if you're lucky enough, you lose sight of it. It's either that or fall into the abyss.

Myrtle's chasm was widening. On one side was her regular old normal life, the one filled with a husband and unrealized dreams, and she tried to remind herself that no, they were not the same thing. On the other side was Tom and everything she convinced herself that having him would bring. The happiness, the love, the potential, the things. How could George compete? The only card he held was familiarity. Often the trump.

As the separation between her two lives grew, so did her misery. It may seem exciting to dance back and forth between options, to taste the whole menu of life's choices, but really it just leaves you exhausted, uncomfortably full and feeling guilty of gluttony.

Gluttony. Myrtle's parents hadn't been very religious in their raising of her and Catherine. Their own strict Catholic upbringings were enough to inspire an atheism that kept them and their daughters out of holy buildings on Sundays. But once, when maybe her parents were out of town or had a prior Sunday morning commitment, her grandparents brought her and Catherine to Sunday morning mass at the gray stone cathedral that the older generation saw as welcoming and the younger as foreboding.

Myrtle was a young teenager, just beginning to become the woman she'd soon be for the rest of her life, and so eager to become her. No thoughts or mourning for the lost child she'd never again know. Just a race to be grown and away from the perceived powerlessness of childhood.

It was at that age that Myrtle sat inside the gray stone welcoming/foreboding cathedral alongside her pious grandparents, half listening to the elderly priest's droning and half daydreaming of friends and boys and all of those very normal things. He—the priest—was speaking of the seven deadly sins, as salacious of a topic to grip the interest of a young teenager as any that Catholicism could conjure. The sins, for the uninitiated or the merely forgetful, are: pride, greed, lust, envy, wrath, sloth, and gluttony.

The priest spoke of these capital vices with the expected disdain of a man in his position, but with an unexpected level of passion that let on that maybe he, too, was aroused a little more than he should have been by these succulent cardinal sins.

Myrtle listened in to his impassioned harangue, counting off each of the seven and evaluating their merits and potential for destruction. Pride, greed, lust, envy, wrath, and sloth were all certainly bad, she thought. She could see how the floating, faceless deity in the sky wouldn't like those and would punish accordingly. While she was a little slower to come around to lust as being so evil, she understood that these people were very much against it and spent most of their lives fighting to quell it. These were all bad sins, she agreed.

But gluttony, that one she didn't get. Excess, more, too much—sure, overindulgence may not be ideal, but deadly? That categorization seemed a little extreme.

The priest's inflamed sermon did not convince her. She left mass with a fleeting determination to avoid six of the seven deadly sins, which she figured would be a good enough effort to please the Lord, if He existed. He wouldn't mind, she thought, if she ate a few extra cookies.

Over the subsequent years, Myrtle would, on occasion, successfully banish greed and wrath and the others, but she never wasted thought nor effort on gluttony. She overconsumed—food, drink, objects, possessions, feelings—but never considered that overconsumption could lead to the starving of her soul. She indulged her physical appetites, which later turned into carnal appetites, without much guilt or consideration of the consequences.

Gluttony's negative consequences, though, are worse than Myrtle imagined. And it's entirely possible that her ignoring of gluttony's deadly sin status was responsible for the predicament she was now in. By allowing herself the indulgences, she deprived her development of self-control. By saying yes to more so often, she said no to less.

Now, a couple decades removed from that sermon, Myrtle's constant desire for more was insatiable. Her self-discipline was, to say the least, lacking. And maybe it's all because she didn't see the dangers of gluttony when a repressed priest hurried through them alongside pride, greed, lust, envy, wrath, and sloth.

You can't have it all. Choices have to be made. And if you can't learn to be satisfied with your present, uncomfortable change will force its way in. It had arrived for Myrtle, in the form of all of the deadly sins manifesting themselves into the one word that defined her present moment—*affair.*

There it was, the affair on one side of her life, across the chasm. And there was marriage on the other. At the very beginning, her relationship with Tom had felt fictional enough to avoid the pain of hurting George and herself. But the realness was catching up to her. The realness revealed the truth—that she didn't have a future with Tom. That he would never disrupt his own life—sacrifice it, really—for her. She knew she was only a distraction to him, and she couldn't throw away a decade-plus of actual love, even if it had become beaten down and lethargic over the years, to be somebody's temporary distraction.

Had she developed better self-control, the choice would be easy. Myrtle should have, and truly wanted to have, chosen the side of her marriage. She wanted to plant both feet firmly on that side of the chasm and watch the rest drift away. She fought for it, in the way she knew how to fight, which was by setting her sights onto something else that was new and different, thus caving to gluttony once again, only in a different form.

"Let's move to California," she said to George.

He continued to change into his pajamas, as comfortable ignoring her words as he was her presence in front of his nakedness.

"We could have a better life there," she continued. "You know we could."

"Our lives are here," he said. Here was almost all he knew. Almost. Besides the small apartment he'd taken up in his young adulthood, the one where he'd taken Myrtle before he took her here, George had only lived in one other place. He didn't know where it was or what it looked like from the inside, but he remembered the cracking brown rectangles that made up its siding, and the pecans falling from the tree that split when you jumped on them. There was the darkest green grass he'd ever see, and ponds that sprang up overnight. And then he was here, in this garage and in the small rooms above it. His family never spoke of the place with the cracked siding and dark green grass, and they made the garage their own. Now it was his own, and to leave seemed as impossible as finding the first home he couldn't quite remember.

"We could move," Myrtle said. "You could get a job painting movie sets, like we used to talk about. And if it doesn't work out, you could always get work in a garage out there. Anything would be better than here. A change of scenery, different people—it would be good for us."

"What's so wrong with here?" George asked.

"Oh, come on. Neither of us are really happy. The city is great, but you never even go. You stay here all day, in this gray, boring place. If you're going to have your head stuck in a car all day, it may as well be somewhere good, like California."

"If my head is stuck in a car all day, it doesn't matter where I am."

"What about me?" she asked. "Don't you care if I'm happy?"

"You've never been to California. You think it's the answer to everything, but it's not. At least here you have your sister."

"It doesn't need to be the answer to everything. A change of scenery, though. The beach, the weather. A chance at a job where you could use your talent and be creative. Don't you want to at least try? To see if you could do better than this?"

"I didn't realize that this was so bad," George said.

"Really? This is what you wanted for your life? This isn't what you told me about when we were younger. You could paint there. You'd be so much happier," Myrtle said.

There hadn't been any extra room when they moved into the garage. His parents' things took up most of the space, and of course Myrtle had her clothes and cosmetics. The closets were full of forgotten things that seemed like necessities, and the garage itself was off-limits. That was for work. There hadn't been anywhere to fit an easel and oversized canvases, and he'd had so many crammed into that tiny apartment. Where did they go? he wondered. He couldn't remember packing them, couldn't remember making the decision to keep or forever throw away the art he once loved. Did he throw his work into a bin with rusting hubcaps and blown tires? Where had it all gone?

"Myrtle, this is ridiculous," George said. "We can't just pick up and move. We aren't moving."

"You won't even listen to me," she said. "This is important. Your wife is unhappy, George. I'm coming to you telling you that something has to change. I can't go on like this. I need you to listen to me."

George sat down at the bottom of the bed. He heard the change in her voice, the pleading trying to disguise itself as diplomacy. He recognized that this was one of those conversations that have repercussions, and his presence was required to make sure the repercussions were minimal. With reluctance and effort, he decided to placate her.

"All right. I'm listening. What's the real problem here?"

"I've been unhappy for a while now," Myrtle started. "I never wanted to come here to begin with, and—"

"Sometimes we have to do things we don't want to do for the benefit of other people," he interrupted.

"I know, and I understand why we came here. But I don't understand why we stayed. This wasn't supposed to be permanent, and yet here we are, what, ten years later? That doesn't matter now. What matters is that we do what we originally planned and wanted. We can still do that."

Everything she'd brought that first day had fit into three trunks and a large suitcase. The trunks were borrowed from friends; the suitcase had been her mother's. After George's father had passed, it made the most sense for them to live there, above his garage. George had worked on the cars with his father for years, and he continued the business so seamlessly that many customers hadn't even noticed that it was the son and not the father who returned their car, functioning and useful once again. The move hadn't been as seamless for Myrtle, who had nothing to continue.

"Our plans were the plans of young, naive kids," George said. "You don't just go to California and make it big. It doesn't work that way."

"I don't need it to be big! I just need it to be different."

"You have all these illusions, Myrtle. That moving will fix everything and that everyone in California leads these perfect lives. They don't. It's not magic. You're smarter than that."

"I know it won't be perfect. You're not hearing me. I am miserable. I am desperate. I cannot do this."

"Or what?" George asked.

"Or what? There's no 'or what.' I'm not threatening you here. I am telling you that I'm miserable and I need your help. I don't know how to fix it here. I feel like I'm too far gone here, and we have to start over somewhere else. It doesn't need to be California, but that seems as good a place as any, and I'm thinking of you too. I want you to be happy, too, and I thought painting made you happy. It used to."

"You can't make a living painting. We need money. Things cost money. Your dresses and books and food and house—they all cost money."

"I'm aware of that," Myrtle said. "Someone is making money painting the movie sets. People are doing this. You could at least try."

"It's easy for you to say from your safe perch where your skin isn't in the game. You can't fail."

"Oh, but you're such a success here?"

She regretted it as soon as she said it. It was one of those things that made perfect sense and needed to be said, but no one wants to be the messenger of a hurtful truth. No one wants to endure the weight of the seconds that follow.

"I make our living," George said quietly.

"And yet, we don't seem to be doing much living."

"You want some glamorous life? Go get it. What's stopping you? Go out and get it."

"I don't want to feel miserable anymore," Myrtle said.

"I'm sorry you're not happy here with me, Myrtle. I don't know what to tell you. I'm working my fingers to the bone for you. Every day. I'm sorry it's not enough for you. But I'll be damned if I'm going to sacrifice the business and life I've worked for. I'm not throwing it all away so you can chase a ridiculous dream that will never happen in California."

He didn't think they'd all fit in the rooms above the garage. It hadn't been a fun place to grow up, and with their own children, because surely he and Myrtle would have children, they would need more space. Maybe he'd add on to the building. Maybe he'd build something in the field out back. He never needed to add any space, though. Their children only materialized as the ghosts that followed them. They didn't take up any space at all, and yet they took up so much.

"Can't you just consider it?" Myrtle asked. "Can't you see how badly I need this? I've stayed here for ten years, and I haven't complained—"

"Oh you've complained plenty."

"Not as much as I should have. Clearly not as much as I should have because we're still here."

"This is our home. This is our business."

"Your business. I don't have anything to do all day. You think that's a luxury, but it's a punishment. I'm trapped, waiting for something to change, but knowing it never will."

"A punishment," George said. "A punishment for what? For marrying me?"

"For being born a woman."

"Oh you poor thing. You poor women, born into a life of freedom from work and worry. I feel real terrible for you, Myrtle."

"You're never going to listen," she said.

"I've listened. I've heard you. You're feeling sorry for yourself because you have to live out here with me. I'm sorry I disappointed you and couldn't give you the life you wanted."

Myrtle hadn't given George the life he'd wanted, either. He felt that they'd both failed at their roles as husband and wife, and he could not stop thinking of the boy he didn't have. Why couldn't he have him?

George was one of those people whose life as it appeared on the outside matched how it actually was on the inside. He thought of himself as a simple man, and that's exactly what anyone passing through would think, too, if they thought of him at all. His relationship to gluttony was the same as his relationship to most of the sins—the smear campaign had worked. So long as he kept his head down and avoided all that he'd learned to be bad, life would be as good as it could be, which wasn't really very good, but as that's about what George expected anyway, he didn't see any fault in accepting most things just as they were. It was only his lack of children that he ached for.

Accepting things as they were, to Myrtle, was a sort of suicide. Weren't we put on earth to strive for the best possible life? Wasn't it our obligation as the living to at least attempt to seize every opportunity for greatness? Wouldn't taking things as they are be an insulting affront to all that could be?

The funny thing, or the ironic thing, or the tragic thing, was that the striver and the acceptor shared the same life. The desire for and the rejection of more led them each to the same place. Their home represented such different things to George and Myrtle, and the bridge connecting their opposing perspectives had been cremated through years of marriage and inertia.

"You didn't disappoint me," Myrtle said. "You're not hearing me. I'm not blaming you for my unhappiness, but I'm trying to do something about it, and you're not willing to help."

"What you think will help will only hurt us."

"It's worth a shot."

"Give it up, Myrtle."

"You already have, George."

Myrtle's words couldn't hurt George anymore. He didn't much care what she thought of him, because he'd come to not respect what she thought of anyone. And any care that did remain, any sharpness she could muster to sting him, could easily be dulled by the spirits he couldn't live without.

Seeing she couldn't get to him only made her meaner. Her weapons—attacks upon his skill, his decisions, his character—got stronger. Like any two creatures thrown together into captivity, they'd learned to adapt.

It was easy for George to abandon the conversation for sleep. It was more difficult for Myrtle. She'd never before felt more justified for having an affair, and yet the guilt endured. Except it was no longer quietly hissing in the background, a truth she'd learned to ignore and to live with. The guilt was now honking incessantly, blaring over any rationalization her brain could devise. It was maddening, and Myrtle thought that yes, this is how it happens. This is how people lose it, how reality slips away.

The two seemed equally impossible—recommitting to her life with George and forcing something that could never really be with Tom. But only one of these options was truly beyond her control. She knew that was the one she had to give up.

Even knowing that nothing would change with George, she made the decision that moment, staring out the bedroom window at the dimmed, dark face of Dr. T. J. Eckleburg, hypnotized by the way the yellow glasses still glowed in the night, to end things with Tom. They looked like two gigantic halos, the glasses, floating in the sky, searching for the cherub heads they'd crown. She would miss the fantasy, but not the guilty anguish of existing in two worlds at once. The golden halos and Tom's dark hair clashed in the night outside. One symbol actually there; the other imagined.

Of course it was the "right" thing to do, as judged by society and religion and good people out there making good choices. It was also the kindest thing she could do for herself. Lying didn't come easy to her, and living, always, with such a big lie, was even more difficult. She could at least remove this burden, she thought. She could give herself that.

As Myrtle laid there in the dark, castigating herself with the mercilessness that we only reserve for ourselves, so much became clear. She saw that George wasn't the only one looking to a state of intoxication to remedy life. She understood his addiction in a way she never could before meeting Tom. She forgave George his weakness, even as she couldn't forgive herself hers.

She saw her relationship with Tom as it really was. They were not star-crossed lovers kept away from each other by circumstance. It was not romantic. Their affair, at least for her, but probably for him, too, was a means of covering up all the mistakes they'd made that led them to that point. Escaping into him allowed Myrtle to avoid facing the life she'd created, to avoid taking responsibility for the role she'd played getting there.

Her resolve to end the relationship with Tom was strong. The efforts she'd put in to mend her marriage to George felt so real. But she was tired and it was late and her well-intentioned consciousness was losing the battle for wakefulness. She hoped she'd rise up in the morning with this same heightened state of motivation. She knew that she must, because weathering the highs and lows of an affair were too much for a woman accustomed to living in the flat plains of monotony.

She wouldn't remember it, but Myrtle dreamed that night of a golden palace with a never-ending staircase. As can be the case in a senseless dreamworld, she saw the dwelling's beautiful exterior even as she trudged up the stairs hidden away inside, aiming for an unknown destination but never reaching it.

When the sun lit the room the next morning, the dream was gone, as inaccessible as anything she'd never experienced, except this was something created entirely by her, for her, and then—zap!—it was sucked away from her consciousness forever. Where do all of our dreams go? What is the purpose of spending one-third of our lives thinking up wild places and scenarios that are destined to disappear? Such is the futility of trying to help ourselves.

The bad feeling crept up on her. Layer by layer, Myrtle remembered the hopelessness of her future with George, the foolishness of believing in the possibility of an actual relationship with Tom, the guilt she'd thoroughly earned, and the pain she was about to incur by weaning herself off her source of intoxication.

The words of what needed to be done arrived quickly, strung together so effortlessly yet so effectively that Myrtle could not wait and risk losing them. There was courage in the hazy state between sleep and awareness, and Myrtle needed every advantage she could get. She was about to castrate her hope. She'd plant her feet on one side—the side of her marriage—and allow Tom and the life he represented to drift away.

Before too much of the day's light could scare her back into indecision, she made the call, ready to hear the "Buchanan residence" announcement on the other end, and ready to inflict intense pain upon herself in an attempt to preserve what remained of her dignity.

"Hello?" It wasn't the deep male voice of the usual gatekeeper. The woman who answered spoke in a honeyed, throaty tone, and Myrtle knew without question that it was Daisy.

Daisy, who casually possessed what Myrtle most wanted. The woman she envied, hated, and revered. They were finally connected, via the receivers in each woman's hands. Myrtle wanted to know everything about her, to strike up a friendship and make Daisy love her. She also wanted to punish her, to tell her about Tom and his apartment and make Daisy suffer like she did.

But Daisy, like Myrtle, was caught in the crossfire of Tom's life, and any interaction between the two women would be disastrous. It was women who suffered most for men's sins, and these two would surely suffer. Wanting to simultaneously love and hurt her, Myrtle asked to speak with her husband.

"Hello, is Tom available?" she asked.

"Yes, who may I say is calling?" the honeyed voice questioned back. Myrtle didn't know if the suspicion she sensed in the words was real or imagined.

"This is a secretary at the office. Something came up this morning and we need to reach Tom."

“And which secretary is this?” Daisy pushed.

“My name is Eleanor. Is Tom available? The business is urgent.”

“I don’t know of a secretary at Tom’s office with the name of Eleanor.”

“I’m new,” Myrtle said. “I just started last week.” Daisy must know, Myrtle thought. They were found out. Whatever scorn Daisy was about to shower upon her, she deserved.

“Of course,” Daisy said. “I’ll get Tom for you.”

The scare was enough to confirm that she was doing the right thing. Their treachery was real—to Tom’s household as much as to her own. Myrtle may have felt that she’d already ruined her own life, but at least she could feel decent about not ruining the bystanders’ lives too.

“This is Tom.”

“Tom, I’m sorry to call so early,” Myrtle said. “I’m sorry to call at all.”

“Eleanor, this must be very important for you to interrupt me at home,” Tom said, clearly annoyed.

“It is. I couldn’t wait any longer.” The words that had seemed so poetic and final in her head refused to come together as anything but trite as she prepared what to say next. “I’ve enjoyed our time together—so much—but we shouldn’t be doing this. I want a real relationship with you, or nothing at all. And I know that you can’t give me that. I don’t blame you—of course I don’t blame you for being married—and I want you to be happy. I want both of us to be happy. But we can’t be happy like this, and so we need to stop. We need to stop, Tom.

I've really enjoyed getting to know you and I'm so appreciative of our time together, but it's run its course. We can't see each other again."

The silence that followed was so long that Myrtle didn't know if she should continue to wait for his response or hang up. Because she needed to hear that she'd affected him, because she hoped he'd try to change her mind, she stayed on the line.

"I understand," he said.

Myrtle was hurt and surprised by his brevity. She didn't have a specific expectation as to what he'd say—unlike so many other imagined moments, she hadn't had the chance to write out a script in her mind as to how this would go—but she did expect more than two words.

"Well then, good," she said. "I'm glad you understand. Goodbye, Tom."

"Goodbye. Take care of yourself," he said.

Myrtle reluctantly hung up the phone.

Had George not started up the stairs just then, there may have been tears, but Myrtle didn't get the chance to fall into a well of self-pity and depression. There was breakfast to be made, a life to keep up. The life, she reminded herself, that she had chosen.

With her clumsy words, the double life was over. Only this one remained. Her feet were planted on the same side now, on the side of George and complacency and the familiar. On the other side of the chasm, the life she wanted drifted away.

CHAPTER 11

SOMETHING WAS UP WITH MICHAELIS, Myrtle thought. His restaurant was busier than ever, and not with the working-class families and hungry city commuters that typically ate there. These new customers were a different sort, rough men and vacant women whose eyes conveyed the loss of missed opportunities. When Myrtle saw them outside the garage—and she saw them more and more—she felt complicit of some sort of crime against them. As if something she had done turned the men so rough and caused the women's souls to vacate their bodies.

"This is strange, don't you think?" Myrtle whispered to George. A trio of women in too-short, silk, sleeveless dresses sat on the curb in front of the garage.

"What's strange?" George asked.

"These women. These people. Have you talked to Michaelis? Why are all these people coming to the restaurant?" Myrtle asked.

"Maybe they're hungry."

"I think something's going on," she said.

"Of course you do."

"It's not good for your business, you know. They're scaring away your customers. Respectable people aren't going to stop here while the likes of them are out in front."

"I'll talk to Michaelis," George said. "Maybe he's running a special."

"Oh he's running a special all right. He's into something seedy, and I don't want it next door," Myrtle said.

"I said I'd talk to him."

George's principal value was service. What service could he, or any other able-bodied man, provide? His service was fixing cars when they broke down and providing the gas to keep them running. That was the beginning and end of his identity as he saw it—fixing cars and selling gas. If anything got in the way of him providing those services, his value, his mere existence even, would be diminished. That's why he headed over to Michaelis's restaurant—to maintain the status quo of his existence.

"George!" Michaelis said in the rolling pitch that made all his words sound like he was having the time of his life just saying them. "Come over here and try this tapioca. This tapioca I'm making is fantastic." He said *ta-PEE-oca*, with all of the emphasis on the "pee" sound, and it thrilled him to do so.

"You're doing a brisker business these days," George said.

"Mouths to feed and dicks to please, right? Really, try this tapioca. You're gonna die."

"You've got a different sort of crowd in here lately. Myrtle noticed."

"Yes, different people. Who cares what sort of people so long as they pay, right?" Michaelis laughed and waved a spoon dripping with tapioca at George.

"Are they coming round for the diner?" George asked. "Or something else?"

"George, my friend, what does it matter? What does it matter what sort of business we all are in? I have the diner, that provides people with food. With energy and—what do you say?—with sustenance! The sustenance to live their lives. You fix the cars and keep it all rolling. And there are other things we need to keep rolling too. You know what I mean, George! You know about those other things!" He laughed at his words, so thrilled to say them.

"I just want to make sure everything's on the up and up," George said. "I don't care what you do in here—that's your business. I just don't like a bunch of questionable people hanging round outside my business."

"It's so sweet, so creamy," Michaelis said, pushing a spoonful to George's closed lips. "What do you think? Do you love my tapioca? Bring some home for the wife!"

"Are we on the same page here? About these new customers?"

"Yes, George, yes. Don't worry so much! Everything is taken care of. Everything is good." Michaelis stopped. "I see. I know what it is you're after! You're a sly one, George Wilson! You sly dog, you! Yes of course, you like the ladies too. And one isn't enough for a man like you. I can help you with that. We are friends. I can help you with the ladies. Tell me what you like. You like the blondes? I bet a man like you likes the big-titted blondes, am I right?"

George's preference in women was irrelevant. His interaction with the opposite sex was, outside of Myrtle, over when he got married. So preposterous was the idea of him being with another woman that he had to stop and think whether he did, indeed, like the big-titted blondes.

"Not interested in a woman," George said. "Just keep them inside, okay?"

"It is all good, George. There is no need to worry, friend. We will bring the girls inside. Harry! Bring the girls inside! See—Harry will bring the girls inside. We will feed the people, food and all the rest they need. Man cannot live on bread alone. Is that the saying? He needs a little extra. I'm giving the extra too. You get it all at Michaelis's restaurant now. You get the food, you get the girls, you get this fantastic ta-pee-oca!"

George thought to himself that never in his life, not on his happiest day, had he felt as happy as Michaelis was right then, making tapioca pudding and selling women.

"Just keep them inside. I've got work to do," George said.

"Bring some home to your wife? I know she will love it!"

"We're good."

"If you change your mind, George. If you change your mind about anything," Michaelis offered, one last time.

The trio of women, currently being wrangled inside by who George assumed to be Harry, glared at George as he crossed their path on his way back to the garage. He, who had not touched another woman since Myrtle; who may have had vile thoughts of his own, but who didn't pose a threat to them. The women glared at him, of all the men to glare at.

"What happened?" Myrtle asked. "What's he running over there?"

"It's taken care of," George said.

"What does that mean? 'It's taken care of'?"

"It means it's taken care of."

"What's he doing with these people? Are they gonna stop coming around here?" Myrtle asked.

"It's his business. They'll stay inside, but it's his business."

"They'd better stay inside. It's not good for our business."

While George had been talking to Michaelis, Myrtle had done what she'd been doing since the morning three days ago when she'd called to end her relationship with Tom: resisting the urge to call him back, telling him she'd changed her mind.

The desire to see him again was so strong, and the exhilarating feeling of being wanted by him so tempting to recapture, that she'd had to start training her long-dormant self-control to somehow bulk up in a hurry. She felt she was in a constant battle against her own inability to curb her appetites, and she didn't know for how long she could keep up the resistance.

She'd chosen George, and over the past few days she'd made an effort to rebuild their relationship. She forced herself to initiate sex not once, but twice, and she asked him questions about the cars he fixed and the people who came by. George's response to all of these efforts was the same: he answered as quickly and with as few words as possible.

Because her marriage was not improving after all of three days' worth of efforts, Myrtle put herself in an even riskier position than ever. Now she was a martyr. She'd sacrificed her lover for George's benefit, and he didn't even seem to appreciate it. Minute by minute, the ideas that she deserved Tom crept back into her mind. She'd tried and failed with George. By not matching her efforts—which George, poor fellow, didn't see as anything but annoyances—he may as well have granted her permission to have an affair.

George, upon returning from Michaelis's restaurant, strode to the back of the garage, where a rusty metal folding table held boxes and papers and other things that Myrtle never needed to look at. From one of the boxes he pulled out a bottle of whiskey, new, but still mostly empty. He drank from the bottle's smooth glass lip, a long, burning swig that replenished the power he'd lost to Myrtle and, that morning, to Michaelis.

He didn't realize that Myrtle could see him. Myrtle didn't realize that he couldn't see her. Neither wanted to be in that moment—George so beaten down by years of acquiescence that he needed alcohol to remind him he was a man; Myrtle, fresh off the decision to choose him and return to their declining marriage, only to realize with George's gulp that she'd made the wrong choice.

And then Tom walked in.

Right as George opened his watery eyes. Right as Myrtle opened her mouth to chastise him for drinking so early. Right as the whiskey warmed the full length of his esophagus, radiating out to his limbs and floating up to this head. Right as Myrtle had given up.

Tom walked into Wilson's Garage.

The stranger and the lovers all saw each other at roughly the same time—it wasn't a large garage—but only the stranger knew what to say. The lovers, having spoken so much before, felt far more weight upon whatever words they'd choose now.

"Can I help you with anything?" George asked, walking toward Tom as if he was anyone. Most definitely not as if he was the man with the power to wreck his life while undressing his wife.

Tom took a few moments to answer. He looked around—at Myrtle and at her greasy, junk-filled surroundings—gathering superiority with each second that passed. He'd arrived there, not desperate really, because a man like him in his position rarely felt desperation, but more, well, hopeful in a sad way. Hopeful because he was accustomed to securing what he wanted, and sad because he couldn't control that which he wanted.

"I've got an old car I want to get rid of," Tom said finally, speaking directly to George but studying Myrtle. "Someone told me you buy and sell these things. Is that right?"

"Sometimes," George answered, not noticing the intensity of Tom's eyes upon Myrtle. "It depends on the car. Let's have a look."

While George strolled out front to appraise the car, Tom hurried to Myrtle.

"I miss you," he said.

"How did you find me?"

"Come with me to the city. Get on the next train and meet me at the apartment."

"I can't," Myrtle said.

"Yes you can," Tom said, knowing she, like most, would ultimately fulfill his wishes. "I know you want to see me too. We don't have time. Get on the next train."

It had already been decided for Myrtle. Whether by George's swig, Tom's insistence, or maybe even way back in Tom's first lascivious gaze on the subway. It was decided, and she would meet him. Remember, Myrtle was not practiced in self-control, and when that inexperience meets dire insecurity, what can happen but fruitless attempts at fleeting happiness? Like most people, she didn't see her downfall for a downfall.

"This looks like something I might be able to do something with," George told Tom as he met him at the vehicle. "How long have you had it? Any problems?"

Tom saw Myrtle head inside, knowing with a look that she would gather her things and meet him at the apartment. He had won.

"It's four years old now," Tom said to George. "I got a new model at home, and I've been meaning to sell this one. No problems with it; I just wanted the newer model."

"Sure, sure. It looks pretty sound. I could probably offer you three hundred for it," George said.

"I was thinking closer to four."

"I doubt I could get four hundred for it even after tinkering with a few things. Three ten is the highest I can go. The dealership wouldn't come close to that."

"All right, I'll think it over," Tom said, seeing Myrtle, as he expected, emerge from the door with bag in hand.

"Three fifteen," George said. "Let's make a deal."

"Sounds fair. I'll come back another time," Tom said, opening the door of the car he'd never sell to George.

"George, Catherine just called. She's terribly sick and needs me to come help," Myrtle said, pushing her way between the two men, brushing against Tom but keeping distance from George.

"Myrtle, I'm in the middle of something," George said.

"I'm jumping on the train. I'll check on her and be back later."

"Fine, fine." He waved Myrtle off. "Let's go down to the bank and do this. I can get you three fifteen. That's more than any dealership will give you."

"Great, it's yours. I'll come back another time and we'll make the exchange. I don't have the time today," Tom said.

"We can go quickly. The bank's just down the street."

"Another day," Tom said firmly. He made eye contact with Myrtle as she crossed the street to get to the train station.

Tom got into the coupe and drove away, not so much as glancing back at the man.

George stood in the empty lot in front of the garage, looking back and forth between the train and the road upon which Tom had driven away. Turning his head between the wide-open space of the asphalt and the hulking metal body of the train. Back and forth. Alone, back and forth.

Myrtle should have been happy, and she did delight in the proof that she possessed the power she'd hoped to possess over Tom. But mixed with that satisfaction was dread. Not the dread of reuniting with Tom and all that could happen that day, but the dread of what would happen beyond the afternoon. She'd have to choose again, one or the other, and neither choice was a good one. Whichever man she chose would break her heart in a different way. That's how she saw it—that she had just two choices, both of them men.

She would have one last day with Tom, she thought. That's what she'd said before, and yet here she was. She'd soak it all up, remembering to savor the feeling of being with him, being wanted by him. They'd say all they needed to say to each other and then she would go back to George. That was her intention walking into the apartment. Her last day with him. Her last day with the swinging ladies.

"Thank you for coming," Tom said. "I wasn't sure if you would." Tom had been certain she would come, but he thought this was the right thing to say.

"We really shouldn't do this. There's no point. There's no future."

"You sound so hopeless. There are options."

"What are those options?" Myrtle asked. "Are you going to leave your wife and kid? We can't actually be together."

"Things aren't great with Daisy," he said slowly. "I don't know if they ever were. But lately it's gotten worse. She's on me about everything, and every conversation turns into a fight. I've thought about it, Myrtle. I've thought about divorce."

Was Tom lying? He didn't even know. He felt he should get what he wanted, and he felt justified in doing whatever he needed to do to get it.

Myrtle had gone to the apartment to say goodbye. She hadn't thought that anything said or done could have changed her mind, but this certainly did. There's a riddle about expectations—what, when you have them, only disappoint, but absent of them, pleasantly surprise? Myrtle's lack of expectations pleasantly surprised.

"I didn't know it was that bad," she said.

"It is. We're both miserable. We're both pretending. I know we'd be better off apart, but what can we do now? Everyone expects us to be together. Our families, our friends. Nick is always around, and that blasted Jordan who just makes everything worse. Daisy's family is Catholic. They're religious, and she . . . pretends to be religious. She won't consider divorce. I'm not sure what exactly to do here, Myrtle, but I know that there are options. If you feel about me the way I feel about you, we can figure something out."

Tom most likely believed that he loved Myrtle, but he did not for one second believe that the two of them could ever be united in the way he and Daisy were. It was not for a lack of feeling but rather a lack of something far more important to Tom—Myrtle's lack of privilege.

Myrtle, on the other hand, believed, or at least very much wanted to believe, that they could be together, if only Tom had the courage to make it so. Oddly, what was hardest for her to fathom was that he loved her. She thought that maybe he could love her for who she *could* be, but could he love her exactly as she was?

Now Tom was in front of her, offering what she thought she wanted, and maybe she would find out.

"You know I'm crazy about you," she said. "I wish I could start over, have a do-over. If I wasn't married and you weren't.

If we could have a normal relationship and see each other and wake up with each other. How can we do that? That's what I want—to see you and wake up with you."

"That's what I want too. These past few days were awful without you. At least before I could look forward to seeing you again, but not having that, thinking I wouldn't see you again, it hit me hard. It made me realize that I need you in my life, and we can figure out a way to make that happen."

"We'll figure it out," she said, knowing that they would not. When there was nothing to believe in, that's when Myrtle most believed.

He kissed her then, because it was easier than talking about a future they didn't have and more comfortable than expressing feelings and telling half-truths. Actually, the telling of half-truths was fairly comfortable to Tom.

As he pushed her down toward the swinging ladies with the weight of his body, there was a knock at the door. Or rather there were four knocks, done in a singsong way, if knocks could sing songs.

Because the knocks were so cheerfully rhythmic, neither Myrtle nor Tom feared an angry spouse stood on the other side of the door. Annoyed, though, by the interruption, Tom reluctantly got up to see who would be knocking in such a way.

It was the McKees, the couple they'd met on the elevator. The wife, Lucille, wore the same loud floral-print dress, and the husband, Chester, looked even more effeminate and subservient than before.

"Hello! I hope we're not interrupting anything! We saw you coming up the walk from the window," Lucille said.

"She saw you from the window," Chester added. "I don't spend the day spying on neighbors out the window."

"Oh stop! I'm not a spy, I'm just curious. We thought we'd stop by and say hello." Lucille didn't wait for an invitation to come inside from Tom, which, had she waited, would not have come. "What a lovely living room!" she continued. "I just love it. Such an artistic sofa. Isn't it lovely, Chester? So much nicer than the old thing in our living room. And the paintings! You know, I don't mean to be rude, really I don't, and I'm sure you won't think this rude once I say it, but I can't help but think that a photograph of you, Myrtle, a real artistic photograph, would look better on the wall. Chester could take a lovely photograph for you."

"Oh, I don't know," Myrtle responded. "It's nice to see you both again." She stifled a laugh as she caught Tom's pained expression. She enjoyed his discomfort and wanted to prolong it even.

"Chester really does take lovely photographs, and you're such a classic beauty, Myrtle, it would be stunning. Perhaps next time we can have you over. Twelve-twelve remember!" Lucille sat down on the swinging ladies next to Myrtle.

"Yes, I remember. I'll have to do up my hair and makeup real nice for that. I look such a mess today."

"You look beautiful exactly as you are! It's your bone structure. Don't you think she has exquisite bone structure, Chester?"

"She has exquisite bone structure," Chester said, taking a seat himself.

"I was telling Chester the other day, we need to get out more and socialize! He's such a hermit. It would be so nice to have more couple friends," Lucille said.

"We see people all the time," Chester said.

"Dogs aren't people, Chester."

"The dogs are owned by people."

"Chester photographs a lot of dogs," Lucille said.

"That's right," Myrtle said. "I think you told us that the other day."

"He also photographs people, though, and does a remarkable job. We could do dinner and a portrait session. We'd love to have more couple friends."

"Dinner," Myrtle said. "Did you hear that, Tom?"

Tom still hadn't said a word. As he didn't much care to listen to what other people had to say, anyway, he was good at tuning them out. Unless they were his own words, Tom wasn't interested in conversation.

"I'm not much of a cook, but we could bring something in," Lucille said. "It would be lovely, a night with the four of us. How rude of me, I didn't even ask. Are you married? For how long?"

Again, Tom did not care for these people, especially since their social ranking was so obviously inferior to his own. He did not worry about what they thought and hoped that by saying something shocking, maybe they would leave him alone.

"We're married," Tom said, "but to other people."

"Oh," Lucille started. "Well, well, you know, we are open to unconventional couplings, aren't we, Chester? Who are we to judge? Not us, we are very open-minded people. Probably two of the most open-minded people you'll come across."

"It's complicated," Myrtle started to explain.

"No need, no need at all, dear. We understand completely. Modern society! In fact, I find it fascinating. That's the way I hear people are doing it these days, and we are just fine with it. We're just fine with unconventional couplings."

"We were enjoying each other's company when you two came along," Tom said.

"Oh. Well, yes. We should be going anyway. Just wanted to pop in and say hello," Lucille said, clearly disappointed.

"It was nice seeing you again," Myrtle said. And to soften Tom's message, "We'll do something together soon. I promise."

"That would be lovely. Twelve-twelve!"

Lucille's departure was loud and clear—there was no missing the bright red poppies on her dress or the clatter of her bumping into absolutely everything as she left—but Chester seemed to have just disappeared. Perhaps he was hidden by his wife's more conspicuous presence.

"I blame you for them," Tom said.

"I'm not the one who lives here."

"I'd never seen them until you." Tom actually had seen them; he'd just never consciously noticed their presence. They weren't the type of people he consciously noticed.

"Tom, how many other women have you brought here?" Myrtle asked.

"Why are you asking me that?"

Because she wanted to be the only one. Because she didn't want to be just another meaningless receptacle for his pleasure. Because she wanted to feel special. Because she wanted to believe that an ordinary woman like herself could really have the romance novel ending.

"Just wondering," she said.

"All that matters is you. You are the only woman I'm seeing."

"Besides your wife."

"Not funny," he said. "You're the only one I want. Want proof? Ask your friends the McKees. Apparently they see all that happens around here. If they see anyone else—and they won't because there isn't anyone else—I'm sure they'll let you know."

"Good point," Myrtle said.

"I have an idea. To put your mind at ease. Why don't you decorate? Make the apartment more your own."

"Really?"

"Sure. Make it more our apartment rather than just mine," Tom said.

"I'd like that."

It was fitting that Tom offering Myrtle ownership inspired such euphoric feelings in her. Ownership was what she'd been after all along, even if she called it love.

They spent the next several hours discussing a fictitious future and having raucous sex. By the time Myrtle boarded the train that night—still in broad daylight because of the sun's reluctance to leave the sky at this time of year—she viewed her relationship with Tom with more permanence. Instead of ending things, she felt they were just beginning. Their life together awaited, and she thrilled at the prospect. Never mind the details, the hurdles, the spouses, the children. All that mattered to her right then was keeping the high she got when she was with Tom.

But as the giant smoke-spewing vehicle approached her home, Myrtle could once again only see limitations. She saw the garage, and her little window upstairs above it. She saw both being looked over by Dr. T. J. Eckelburg, whose gaze extended to the Greek diner and to the women out in front with their comparatively vacant eyes.

CHAPTER 12

MYRTLE WOKE UP WONDERING how so much time had passed. Her relationship with Tom had gone on for a few months now. No longer a fleeting aberration, the affair had become nearly as big a part of her present life as her marriage. They'd met repeatedly throughout the spring and into the scorching summer. Over the same time, George was drinking more and more, which helped Myrtle justify her actions and pacify her conscience.

She didn't much worry about George finding out, both because he was rarely in his right mind to figure anything out, and because she had a premonition that she'd already lost everything anyway. She would, in just a couple months' time, be proven correct.

She didn't know, though, that she was wrong about what she had lost. Both she and George saw their lack of children as a loss, one that foreshadowed an entire life of loss for them together. Without the family they'd expected, they hadn't stood a chance. The purpose and the meaning that those squirming little bodies magically provide. They tried not to think about it. It was too painful.

It was strange that she didn't feel more guilty about the affair. Yet another testament to our brains' ability to rationalize just about anything. Before you judge her harshly for this, remember that yours could do the same. It probably already has. It's all a part of the inexhaustible variety of life.

Myrtle was cleaning up lunch on that early July Sunday afternoon when she heard Tom's commanding voice mingling with George's meeker one below in the garage. Hearing Tom, here in her home environment, had happened enough that it was no longer jarring.

"Hello, Wilson, old man. How's business?" Tom asked.

"I can't complain," George said. "When are you going to sell me that car?"

"Next week; I've got my man working on it now."

"Works pretty slow, don't he?" George asked.

"No, he doesn't. And if you feel that way about it, maybe I'd better sell it somewhere else after all."

"I don't mean that. I just meant—"

Myrtle interrupted the conversation between her two lovers. She didn't like that the two had any sort of relationship at all. It wasn't because she was worried about George catching on or Tom taking sympathy upon the jilted husband. No, it was more out of jealousy. She resented that Tom gave himself so much power not just over her, but over her husband as well. Meanwhile, he wouldn't allow her to so much as mention Daisy's name.

"Get some chairs, why don't you, so somebody can sit down," Myrtle said to George.

She noticed that it wasn't just the three of them there. Tom had brought along someone else, a young man who looked so innocent that anyone less so might be inclined to force all of their secrets upon him, just so he could stop looking so virtuous.

"I want to see you," Tom said to her while George went inside for more chairs. His breath was hot and flavored with whiskey. "Get on the next train."

The sweet, sharp smell instinctively revolted her, and Myrtle had to remind herself that she wanted the man from whom this breath escaped.

"All right," she said.

"I'll meet you by the newsstand on the lower level," Tom instructed.

By the time George emerged with the chairs, no one remained to sit on them. Myrtle had gone upstairs to pack a bag for the city, and Tom and his guest had already begun their walk across the dusty road to the train station. George stood there, chairs in hand, for much longer than was necessary to realize he'd been left alone. For those with delicate dispositions affected by the sight of such pitiful things, they would most certainly be affected by the sight of George standing alone, confused and embarrassed.

When Myrtle breezed by, avoiding eye contact as she told him Catherine had an emergency she needed her for, she visualized him as he'd been the previous night—so pathetically drunk that his eyes couldn't focus and he smiled stupidly. The thought repulsed her. And here George had thought that he'd been the one getting away with something.

Myrtle was surprised to see Tom at the train station—he usually drove his coupe into the city. She started toward him and his young friend, but Tom stopped her with a warning look that reminded her, just in case she could ever have forgotten, that he controlled the situation. She waited dutifully to board a car separate from the men, feeling both excited and humiliated.

Myrtle wondered who the man was with Tom. He wouldn't be the first of his friends that she'd met, but he was the first to venture into the Valley of the Ashes with him. That must mean that he was either someone he trusted very much, or someone whose opinion he cared for very little. Or, remembering the other man's face, both.

The train did a sort of waltz as it pulled into the city station. Chugging ahead and stopping abruptly, then creeping forward slowly before rhythmically halting. Tom and the man waited for her on the platform, and Tom held her arm as she stepped across the space between the vehicle and destination.

"Myrtle Wilson, meet Nick Carraway," Tom said. "He's a distant relation of Daisy's, a good chap. We've been having some fun taking him around while he's here this summer."

Tom had become quite comfortable with Myrtle, and so naturally he had that human impulse to insert discomfort into his comfort. Perhaps that's why he brought Nick that day. A hostage to Tom's subconscious self-sabotage.

"It's nice to meet you, Mr. Carraway," Myrtle said.

"Please, call me Nick," said the man with the innocent face. "The pleasure's all mine."

"Where is it you're visiting from?" Myrtle asked.

"I'm from Minnesota. I'm here learning the bond business, trying to get into the stock market action. Tom and Daisy have been invaluable."

Myrtle felt uncomfortable that he was a blood relative of Daisy's. Blood is thicker than water, and all that. She didn't know what that meant, from Tom's viewpoint. Was he trying to get caught? And would getting caught mean the end for their relationship, or the beginning?

"Pick something out," Tom said, nodding toward the corner newsstand. "Is there anything you need for the apartment?"

"Now that you say it, I could really use some perfume. There's a drugstore just over there," Myrtle said.

From the newsstand, she picked out a movie magazine and the latest *Town Tattle*, a gossip paper. At times she flaunted the fact that she wasn't cultured and wealthy like Tom. It was almost a test. Would he still want her when she read trashy novels and gossip rags? She dared him to love her for, or in spite of, her crassitude.

After the drugstore, where Myrtle selected a name-brand cold cream and didn't even look at the price of the perfume in the fanciest bottle, the three hailed a lilac-colored cab at Myrtle's choosing. Tom appeared to enjoy indulging Myrtle in front of his friend.

Stopped at a crossing on the drive over to the apartment, Myrtle spied a gray old man with a basket of puppies swinging around his neck. She and George had never had a dog—they didn't have the space—and without giving it any real thought, she determined that she and Tom should have one of these puppies. The idea of owning a pet with Tom had truly never occurred to her before seeing this old man hunched over with the weight of writhing little runts. In fact, it wasn't even that she wanted a dog so much as she wanted to see if Tom would allow them to purchase and keep a living thing together. She was sort of joking when she said, "I want to get one of those dogs. I want to get one for the apartment. They're nice to have—a dog."

She thought back to the dog who'd appeared in her kitchen window, how he pulled his man forward. Pulling men forward was something she desired.

Instead of rejecting her idea as she'd anticipated, Tom asked the cab driver to stop, and rolled down the window so Myrtle could talk to the dog peddler. Her bluff called, it now became imperative that she succeed in procuring one of those poor creatures.

"What kind are they?" she asked the dog man.

"All kinds," he said. "What kind do you want, lady?"

"I'd like to get one of those police dogs; I don't suppose you got that kind?"

The old man sifted through his basket of fur, lifting up a puppy the color of his own smoke-colored hair by the scruff of its neck.

"That's no police dog," Tom said.

"No, it's not exactly a *police* dog. It's more of an Airedale. Look at that coat. Some coat. That's a dog that'll never bother you with catching cold."

"I think it's cute," Myrtle said. "How much is it?"

"That dog? That dog will cost you ten dollars."

Knowing the puppy was his most powerful sales tool, he handed it over to Myrtle, who pressed the dog against Tom's face for licking.

"Is it a boy or a girl?" she asked.

"That dog? That dog's a boy."

"It's a bitch," Tom said decisively. "Here's your money. Go and buy ten more dogs with it."

"Thank you!" Myrtle said, surprised that her impulse had been rewarded. "Look at this little guy! What are we going to name him?"

The puppy, who'd just escaped one irresponsible owner only to replace him with two, ran back and forth between the cab's windows, running over all three of their laps with sharp claws and complete disregard.

"Petunia," Tom said.

"He's a boy," Myrtle said. "Aren't you a little boy? Tom Junior. TJ."

Tom, in his fairly intoxicated state, found this humorous rather than insulting.

"A fine specimen to carry on the family name."

"Hold on, I have to leave you here," Nick said, tapping the glass between them and the driver as the cab rolled up to Fifth Avenue.

"No, you don't," Tom said. "Myrtle'll be hurt if you don't come up to the apartment. Won't you, Myrtle?"

Myrtle didn't really want Nick there, but seeing as Tom did, she made herself agreeable.

"Come on," she said. "I'll telephone my sister Catherine. She's said to be very beautiful by people who ought to know."

"Well I'd like to but—"

"Keep driving," Tom said.

Nick looked dejected, but he didn't offer any more words of protest. He'd had enough experiences with Tom to know that when someone else's desires went up against his, Tom's would usually prevail. And if they didn't, it came at such a high cost to the opposing victor that surrender would have been preferable.

"We'll have a good time," Myrtle said, trying to win over Nick. "You'll like Catherine. She's a lot of fun and probably around your age. She can tell you about all the fashionable parties. She's quite the gal about town. You could probably go with her sometime, if you wanted to."

"That's nice of you to offer on her behalf, but I'm not much fun at parties. I don't drink much, and I'm afraid that I'm just not very interesting," Nick said.

"Oh, that can't be true. Everyone has something interesting about them. It may not be interesting to you because you're so used to it that it's just another part of you, but to others, it's fascinating." Myrtle had learned this from Tom. He'd taught her about her own fascination.

Getting the dog into the apartment was a struggle. Little TJ seemed to instinctively know that his new owners were solely focused on themselves and could not provide the sort of stable home life for which he was bred. So he decided, if dogs could make conscious decisions, to escape. Outside the apartment building he leapt out of Myrtle's arms and ran down the sidewalk. If he hadn't made the fateful mistake of stopping to pee on a lone tree, he would have surely outrun Tom, who chased after him, and gotten away forever.

He continued to squirm inside, this time writhing against Tom's much bulkier arms and firmer grip. The fight was strong in TJ's youthful little puppy body, and discovering that his arms and legs were no match for his new captor, he employed his teeth. He ripped into the skin taut across Tom's forearm, causing his victim to curse and drop him.

Off TJ ran, darting around the lobby, sliding across the marble floor. Scared by the commotion he caused and all the human bodies pursuing him, little TJ's bladder betrayed him once again. The doorman scooped him up and returned him to Myrtle.

"TJ! You bad boy," she said, laughing. "Don't you want to see your new home? We're going to take good care of you. Don't you worry." Myrtle felt that TJ did have cause for concern, but, like many new parents, she pushed down her feelings of being caught quite off guard with this new creature to care for and instead convinced it that it was in capable hands.

"Damned dog. Why the hell did we get a dog anyway? Who's gonna take care of it?" Tom asked.

"Don't listen to him," Myrtle said. "You're going to love your new home."

Inside the apartment, TJ ran around unattended. Tom, Nick, and Myrtle were distracted by a bottle of whiskey, and the dog celebrated this freedom by peeing on Tom's shoe.

"I've only been drunk once in my life," Nick insisted.

"Where did you find this innocent boy?" Myrtle asked, not drinking much herself, having more secondhand experience with whiskey than anyone wants to have.

"Come 'ere and sit on my lap," Tom slurred.

Myrtle complied, reaching for the phone receiver to call and invite over Catherine and—in spite of Tom's protest—the McKees. Meanwhile, Tom rubbed his hands across her tight brown dress, kissing her neck and shoulders. Nick looked on uncomfortably and gulped down more whiskey.

"Do we have any cigarettes?" Myrtle asked.

"I'm out," Tom said, hands sliding above her waist.

"I'll run out and get some," Nick volunteered, anxious to get away from the increasingly racy situation happening on the couch next to him.

As soon as the door shut behind him, Tom and Myrtle headed to the bedroom. Tom was drunker than Myrtle had ever seen him. She wondered why, considering George's irresponsible relationship with alcohol, she was so turned on by Tom's loss of control. She quickly stopped wondering and instead gave herself over to the aggressive, rowdy partner in bed with her. They both forgot Nick had ever been there and seemed surprised to see him back on the swinging ladies when they emerged from the bedroom.

Catherine was the first to show up, going straight for a lipstick on the vanity before leaving most of it imprinted on a drinking glass. She'd been here before, anxious to follow her big sister in her new adventure. She made herself so comfortable so quickly, and demonstrated such an air of ownership, that Nick assumed she lived there.

"Live here?" Catherine laughed incredulously. "No, darling, I'm afraid I share a room at a hotel with my girlfriend. No glamorous life for me."

"It's probably safer that way," he said.

"I don't know about safer with two women living in such close proximity to each other, but we haven't killed each other yet."

The McKees came over soon after, rapping on the door with another rhythmic knock. Instead of forcing someone inside to get up and answer the knock, Lucille took it upon herself to let her and Chester in. Similarly, they didn't wait for introductions but announced themselves to the two new faces in the room.

"I'm in the artistic game," Chester explained to Nick, who did his part to avoid staring at the white spot of shaving lather left behind on Chester's cheekbone.

"Chester has photographed me 127 times since we've been married," Lucille said.

"Interesting, 127 times," Nick said. "Are you sure it's not 128? Or 126?"

"Exactly 127," she replied. "I make a note of every one."

"I also photograph dogs," Chester said.

Nick nodded and drank more whiskey.

"I like your dress," Lucille said to Myrtle, who'd changed into a cream-colored chiffon dress that Tom had paid for. "I think it's adorable."

"It's just a crazy old thing," Myrtle said. "I slip it on sometimes when I don't care what I look like."

It was the nicest dress Myrtle owned, and she knew she looked great in it. But in this apartment, with these people, Myrtle fell into the role she thought she needed to play to fit into Tom's world. The role of a jaded woman, much more sophisticated than herself. Merely playing it was her way of marking her territory. Like little TJ, who'd been forgotten about by everyone but Myrtle already.

"But it looks wonderful on you, if you know what I mean," Lucille continued. "If Chester could only get you in that pose, I think he could make something of it."

"I should change the light," Chester said. "I'd like to bring out the modeling of the features. And I'd try to get hold of all the black hair."

"I wouldn't think of changing the light! I think it's—"

"Shh!" Chester, too, was playing a role. That of actual, realized artist. Tom was bored with them both; Chester's faux photograph composition and Myrtle's posing while pretending not to be posing.

"You McKees have something to drink," Tom said. "Get some more ice and mineral water, Myrtle, before everybody goes to sleep."

Myrtle dutifully went to the kitchen as requested. She'd taken her fair share of swigs that afternoon, but not so many that she'd forgotten her status. This was not her husband. This was not her home. This was her acting in a scene that would not end well.

She heard Catherine talking loudly to Nick, the way she usually did when she wanted to sound impressive. She was telling him about a party at that man Gatsby's house. The one with the giant house with the swans in the pool. Myrtle thought she heard Nick say that he lived next door to Gatsby, but that couldn't be right. A man with swans in his pool doesn't live next door to a man like that.

"Ask Myrtle," Tom said to the McKees as Myrtle returned with a tray of ice and mineral water. "She'll give you a letter of introduction, won't you, Myrtle?"

"Do what?" Myrtle asked.

"You'll give McKee a letter of introduction to your husband, so he can do some studies of him. *George B. Wilson at the Gasoline Pump*, or something like that."

Tom laughed at what he thought was a very clever joke. He thought it was hilarious to further demean the man whose wife he was sleeping with. It wasn't out of cruelty, though, as much as it came from a deep-rooted, latent insecurity in himself. Actually, much of it may have been out of cruelty.

Myrtle didn't like Tom speaking about George in this way. For one, if he was making fun of George and his position, she'd be guilty by association. She led the same life as George, that life that Tom found so easy to ridicule. This kindredship to George didn't make her any more sympathetic to him, though. No, it made her want to distance herself further from George and working-class life and the air choked with ash because its residents couldn't afford to simply make it go away. She filled in that distance she longed to create from George with disdain and scorn.

Tom was so pleased with himself and the words he kept saying that he didn't notice Myrtle wasn't a part of his audience. She was trying to listen in on the whispered conversation between Catherine and Nick. Myrtle was surprised to feel a pang of jealousy—just as hushed as their whispers, but a pang nonetheless.

"Can't *stand* them," Catherine said to Nick. "What I say is, why go on living with them if they can't stand them? If I was them, I'd get a divorce and get married to each other right away."

"Doesn't she like Wilson, either?" Nick asked.

In this setting, this apartment that she'd accented with doilies and lace and other things that she thought belonged but didn't, she was not the wife of a struggling garage worker. No, she couldn't be. Because if she was that, she certainly couldn't have all of this. George was an offering she made in exchange for all that lace.

"He's low-class, abusive, a drunk," Myrtle erupted, loud enough so Tom would hear. "He's a disgusting, weak little man, and it's beyond me how I got stuck married to him."

She said this out of fear of losing Tom. Out of fear of ending up alone when she didn't know how to be alone. Out of fear of having wasted the only life she'd have the chance to waste. Out of fear of going back to the way things were. She did not say this because she honestly believed the words, but because she believed more in her fears.

"You see, it's really his wife that's keeping them apart. She's a Catholic, and they don't believe in divorce," Catherine said.

"I almost made a mistake too," Lucille said. "I almost married a little Jew who'd been after me for years. I knew he was below me. Everybody kept saying to me, 'Lucille, that man's below you.' But if I hadn't met Chester, he'd of got me for sure."

"Yes, but listen. At least you didn't marry him," Myrtle said.

"I know I didn't."

"Well, I married him. And that's the difference between your case and mine."

The room spun slightly for her. It wasn't the alcohol that made everything blur into a sort of unreality. It was her unreal words, the ones she hated herself saying, but yet couldn't hold back.

"Why did you, Myrtle?" Catherine asked. "Nobody forced you to."

She saw George's long ago painting of Manhasset Bay. The puffy green trees, the strokes that made the ocean ripple like a sheet in the wind. She hadn't seen it in so long. Where had it gone?

"I married him because I thought he was a gentleman. I thought he knew something about breeding, but he wasn't fit to lick my shoe," Myrtle said.

"You were crazy about him for a while," Catherine pressed. Myrtle didn't like her boldness.

"Crazy about him! Who said I was crazy about him? I never was any more crazy about him than I was about that man there." Myrtle pointed at Nick, who, in his drunken state, couldn't figure out what he was being blamed for. "The only *crazy* I was was when I married him. I knew right away I'd made a mistake. He borrowed somebody's best suit to get married in, and never even told me about it, and the man came after it one day when he was out. 'Oh, is that your suit?' I said. 'This is the first I ever heard about it.' But I gave it to him and then I lay down and cried to beat the band all afternoon."

Myrtle actually loved that George had cared enough to borrow a nice suit. He'd told her it was because he wanted to look at least a fraction as nice as he knew she would on their wedding day. She hated that she'd used this sweet memory against him, weaponizing not the man he'd become but the man he'd been, who she'd so willingly fallen in love with. Why had she done that? To make herself look superior? She knew that when she said things like that, it only made her look worse. Mean, patronizing, money-grubbing. She continued to say things like that, though, because sometimes our eagerness to do better lags infinitely behind our egos.

Tom opened up another bottle of whiskey. Myrtle couldn't figure out where it had come from. Her sense of time had become a bit warped, but she was certain no one had left the apartment to procure it. Did he have bottle after bottle stored away somewhere? She thought herself familiar with the apartment and its contents, but these regenerating whiskey bottles proved otherwise. She felt herself becoming paranoid. Where had that bottle come from?

"None for me, thanks," Catherine said as the new bottle made its way toward her. "I feel just as good on nothing at all."

Nick had drunk himself to the point of not believing he was drunk at all, and so he took three drinks from the bottle and poured some into a glass for good measure. He and Chester had moved adjacent to one another, sharing looks and a tone that made everyone else a little uncomfortable.

Sandwiches appeared out of thin air, or they may as well have, as that was as valid of a possibility as any in their current state of intoxication. Myrtle pulled her chair close to Nick's and, feeling nostalgic, told him a highly romanticized version of how she and Tom had fallen in love at first sight on the subway.

"'You can't live forever,' I told myself. 'You can't live forever.'"

They smoked and drank and poor little TJ made do on sandwich crusts and ham that Myrtle fed him and water thoughtfully set out by the delivery boy. Myrtle hugged and squeezed him and thought he was the cutest thing she'd ever seen. She probably should have gotten a dog long ago, but not now. Maybe it would have eased her and George's loneliness, acted as a proxy for the child they couldn't have.

Shortly before midnight, Myrtle went into the bedroom to get some headache medicine from her purse. As she bent down to grab it, she saw something white peeking out from under the dresser. It wasn't wedged way back, like it'd been hidden there for months, but rather just barely under, as if recently kicked to the side. She pulled it out. It was a cotton stocking, the kind from the drugstore, the kind that she wore. But this was not her stocking—she was sure of it. Never once had she emerged from this apartment stockingless, and also, women inherently know their own stockings. This didn't belong to Daisy, either; she wouldn't wear cheap drugstore stockings. No, this was another woman's stocking.

Her short-lived confusion evaporated into panic. Her heart pounded, her breath quickened, and the bats filled her stomach again, flap, flap, flapping. Beating their wings inside her, trying to escape the confines of her body.

Tom came in after her. “There you are,” he slurred.

“What is this?” Myrtle demanded, holding the foreign stocking, unable to put it down.

“What is what? A stocking?”

“It’s not mine, Tom!” Myrtle yelled. “Whose is this?”

“I don’t know, it has to be yours. No one else has been here.”

“It’s not mine,” she yelled again, pulling on it, stretching it to its limits.

“It has to be yours,” he said.

“Whose is this? Who was here? Who did you bring here?” Myrtle was desperate to believe Tom, that the stocking was her own. But she knew he was lying. She knew that this cotton stocking represented the end of her fantasy life. Livid, hurt, betrayed, she reached for the only thing she could think of at that moment.

“I’ll tell Daisy!” she shouted. “I’ll tell her everything! About me, and her.” She ran out of the bedroom and into the living room, tripping over the bottom of her chiffon dress on the way.

“Shut up, Myrtle. Don’t you say her name,” Tom said.

“Oh I’ll say it all right. I’m going to tell Daisy everything!”

“Shut up!” he shouted. “I told you not to say her name.”

“Daisy! Daisy! Daisy! I’ll say it whenever I want to! Daisy! Dai—!”

With a flick of his enormous hand, he cut her off, smacking her hard across the face. The force broke her nose. The physical pain was so intense that Myrtle forgot, for at least the first few minutes, her emotional anguish. Tom had never hit her. She’d thought that these sorts of things were different in his world. As if violence was monopolized by the poor.

The rest of the party had been pretending to ignore the commotion, but there was no ignoring Myrtle's cries, nor the blood flowing out of her face. Catherine and Lucille rushed her to the bathroom, unsure what, exactly, they could do to ease her pain, but assuming that the answer lay somewhere near water and towels.

Confronted with the liquid, ruby-red consequence of his abrupt action, Tom was so very sorry. He said so, over and over, while the other men, unsure as well of what they could do to help, decided instead to leave together.

"I'm so sorry, Myrtle," Tom said. "I didn't mean to hurt you. It just happened. It was an accident. I didn't want to hurt you."

He'd brought another woman here. She was not special. The blood falling from her was only the physical manifestation of how he'd hurt her that night.

The women continued their attempts to remedy the situation via wet white towels staining red. Eventually the blood's surge decelerated, and they gingerly walked Myrtle to the couch. She was tired, she said through slowing tears. She only wanted to lie down and forget about everything. They thought she meant the broken nose, but it was everything else she wanted to forget.

Still cognizant enough to preserve the swinging ladies beneath her, Myrtle unfolded her *Town Tattle*, placing its pages all around her head like a typography-covered lion's mane. She lay there, gossip pages and towels all around, blood still leaking out of her body.

"I'm so sorry. I'm so sorry," Tom repeated.

Catherine glared at Tom between pitying glances at Myrtle on the couch. "I can get you to my place," she offered.

Myrtle wanted to leave this apartment that was no longer hers. It belonged to another now. Did this woman notice the swinging ladies? Had they, too, betrayed her? She didn't say a word, and she didn't look at Tom. She got up, grabbing one last towel, and headed for the door.

"I'm sorry, Myrtle—don't go," he said. "We'll get this taken care of. I can send for a doctor. I didn't mean to."

"But you did," Catherine said.

The sisters left, closing the door on a Tom who was unrecognizable compared to his earlier cocky, commanding self.

Myrtle pretended to sleep during the taxi ride to Catherine's hotel. Catherine knew she was faking but let her. There was nothing for them to say to each other tonight anyway.

By the time they'd reached Catherine's, the blood had stopped. The large quantity of alcohol that Myrtle had consumed that day worked in her favor to numb the pain and knock her out. This wasn't the first time she'd been hit by a lover, and, even though the end of her life was quickly approaching, it wouldn't be the last.

Myrtle fell asleep wondering what would happen to little TJ.

CHAPTER 13

THERE'S SOMETHING THAT CHANGES inside a woman after she's physically hurt by the man she loves. The love doesn't end, because she loves deeper than that, but to reconcile his abhorrent action with her benevolent feeling, she must create a new space inside her capable of compartmentalizing the two. They can't coexist, the violence and love, but love is so violent that forgiveness comes too easily.

She emerges from the event with a new compartment, one she couldn't ever fathom having before, but now it's just another part of her. She has learned to accept this, just as earlier in her life she learned to accept other impossible things, like that people don't live forever and her love would not always be returned.

Myrtle couldn't remember the first time George had hit her. She couldn't remember the first time she saw her father hit her mother, either. Her memories didn't always arrange themselves in neat chronological order anyway, so they weren't to be trusted.

Myrtle hated Tom, but she also loved Tom. Would she remember this, the first time Tom had hit her? Would there be others?

Catherine awoke first the next morning. When she opened her eyes and saw her sister's purple, swollen nose, she gave thanks, for maybe the first time in her life, that she was not tangled up with a man. After so many years chasing what Myrtle had, she was finally relieved to be without it.

When Myrtle stirred, she brought her some ice wrapped up in a rag and gently arranged it around her nose. "You probably shouldn't look in the mirror anytime soon," Catherine said.

"Does it look that bad?" Myrtle asked.

"Maybe worse," Catherine said. "You're never going to see him again, right?"

"I'm never going to see him again."

The thoughts that Catherine didn't want to acknowledge were the ones that were happy that her sister's relationship with the unattainable, socially superior man was over. It didn't seem fair that Myrtle was able to make two men fall in love with her when she couldn't even inspire the love of one. She would never say this, of course, or even allow herself to know that she really believed it, but she did feel this way and now, as a result, she felt relief. Myrtle was back to being loved by one man, at most. And there was also the new relief felt from being loved by no one at all.

"This is what I get for cheating. This is what I deserve," Myrtle said.

"Bullshit. No one deserves that. You most certainly don't deserve that. If anyone deserves it, it's him. I hope someone punches him in the face today. Hard."

"I'm never going to see him again."

"Was it really because you said her name?" Catherine asked.

Myrtle realized that Catherine didn't know about the stocking and Tom's other woman. She was about to tell her but stopped. She'd told Catherine everything, but the embarrassment hushed her. Myrtle would never see Tom again anyway, she resolved. She wouldn't tell Catherine that he had been with another woman. She wouldn't admit that defeat.

"He didn't want me to say 'Daisy.'"

"Meanwhile he could ridicule George all he wanted," Catherine said. "Asshole. Hypocritical asshole."

"Nick is Daisy's cousin, you know," Myrtle said.

"Nick?"

"The guy you were talking to all night."

"Oh right. I got a funny feeling from him. He definitely wasn't interested. Probably a good thing based on the company he keeps."

"I wish I could undo this entire thing," Myrtle said. "Go back to that first day on the subway and miss the train."

"But you learned from this," Catherine said. "Every experience we have shapes our futures in some way, even the smallest ones. Ripples in the pond, and all that."

"You're being a little overdramatic again."

"Your lover broke your nose last night and I'm the overdramatic one?"

"I did learn from this," Myrtle said. "I learned that I can't trust myself or my judgment."

Myrtle had thought that the scariest thing in the world was that love changes. But not being able to trust herself felt even scarier. Maybe the two fears were related. Maybe Myrtle made up an entire connection out of loneliness, out of love changing, and not being able to trust herself to deal with its fallout.

"You don't have to stay married to George, you know," Catherine said. "I could help you find a job. You could live with me. It could be fun."

Both women knew the impossibility of Myrtle going anywhere but back home to George. Catherine's offer was kind and practical, but those aren't the types of offers anyone is looking for.

Myrtle had always done the right things, in the right order, including getting married. That—marriage—was supposed to be the finish line, the end to the loneliness. But she'd gotten married at twenty-three, so how could that possibly be the finish line? Something has to come next, and it does. Humans are lonely for reasons other than their relationship status.

"Here I felt like a failure all this time for not being able to con anyone into marrying me," Catherine said. "Maybe I was onto something all along. Or maybe I'm just stubborn and needy and couldn't con anyone into marrying me."

"What am I going to tell George?" Myrtle asked.

"You tripped and fell," Catherine started, the lies coming as easily to her as anyone else, and why shouldn't they? "We were going down the subway steps and you missed one and fell flat on your face. The impact with the hard ground broke your nose."

"At least I never have to see Tom again," Myrtle said. "I don't have to lie anymore."

The lie she was talking about was to her husband—about where she was going, what she'd done. But Myrtle's biggest lies were to herself, in her daydreams and fantasies, and in the role she played when she was with Tom. Myrtle had faked her present and her future for so long that she didn't know how to face her truth. She didn't know herself without the lies that made her life a little more palatable.

She left Catherine's hotel to return to her life above the garage; each place where the sisters rested their heads suspended above the ground. It felt like a long train ride home to Myrtle. While one metaphorical weight had been lifted, it seemed like a new, heavier one had settled into its place. Uncertainty often feels like that. Or was it the certainty of knowing what the rest of her years—just months actually, but Myrtle expected years—would feel like that weighed so heavily?

Never again, she swore, would she chase things that hurt her. She'd deviated from the relative safety of her known path; she couldn't act surprised when she encountered danger elsewhere.

Besides worrying about George's reaction and trying to push down the intense disappointment she felt over Tom cheating and the end of their relationship, Myrtle was embarrassed by her nose, which she attempted to cover with an ice pack Catherine had given her. She looked hideous, she thought, and the stares she got from her fellow passengers didn't help her concerns. She still worried so much about the approval of strangers.

She deserved all of these uncomfortable feelings, she thought, and her punishment now was to endure them. But she wanted to endure them at home. Home was familiar; it allowed her to relax her strained posture. Home would not require her to censor herself. Home, after all, had already completed the censoring of herself long ago.

As she descended the train at her station, Myrtle saw Michaelis waving his stocky arm at someone, gesturing for them to come his way. Myrtle hid behind a group of workers, not wanting to rehearse her lie to Michaelis before performing for George.

The man Michaelis was waving to was a Black man, which didn't much bother Myrtle, but he was very large—even larger than Michaelis. Unlike Michaelis, the man's largeness was firm, as if ready to crush anything that got in its way. His body looked like it consisted of multiple round, dark-gray rocks strung together to make a man. It was covered in a white suit that may have made him appear even larger. He did not smile at Michaelis's enthusiastic greeting. He did not seem to acknowledge the young Greek at all, but still he followed him across the street to the row of dusty yellow buildings.

Outside the diner stood a small group of women, dressed in the sort of way that makes onlookers wonder what kind of lives they'd led to bring them there. Myrtle pitied them. They shared the same struggle.

The women ignored Myrtle, but the gigantic blue eyes of Dr. T. J. Eckleburg did not. Today they seemed to be mocking her. Casting their supercilious stare upon her and all that she was as she went to find her husband and explain away the broken nose her lover had given her.

George was inside the garage, sitting at his desk in the back, next to the folding table that held the boxes that held the whiskey. He was engrossed in paperwork and didn't hear Myrtle come in. Her approach startled him, even more so when he saw her nose.

"My God! What happened?"

"It was an accident," she said, almost robotically. "I tripped and fell going down the subway stairs and I landed on my face."

"Did you see a doctor? It looks horrible!"

"No, I'll be fine. It's not bleeding anymore."

"Were you alone?" George asked. "Was Catherine with you?"

"Catherine was with me," Myrtle recited. "She helped me. It happened last night. I'm feeling better today, it will be fine."

"That must have been some fall," George said. There was relief that he hadn't caused this injury. He'd always regretted hurting her, always swore to himself that the next time would be different—all the usual stuff that usual people do. He was so meek with men, but hitting Myrtle felt like a gross power he'd earned by marrying her. It wasn't a power he wanted, but still he felt that it was his.

"You put ice on it?" he asked.

"Right now I just want to rest," she said. "I didn't get much sleep last night and I'm looking forward to resting now that I'm home."

George rarely touched his wife these days, and he didn't want to make things worse by inadvertently hurting her further, so he kept his distance. He thought he was helping.

He didn't even question the story, Myrtle thought upstairs, partially relieved and partially annoyed. George was either too stupid or too checked out to question her. She couldn't decide which was worse.

George was her only option now. Tom had shown her, with violent certainty, that what she'd thought they'd had was an illusion, simply wishful thinking on her part. He'd had another woman, maybe more, and she'd never been as important to him as she'd hoped. Violence was everywhere, but at least George was faithful.

Myrtle felt used and foolish and guilty, but she also felt sick. Nausea bubbled up inside and then clung to her body. She tried eating and drinking and sleeping, but she couldn't shake it.

The feeling stuck around all day and night. While cooking dinner, the smell of the pork chops choked her, and she ran to the kitchen sink to throw up. The force of the vomiting caused her nose to begin bleeding again, and even amidst the physical misery of throwing up with a newly broken nose, Myrtle laughed at the fact that her situation had become even more pathetic. There was not much else she could do. She laughed more. And more. She laughed through the bloody paper towels she dabbed under her nose, and she laughed through the battered image of herself she saw reflected in the window.

She tried to eat dinner with George, but she was unable to keep anything down. It had been years since Myrtle had gotten sick like this, and the strong waves of nausea were unlike anything she remembered experiencing. George continued to keep his distance but tried to help by silently leaving cans of ginger ale he procured from Michaelis for her to drink.

The next morning was just as bad. She was awoken early by the urge to throw up, and any sort of movement made the urge return. For that reason, she was still in bed when Tom drove up to the garage.

Unused to feeling bad about his own behavior, the previous day had been hard on Tom. Self-reflection was fairly foreign to him, and he bumped up against some very difficult truths about himself. He probably didn't quite feel bad enough to make any lasting changes, but he was eager to tell Myrtle he planned to do so. He needed her forgiveness to make his own guilt lessen. He needed her back to make his own life more bearable.

Seeing that George was the only one in the garage, he surmised that Myrtle was upstairs. He spoke loudly, both because he always spoke loudly and also because he hoped his voice would carry up through the open window and into her ears. He was desperate for her, which may have been a victory for Myrtle had it not cost her a broken nose to earn it.

"You're back," George said. "You ready to sell me that car?"

"That's what I wanted to talk with you about. I'm just about ready to make the separation." It wasn't George Tom was speaking to, but Myrtle, invisible up above. He said it again, louder. "Yes, just about ready to make the separation. I wanted to talk with you first."

"All right, let's talk," George said. "Three fifteen is the most I can pay for it. I can get you the money right now."

"Sure, that's fine. Not today, though." Tom had expected Myrtle to come down right away. She hadn't, so he continued the conversation with George, its only purpose now to succeed in getting the other man's wife to sleep with him again.

"Not today? Then when?"

"What's the rush? I'll sell it to you, I give you my word. There's no hurry."

"A car like that, that's a summer car. I need to get it fixed up real fast so someone can enjoy it this summer," George said.

Tom had expected to see her, her presence alleviating his guilt, which he didn't quite understand as guilt. He only knew that there was a bad sensation in his body, and he needed to see her to get rid of it.

"There's lots of summer left," Tom said. "Plenty of time. The world isn't going to end this summer anyway."

"So when then? I'll get the money from the bank and have it ready for you when you come back."

Still no sign of Myrtle. "I'm just about ready to make the separation. Just about ready."

Tom had strategized this yesterday. Those exact words, he figured, would be the ones to get her back. There were no doubts in his mind. Like a football play he'd practiced with his team that went off perfectly in the big game, he'd assumed that this play, too, would be perfectly executed against his opponent. It could erase the other women and the violence—two parts of him that Tom would never actually erase.

"Come back day after tomorrow then with the car," George said. "I'll have the money."

"Day after tomorrow," Tom repeated. "All right, day after tomorrow. I'll return day after tomorrow." Without Myrtle's presence, the bad sensation remained. It may have even gotten stronger. Nothing in his world could make it go away; that's why he always entered the worlds of women like Myrtle in the first place.

Myrtle had heard every word. She couldn't have tuned him out if she wanted to. Two strong emotions—love and hate—jostled within her, amplifying every action he made, every word he spoke. Love makes us single-minded. So does hate.

She heard his words; she knew he was signaling her. Myrtle was not yielding that day, though. What she gave him was a look out the window as he was leaving. She let him see her, swollen, sickly, miserable. They locked eyes and she held his pleading gaze, strengthened by her pain.

It was then during that look that she put it together. The lateness, the sickness.

She was pregnant.

CHAPTER 14

In October 1908, Myrtle Daniker had no idea what lied ahead of her. She entered the party barefoot, because the weather was still perfect enough that you could patter around a fall garden party without shoes, and also because the heel had snapped on her white pumps on the walk over, prompting her to abandon them next to a changing maple tree rather than hobble around all night. She told herself the look made her seem more bohemian, cool, and carefree. Her younger sister, Catherine, two shoes firmly strapped to her own feet, agreed.

The grass was only slightly damp, not because it had rained at any time during the previous few days, but because that grass always had a bit of a sheen, a half-wet, half-dry film that coated its luscious, kelly green blades. It was soft and comfortable on her bare soles, more comfortable than any of the other young women felt, their block heels sinking into the ground. Bohemian, cool, and carefree, she told herself again.

This party was in honor of Sheryl Bainbridge's birth. Sheryl's family was just well-off enough to throw a rather large party for their daughter's twenty-first birthday, but not well-off enough to throw it at one of the city's more fashionable indoor venues. So her birth was being celebrated at a Long Island public park, with cake and refreshments enough for every young person within a three-block radius of the lovely, tree-lined square.

Myrtle and Catherine had tried to convince their father to buy them new dresses earlier that year, but he'd refused. Had their mother still been alive, they would have had a powerful ally aiding their cause. Instead, they wore dresses that everyone had already seen them in, and, at least in Myrtle's case, shoes whose heels refused to remain erect for even one more step.

The young ladies circled the park, dropping in and out of conversations like verbal yo-yos, flinging themselves in before abruptly fluttering out. Myrtle looked around for young men looking at her and made proximity to them her criteria for which conversations to cast herself into. Catherine followed.

"Myrtle," her father had said rather hesitantly to her a few months back. "Your mother was a few years younger than you when we got married. Your cousins are all married or about to be. I know you don't want to live here with me forever, now. What do you think? Are there any special beaus in your life you're not telling me about?"

Her cheeks flushed, both when her father began that awkward conversation, and now, thinking about it at the birthday party of Sheryl Bainbridge, who was engaged to be married to Stewart Jeffrey the next summer. Her interpretation of her father's words was that there was something wrong with her, some innate defect, that prevented men from wanting to join their lives with hers. She'd already felt the matrimonial pressure—had been raised to feel it, just like every other girl—long before her father deemed her so past the point of no return that rendered his intervention necessary. He'd died, suddenly and unexpectedly, days later.

Leaning up against a particularly mangled tree, a light-haired, light-eyed man was about to relieve Myrtle of that pressure, if only she'd look in his direction, which she did, because she was looking for men in every direction.

George Wilson did not live within three blocks of that park, but he was familiar with and enjoyed the area. He was interested in all the usual things that men of his generation were interested in, and he intentionally placed himself in situations that would fan the flames of those interests.

Right away he noticed the barefoot Myrtle, and, unlike with the other shoed women and girls at the party, he felt emboldened to approach her. Had her heel not broken on the walk over, she would have looked just like everyone else, and he would have remained leaned up against that mangled tree.

He caught her alone, as was always his approach with women, between stops and starts into conversations and while Catherine was still stuck in one.

"Do you have something against shoes?" he asked her.

"As a matter of fact, I do," she answered. "I have something against their heels breaking on the way to parties."

"That's a shame. Maybe I could try to fix them. Where are they?"

She gave him a dazzling, sheepish smile that he would remember for a very long time.

"I kind of left them on the side of the road," Myrtle said. "I figured, what good could they do me like that?"

"I see. Something has a little hiccup and you leave it on the side of the road. Do you always discard things so easily . . . ?" He trailed off, prompting her to give him her name.

"Myrtle. And I wouldn't call a broken heel a little hiccup! It snapped right in two. I'd break an ankle if I'd tried to walk in them like that."

"How about this, Myrtle. How about we take a walk back to the side of the road where you abandoned those poor shoes. I'm pretty good at fixing things, and I bet I could fix your heel."

Myrtle didn't care much about her discarded shoes, but she wanted to talk further with this blond man who'd taken an interest in her. She yanked Catherine out of her conversation to explain she was leaving but would return, and then slung her right back into it.

On the walk she learned that his name was George Wilson, that he liked to paint, and that he made her feel as vibrant as the fiery maple trees they passed. When they reached the shoes, now partially buried by fallen red leaves, he took the broken one and handed her the other.

"I should be able to hammer that back in," George said. "I'm going to take this home with me and fix it up for you. I'll bring it back to your house tomorrow."

"You don't know where I live."

"Are you going to tell me, or am I going to have to go around knocking on doors with this slipper in my hand, looking for Cinderella?"

"I live just up this street. Seventy-four twelve Bridge Street," Myrtle said.

"Seventy-four twelve Bridge Street. Got it. Your shoe will be as good as new. Should we go back to the party?"

"Sure," she said, returning the able-heeled shoe to the ground beneath the maple tree.

"What are you doing? You're still going to leave the shoe?" George asked.

"I'm not carrying around a single shoe all night! It will be fine here. I'll pick it up on my way home."

They walked back to the party, where they spent the rest of the evening evading anyone's attempts to join their private conversation. George kept the broken shoe wedged tightly into his pocket. Myrtle kept a smile on her face.

It took Catherine three attempts to pry Myrtle away from George. The most interesting thing Catherine had experienced that night was learning that both Barbara Driver and Shirley King had had sex with Stewart Jeffrey, the young man engaged to Sheryl Bainbridge. The excitement of that revelation, however, was short-lived, and she wanted to go home.

"I'm very happy to have met you tonight," George said. "I'll see you tomorrow, Cinderella."

On their walk back home, Myrtle filled Catherine in on George and all they'd talked about. She loved that he was an artist, that he seemed kind, and, perhaps most of all, that he was interested in her. Catherine liked seeing her sister happy again. It had been a depressing summer for their family after their father died. They were only recently getting back out into the world and living life as usual. Catherine always followed Myrtle, lagging a little behind, so seeing her sister happy again surely meant that her own happiness would follow. Just a little behind.

When they reached the spot where Myrtle had left the shoe, it was nowhere to be found. The functional, heeled shoe was gone. But George came to her house the next day, just as he'd said he would, with the broken shoe fixed as good as new.

They started seeing each other frequently. In the fall they'd take long walks around Myrtle's neighborhood, talking about their friends and families, and sometimes their ambitions. They talked the way young people do about such things, in long-winded, optimistic bursts that more closely resembled poetry than anyone's actual life. When the weather became colder, George took Myrtle to a neighborhood restaurant, where they fell in love over hamburgers, Coca-Cola, and well-intentioned, but still false, promises.

"I want to see your paintings," Myrtle said one day that winter.

"They're really nothing to write home about."

"I bet they're great. Certainly better than I could ever do. I can't even draw a proper stick person."

"I can't draw people, either," George said. "At least not people who look like people."

"What are your paintings of?" Myrtle asked.

"Landscapes mostly. The ocean, parks. I actually did one of the spot where you left your shoes. The night we first met. The leaves were changing color and your little white shoes, getting buried beneath the falling leaves."

"Really? You painted that?"

"I did," George said, a little embarrassed that he'd let on that the scene had made such an impression. "The leaves were a really nice color then."

"I want to see it!" Myrtle said excitedly. She hadn't known until that moment that she'd wanted to be someone's muse, but she very much did. She wanted to be the sort of woman who inspired a man to paint her shoes.

"It's really not that great. Nothing special," George said.

"My shoes made it into a painting, I think that I deserve to see it."

"All right. I'll take you to see it sometime."

"Right now!" Myrtle said. "Let's go see it now. What else do we have to do? Plus, I've never seen where you live."

"Now? I'm telling you, it's just a painting. My place isn't anything great, either."

"I don't care," Myrtle insisted. "I want to see where you live and what you do. You've seen everything to do with my life, I want to see yours."

"All right," George said. "Let's go."

It wasn't snowing, but it was cold out as they made the nearly one-mile walk to George's home. He lived alone in a very small studio apartment that just happened to be set above a mechanic's garage. This wasn't his father's garage, though, but rather a coincidence that almost stopped George from taking the apartment. There weren't a whole lot of places that fit his low budget, however, so he signed the lease and moved in.

Myrtle didn't care much about the studio's lack of size and rooms. She was taken by the more romantic aspects of an aspiring artist living and working there alone, creating paintings in his own space. She was younger then and didn't yet realize that aspirations are meaningless if not fulfilled; that small spaces will eventually lose their romance.

She'd already started falling in love with George by the time they first visited his home, but seeing his work added a depth to her love that she'd never before experienced. His colors were ripped from reality, earthy and saturated, and the raised texture cast small shadows that made everything seem that much more real. His pictures felt tranquil, but sad. It was as if his paintings, so colorful and alive, plunged into her heart and scooped out a new chamber just for them. A gallery in her expanded heart, guarding George's art and dream.

Her favorite was the precise, layered painting of Manhasset Bay. The one where the ocean rippled like a silk sheet caught in a breeze, and the puffy trees bled every shade of green into one another. Seeing it made her feel safe, like nothing could harm her so long as her eyes remained fixed upon its ripples and leaves.

"They're incredible," she said. "I thought they'd be good, but I didn't realize they could be this good. You're really talented, George. You can do this, you know. Be a painter and earn a living at it."

"I don't know about that. It's just something I enjoy doing."

"Yes, and you're really good at it."

George's heart expanded too. The woman he loved appreciated his paintings. Very few people had ever seen them; his family's practical reaction to his improbable hopes had made him reticent to share them with others. But Myrtle understood.

Myrtle didn't think he was wasting his time creating the exact moody red hue for a changing maple tree.

As is usually the case with two people in love, George and Myrtle's relationship raged onward, burning down everything in its course. Unstoppable, as feelings are. Until, that is, they evaporate, leaving behind nothing but the ashy remains of a love its owner is desperate to recall, but cannot conjure. These evaporated feelings can't be recaptured; one can only find a new love in order to feel unstoppable again.

But that winter and spring, George and Myrtle still raged onward. They erased, for each other, the lives they'd led and the disappointing lives they'd settled into. More than anything, maybe, love erases.

They dreamed up the kinds of plans that only young people in love can dream up, which is to say, the best kinds of plans, but ones that only so rarely come to fruition. When they had sex for the first time—on the floor of George's studio apartment, beneath the painting of her shoes—the experience was so erotic that Myrtle came before he entered her, and then again after he did.

That studio, which hadn't felt that small to Myrtle the first time she walked in, started to do something funny as their relationship progressed. Like a puppy's crate that seems to shrink as the puppy grows bigger, so did George's apartment. As their love grew, the apartment appeared to get smaller and smaller in comparison. By summer it felt claustrophobic, like trying to stuff a full-grown Great Dane into the crate it had nestled cozily into as a puppy.

Neither George nor Myrtle saw this as a warning sign. To them, the imagined shrinking of the apartment felt real. Falling into an all-too-human pattern, they assumed they needed more. More space, more love from each other, more commitment.

And so George asked Myrtle to marry him.

"Where will we live?" she asked him one day, not too long after they became engaged.

"We'll have to get a bigger apartment," he said.

"I could work," Myrtle volunteered. "I wouldn't mind being a teacher."

"No. No wife of mine is going to work."

"Why not? I'm good at math, and I could teach it. It could be fun. Plus, my income could allow you to focus on painting and getting into galleries. It could help kickstart your painting career."

"No," George said. "I'm not going to live off of my wife's money. Painting isn't a career. I'm going to go to work and take care of our family the way my dad took care of his family, and the way your dad took care of your family."

"What am I supposed to do all day while you're working then?" Myrtle asked.

"There'll be kids, and things to tend to around the house."

George said this with the certainty of stating that the sky is blue. Myrtle didn't question how their lives would go anymore. She'd done her job—gotten a man to want to marry her—and now the message was clear that she was to allow him to do his. Her father would have been so happy, she often thought to herself.

Inevitably, summer morphed into fall again, and fall into winter. Neither George nor Myrtle had paid much attention to the leaves' changing colors that year, and before they knew it, the leaves had jumped ship, revealing barren gray branches that looked far more dead than alive.

Myrtle was twenty-three and about to be married. She'd expected to feel differently. She should have been giddy and hopeful and happy, and it wasn't that she wasn't these things so much as she was other things too. She was also doubtful and morose and nervous. She didn't realize it at the time, but she really hadn't thought her impending marriage through. She'd felt it, yes, but she hadn't really *thought* it. At twenty-three who's thinking about thirty-three, let alone seventy-three?

Something she couldn't shake was the image of the man who'd saved her from the bees the summer after her father had died. That creased, tanned face; those strong, veiny arms waving the hoe to shoo them off. The unnamed hero who'd materialized and disappeared, just as tens of thousands of other people must have done over the course of her life, but this one she fixated on, obsessed over. Who was he? Where could she find him again?

His face became so much of a preoccupation that she decided to walk that trail again, through the empty fields she'd wandered after her father's death. She didn't fear the bees—she figured they wouldn't be out in wintertime—but even if she had, she would have welcomed them if it meant resummoning that man.

The path looked much different now, but she still knew exactly where to go. She gazed detachedly at the mass of web-like twigs, jutting off from their trunks. In one, she saw a dark ribbon, swaying with the breeze. As she got closer, she realized that it wasn't a ribbon at all, but the tail of a dead squirrel, hanging from a branch like a rogue piece of twine, or any number of other non-alive things that could have so easily become tangled in that crush of brittle twigs. It was thick and full and the instant she recognized the object as part of a dead squirrel, she turned away. If there really are only two types of people in this world, they are surely those who turn away, and those who look for the rest of the body.

When she arrived at the hill over which the gardener had arrived and later ascended, she truly believed she'd see him. Intellectually she knew how improbable it was that he'd be there, not only because of the time of year, but because people don't just stay in one place, waiting for someone else to recapture their lost moment in time. Yet she had a strong premonition that he would be there. She felt herself getting closer to him with every step she took down the path. There was a certainty there that she lacked in pretty much every other area of her life. She would see the man again that day.

So it was a very strange sight for her to see a hill completely devoid of life. He wasn't there. He would not appear. She'd been expecting him to change her direction, to alter her future in a way that she couldn't, or simply wouldn't, put into words. But he was not there to do so, and her return home was spent processing the shock and disappointment of losing a memory that never really was.

Often we believe that the most critical stages of our lives are made up of a series of presences, or rather, the opposite of absences. In Myrtle's case, and in most people's if they'd look, this important time was punctuated by an absence. The man's lack of existence in the time and space that Myrtle willed him to be present set off the course of events that would now become her life. Had he been back on that hill that winter day, Myrtle convinced herself, she would not have married George. She couldn't explain why or how that extreme decision would have been made simply by seeing the gardener; she just knew that it would have.

But again, she didn't see him, and his absence led her directly back to the well-trodden path of matrimony.

She married George, the young man who'd noticed her barefoot at a party, who fixed her shoe, who made her feel as vibrant as the fiery maple trees they walked among, who called her Cinderella. The young man who would never subject his art to society's rejection, who would take up his father's business out of loyalty and fear, whose passionate feelings for her would wane over the years until they were unrecognizable to them both. She married George, and things would not go as they planned.

In February 1910, Myrtle Daniker had no idea what lied ahead of her.

CHAPTER 15

MYRTLE WAS PREGNANT, and she knew it wasn't her husband's baby.

This was the only situation she truly needed to avoid, and yet she hadn't avoided it. If she was to keep as many innocent victims out of her affair as possible, then creating a new innocent victim was the absolute last thing she should have done. This is what she thought, over and over, in the weeks of sickness that kept that baby growing.

Yet in between that guilt and uncertainty danced the happiness of potential. She was going to be a mother. She was going to finally receive the gift she'd resolved to never herself getting. The circumstances were not ideal—her husband was not the father and the father could never be her husband—but somehow she believed that everything would work out in a way that left everyone better off. She and George would have the child they'd so intensely wanted, and maybe that little life would be enough to right their wrongs. Tom could remain out of the picture; he'd already given her that which George could not anyway.

This was optimism in its purest, most delusional form. For one, Tom was not staying out of the picture. He'd called at least twice and come by the garage another time in the weeks that followed their last night at the apartment. She'd hid herself away during his attempts at contact, but she knew she'd have to face him again eventually. It was as inevitable as the developing baby inside of her. As her stomach grew, so would her need to see Tom. But that could wait, she figured. For now she'd gather her strength, like storm clouds swirling dangerously over an unsuspecting, empty ocean.

For another, things with George remained just as bleak and futile as ever. Of course it did; people can't change as easily as they're created. That's one of the more unfair elements of life.

George continued hammering and fixing and filling. These efforts, while not insignificant, he made on behalf of other people and the vehicles that he would himself never own. With so much effort being poured out of him for others, there was nothing left to give to himself nor to the woman hitched to his existence. He was empty, exhausted. He must have forgotten, somewhere down the line, that this was his one shot at living, and maybe it isn't prudent to spend that life in a constant cycle of fixing things destined to die. Or maybe he had it exactly right in doing his part to delay that destiny.

Myrtle alone knew she was pregnant, and while she may not have exercised much sense during the events leading up to this situation, she had enough patience now to understand that sharing her status should wait. Not George nor Tom nor even Catherine needed to know she was pregnant just then. It would become apparent soon enough, so she decided to selfishly guard her secret between her and her child for as long as it'd be physically plausible to do so.

But the clues were telling. Her sickness didn't abate, which, after going on for weeks, led George to allow himself just enough hope to let the idea of fatherhood slide into his thoughts once again.

"Myrtle," he said bravely one morning, "is it possible you're pregnant?"

Already consumed by sickness, there was no room left in Myrtle for more lies. She looked at George with her glazed eyes, pale skin, and cracked lips. "Yes," she said. "I think I am."

"Oh my gosh! Oh my gosh! I knew it! I can't believe it! I knew it!"

His elation made her laugh, before making her cry. This poor man, she thought. This poor, happy man.

"Oh, honey! This is the best news you could have given me!" His smile was so, so wide. "Why didn't you tell me sooner? Have you been to the doctor? When did you know?"

Myrtle's comingled laughter and tears seemed answer enough for George.

"Do you know when it will be born?" he asked. "This is incredible news! Incredible!"

"I don't know much. I have not seen a doctor," she said weakly.

"We will have to make an appointment for you. This is incredible."

Nothing could have cut her deeper than that sort of happiness. To raise his spirits so high, to give him the child he'd dreamed of for so long, but for it to not really be his—could she do it? Would he know? The deferred pain of her prior treachery was intense. It was everything that that sort of pain should have been.

She'd originally thought that she would pretend the baby was George's. She'd let him believe himself the father, but seeing him now, like this, that seemed too cruel. Myrtle was caught between loving him enough to not let him play the fool, and loving him just enough to give him the child he so deeply desired.

"I'm sorry you've been so sick," he said. "Is there anything I can do? That means the baby's healthy, right?"

"I don't know what it means. I don't think there's anything that can help me. Just time. It should go away after the first trimester, I think."

It was the first time she'd spoken about the pregnancy aloud, and she enjoyed the flippant sort of gaiety she felt talking about it. That was an unanticipated joy—talking about the baby.

"I wonder if it will be a boy or a girl," Myrtle mused.

"I don't even care. I bet it's a girl," George said.

"I always wanted a girl."

"I know you did."

"We'll have to get a crib."

"Where will we put the crib?" George asked. "I don't think three of us can fit up here. We'll have to build a bigger place. Maybe out back, in the field."

He would have built it, a home for the three of them, but that baby never would require extra space, or anything at all from George.

"We can't just build a place," Myrtle said.

"We'll figure it out. I'll figure it out. You just rest and don't worry about it. I can't believe it. I just can't believe it," George said, his smile never leaving his face.

This child would be the living, breathing proof of the horrible thing Myrtle had done. And yet it would be so wanted and so loved. Her emotions ricocheted through her body, her self-hatred sounding off loudly in her head, her excitement a soft flutter in her stomach. There was too much to think about, too much to feel.

Luckily the nausea was there to dull the thoughts and feelings, at least for a while. We can only process so much before we shut down. Even the most parched dirt will flood when enough water infiltrates it. Myrtle was flooding.

Summer careened forward, with a sun that burned hotter than Myrtle ever remembered it burning. Eventually the waves of nausea slowed, the tide pulling itself in more slowly, showing signs of its eventual stillness. Myrtle was grateful for the easing of her symptoms, but in their absence emerged a rising hysteria.

George would find out. He would leave her alone with the child. And then what would happen to them? These fears were difficult to suffer during the day, and they panicked her at night. Sometimes she'd scream in her sleep, mostly sounds that George couldn't decipher, except for "Come back! Come back!" Other times she would wake up in the darkness, barely able to breathe, gulping for air and feeling around for her baby.

Through her spiraling panic, she saw the need to shield herself from imminent risk, from her fear that George would leave her and the child. Longing for safety, she craved the security Tom could provide, if he'd only do so. This is what Tom represented in her moment of weakness—an insurance policy that, she believed, would leave her with something when her marriage ended in nothing.

That's how she arrived at the telephone set while George was out purchasing whiskey under the guise of purchasing gasoline. The mounting paranoia, the hot sun, the drifting sickness, and the need for a man to eliminate the inevitable risks of living. Don't dismiss explanations as excuses.

It had been nearly two months, but the digits of his telephone number were tattooed deep in Myrtle's brain, so there was no need for physical, written evidence. She placed the call without a thought of the consequences, without a hint of sadness toward the hard-earned solitary time she'd throw away with the phone call. She wouldn't turn back when she heard the faraway, floating voice on the other end. The magic of technology made feel unreal the very real actions clicking impending disaster into place.

"Buchanan residence," the deep voice spoke.

"May I please speak with Tom?" she asked, wavering, but only a little.

"One moment. May I ask who's calling?"

"Myrtle, from his office."

"One moment."

She wouldn't tell him over the phone. She needed to see and feel his reaction face-to-face. Her news would alter everything. Or, as she just now realized, maybe it would alter nothing.

"Myrtle, is that you?" Tom asked, sounding nearly as panicked as she felt.

"Yes," she said, steadying her voice, unsure what to say. What words of hers could she trade for his commitment?

"I'm so glad you called," Tom said hurriedly. "I hope this means you'll accept my apology. I'm so sorry, Myrtle. I've been going crazy without you. I never wanted to hurt you, and it will never happen again. I promise you."

He spoke in rushed, hushed tones that made Myrtle think that Daisy must have been close. She longed for the closeness of Tom, of Daisy, of anyone.

"I know that you're sorry," she said, just as quietly. "You had somebody else."

"I hate myself for doing that to you," Tom said. "She's gone. There's no one else. Please let me make it up to you. Can we see each other again and try to get back to how we were before I fucked it all up?"

It was this man's baby inside of her, a man who already had a child, a wife, and an entire life disembodied from hers. But it was that life that Myrtle wanted, and maybe the child inside of her would help her get it, could help Myrtle unzip herself from her own disappointing skin and climb instead into someone like Daisy's.

"Yes," Myrtle said. "I have something I need to tell you. I want to tell you in person."

"Wonderful," Tom said, just steps from Daisy. "Thursday at the apartment? Around lunchtime?"

"Sure, Thursday at lunchtime."

"Thank you for giving me another chance. I think we have something really special here. I hate that I almost ruined it. I really do."

"I'll see you Thursday," she said, replacing the receiver.

"Was that the doctor?" Myrtle jumped at the sound of George's voice. Her time without Tom had made her forget the panicked, terrified feeling of nearly being found out. She was reminded by the tickle in the back of her hands, the blood stopping its course out of fear.

"Yes," she lied, because what else was she supposed to say? "I made an appointment for Thursday."

"Great. Is that something the father usually goes to?" George asked.

"No, I don't think so. Just routine. Probably very boring, where they'll check me out to make sure everything is going the way it should."

"Okay," he said. "I don't mind going along."

"I'll be fine—you stay here. I'll probably make a day of it, since I'll have to go into the city anyway. I'll visit Catherine and come back that evening."

"All right." He descended beneath the metal blanket of the Chevrolet's hood, his expression—did he look disappointed? Suspicious?—blocked from Myrtle's view.

She'd succumbed to her moment of weakness, and yet everything still seemed fine. She'd escaped unscathed, she told herself, almost as a congratulations, but also as an apology. A euphoric buzz welled up inside her, energizing her, propelling her blissfully forward on her fatal track. It took her a minute to understand that the excited feelings were for Tom, and when she remembered that, the buzz shriveled back into its invisible hiding space, punctured by the dependency she reluctantly harbored.

Making dinner that night, while gazing out the window where the little dog had been but had never returned, Myrtle accidentally cut herself. She didn't run for a towel, though, or turn on the faucet. She watched herself bleed. The blood slowly oozing down her finger, into her palm. It stung, but she wanted it to sting. At last, as the thin crimson stream reached her inner wrist, where turquoise tubes throbbed more blood upward, she turned on the faucet and poured cold water over her sliced hand as calmly as she cleaned the dishes each night. Eventually the blood stopped coming, deciding instead to sink back into her flesh.

On Thursday morning, George woke up early to prepare their coffee, an effort made as a sort of offering to Myrtle and the baby. He believed that boiling water and straining ground coffee was taking care of his family.

"Let me know what the doctor says," George said as Myrtle hurried out of the garage.

"I will." Myrtle looked back at George's excited face and stopped. This was the man she had fallen in love with, a man capable of emotion and care, even though he'd hidden it for so long. And all it took for her to find him again was becoming pregnant with another man's baby. Had she known that walking away right then would hasten the end of her life, she surely would have stayed. She nearly stayed anyway.

Her stomach was still flat, or at least as flat as it had been before becoming pregnant. There was no visible indication that a fetus curled up inside her, deep within her tissue and organs. She didn't need to tell Tom. She was nervous to. Nearly everything to do with Tom made Myrtle nervous, but informing someone that their genes had been passed onto another little human being was an especially delicate task. Their being married to other people twisted things even further away from a place of comfort.

When she got off the subway in the city, Myrtle didn't recognize the buildings outside. She kept glancing around, searching for something familiar to latch onto, but finding nothing she knew. The heat reflected up off the white sidewalk, almost mummifying her, melting her thoughts with a fever that was equally likely to be real or imagined. Finally she realized that she'd gotten off the subway a stop too early. This was not Tom's neighborhood, or rather, not Tom's clandestine affair neighborhood. This was an innocent place, with no meaning whatsoever to Myrtle.

She couldn't decide whether she should get back on the subway and ride it to the stop she knew, or if she should walk the remaining blocks to the apartment. She sat down on a wrought iron chair outside of a coffee shop, astonished at both the heat and her inability to make such a simple decision. The apartment couldn't be more than ten or eleven blocks away, and the subway was so crowded. If only it wasn't so hot. She, like most everyone in New York City that summer, blamed everything on the heat. Myrtle reluctantly returned to the subway, riding it to the familiar stop where she'd encounter the boiling air again, but would be closer to her destination.

When she made it to the apartment, sweat beading on her forehead and her hair matted against the back of her neck, the first thing she noticed wasn't that Tom was there, but that TJ was gone. She'd expected to hear the puppy's yapping when she knocked on the door, to see his wobbly, furry body bouncing up and down when she entered, but the little dog wasn't there. A flash of grief hit her, as she believed that Tom had let him die. Whether intentionally or by negligence, she was convinced, in that flash, that her lover's actions resulted in the death of the animal for which they'd assumed responsibility. This did not bode well for telling him that they'd soon be responsible for a child.

"Are you looking for the dog?" Tom asked, disappointed that she didn't look excited to see him. "I gave him to the McKees. They were only too eager to take that little mutt. Don't look so sad. You can visit, I'm sure."

Myrtle looked bewildered as the flash of grief dissipated into confusion. She wondered, quite earnestly, why she was there.

"I missed you so much," he said, taking her body gently in his arms. Like earlier, when she exited the subway a stop too soon and couldn't decide whether to walk or ride, or maybe like for years, Myrtle couldn't make a choice. She couldn't decide not to yield to him, and so she did. They fell back into the unspoken language they best knew as a couple. Myrtle remained silent while he kissed and undressed her. Tom showed her he needed her forgiveness and acceptance.

But he'd brought someone else here, to that bed. Daisy hadn't been enough, and why would Myrtle have ever thought that she, with her lack of everything that Daisy had, could be enough herself? For men like Tom, though, it wasn't a matter of women being sufficient so much as them being so insufficient on their own. But Myrtle couldn't know that, and so she thought jealously of this other woman who'd been in the bed where she lied, and how she'd gotten there because Myrtle and Daisy weren't enough.

"We haven't seen each other in a while," Tom said. "How have you been? What have you been up to?"

She wanted to tell him that she'd been sick and miserable because she was pregnant with his baby. That her nose kept on bleeding every time she threw up at the beginning because he'd hit her. That she felt worthless to him because he took another woman here. That she'd been strong, at first, resisting him, but she always knew she'd weaken. She'd tell herself it wasn't weakness, no; it was what she wanted. But what she really wanted was to be able to say his wife's name. Daisy.

"Not much," she said. She couldn't tell him. She couldn't tell him anything at all, let alone that she was pregnant with his child.

"I've missed you," Tom continued. "The way you think and see the world, it's different from everyone I know. You don't think like anyone else."

"No one thinks like anyone else," Myrtle said simply.

"That's where you're wrong," Tom insisted. "*Everyone* thinks like everyone else."

"I'm not that interesting. I sit in a garage—my husband's garage," she said deliberately. "Waiting for things to happen that are never going to happen."

"What sorts of things are you waiting to happen?" Tom asked.

"It just seems that at some point I lost control of my life. Maybe it's just an illusion we have as children, but it seemed like we had choices back then. There were options. Then I grew up and the options went away. Now it's like I'm on a raft, being carried along by a river, and I can't get off. The current isn't even very strong, but still I won't get off."

Myrtle's eyes welled with tears. Tears for her lack of options and tears for her frustration at herself for not being able to make the right choices when presented with them. She couldn't look at herself objectively—nobody can—but still she wondered how she got there.

Tom had expected her to hold a bit of a grudge but to ultimately be happy to see him. He did not expect this. But that was Myrtle's appeal to him. He knew every word out of Daisy's mouth before she said it. He knew what would be served at dinner that night and what everyone would be wearing. Myrtle was something he didn't expect.

"You didn't give the McKees TJ's collar," Myrtle said, wiping her eyes and gesturing toward the dog's collar on the dresser.

"I guess I forgot," Tom said. "They got their own anyway—I saw them walking him this morning. Oh, and they changed his name. It's not TJ anymore. Lord knows what nonsensical moniker they came up with for him, though. Want the collar as a souvenir? A memento of your two hours as a dog owner?"

He didn't mean it as a slight, of course. He was poking as much fun at himself as her, making a joke about their inability to care for another living creature for very long. He was annoyed that she didn't take the remarks with the levity he'd intended.

"That's a mean thing to say," Myrtle said, the tears coming back. "As if it's my fault we don't have the dog. I would have taken great care of him. Still will."

"It's the McKees' now," Tom said. "You should see the way she fusses over him. Like he's a child."

"I *will* take the collar home with me."

"Fine. Never know when you'll want to adopt another dog off the side of the road."

"That's not funny," Myrtle said.

"I didn't intend for it to be."

"I should go."

"Oh come on," Tom said, finally noticing the anger in her voice. "We're kidding around. Who cares about the dog?"

"I did, and you just got rid of him, like he was old bread or something."

"I needed to do something with him. I couldn't take him home—Daisy's allergic to dogs—and I'm not here often enough to take care of him. He has a better life with the McKees. We can visit him if you want."

"I miss him," she said. She did. She hadn't thought about the dog much at her own home, but here she felt his absence. Here there was something missing.

"It's a miracle that you made it this far in life, Myrtle," Tom said.

"Because I miss the dog?"

"Because you're too . . . open to things. You're like a giant sponge, eager to suck up everything around it. And I love you for it."

He'd never said he loved her. She'd craved this so badly before, but now she felt it was too late. Whether it was because she had new insight because of the baby or because he'd betrayed her with another woman, something was different now. She knew she couldn't fully possess his love, and so she'd instead hold onto the knowledge that his child was within her. She would not tell him. She'd instead hold the secret that she could possess.

When Myrtle left the apartment later that afternoon, she grabbed TJ's collar; to her his name would always be TJ. She didn't know what she would do with it, only that she wanted to have it with her. Maybe it was as Tom had said, it was a souvenir, a memento, but not of the dog. It was the physical proof of her time with Tom. A reminder that the feelings she experienced in this apartment really occurred, even when, from the distance of her home above the garage, they felt like hallucinations.

It was almost as if she knew it was the last time she'd ever see that apartment.

CHAPTER 16

SHE PROBABLY SHOULD HAVE put the dog collar in a drawer. Or buried it in the closet or the pantry, where George would never look. There were many places she could have stashed it, should have stashed it, but on top of their dresser was not one of them.

Some will say she did it on purpose, that she wanted to get caught. Others will say it was her mounting hysteria, that Myrtle wasn't in her right mind those days. The truth to why she placed the collar on top of the dresser she shared with her husband could be in the middle of those two theories. Or it could lie somewhere else entirely.

Cocoon-like inside a slip of white tissue paper, the collar had no place in their home. It was a foreign object, a curious object, and when people come across foreign, curious objects inside their homes, equilibriums shift and suspicions arise.

Inevitably, George came across that curious object. When he saw the tissue paper cocoon lying on the dresser, he assumed it was something Myrtle had bought for the baby. Probably a rattle, or maybe a bottle. Most things he saw these days reminded him that he'd soon be a father.

It didn't occur to him that he should not know what was wrapped inside; that he'd be better off not knowing. He did not fathom that anything so small and delicately wrapped could have the potential to hurt him. So when he picked up the small package and carefully unrolled its tissue paper blanket, expecting to see something related to his expanding family inside, it was not so much shocking to George as gently puzzling to find a dog's collar within.

Myrtle sat outside, beneath bubbly, coral-like clouds that dotted the blazing sky. She thought of Tom, she thought of the baby, she thought of many things, but she did not think that this would be the second to last time she'd ever be outside in her life.

"Myrtle, why do you have a dog's collar?" George asked, holding the object away from his body like it was the nocuous thing that it actually was. He didn't yet know what it symbolized, but he feared it. We talk so much about women's intuition, but men have intuition too. George knew that this object would change everything, and he asked her how, in spite of not wanting to know.

Myrtle didn't like lying, at least not to other people. She'd become pretty comfortable with lying to herself. Even those who pride themselves at being authentic and self-aware individuals are exceptional self-liars. They're the most exceptional self-liars of them all.

Myrtle, too, had her blind spots. There were things about herself that she just couldn't see, either because the positioning of the outside world wouldn't let her, or she didn't know she needed to readjust her internal mirrors. With so much unseen, it's impossible to ever be completely honest with ourselves. If anything, this should make us more sympathetic characters, but we get held up with the "character" part, and then the sympathy just won't come.

"That?" she said, forming the lie to preserve her deceit. "That was something Catherine got from her store. I guess it was returned or something and somehow she ended up with it. She asked if I wanted it since she obviously can't have a dog at the hotel, and I said sure. Why not."

"You've never mentioned wanting to get a dog," he said.

"No, but with the baby, maybe we'll want a dog. It's not a big deal. She had the collar and offered it to me, and I took it."

George heard her answer, but his suspicions, vague at first, were swirling into clarity. There was no reason for George to find a collar on his dresser and assume his wife was having an affair. Like in a word search, when you're hunting among all those randomly placed letters for the right sequence, and then—bam! There it is. You can't unsee the word. It's risen from the chaos of the letters and revealed itself to you. There's no going back now; the word has been found and it is forever so. So it was for George just then. The fact that his wife was having an affair rose from the chaos of all the possible random suspicions. There was no going back now. He knew.

Many will judge Myrtle based on this single episode. Her life would be defined by the affair—that quick, deviant event in an existence otherwise full of kindness, goodness, and other traits we don't associate with the kinds of people who have extramarital affairs.

"I'm going upstairs to make lunch," she said, to get away from having to make up more lies.

George let her go, let her lie to him, let her devastate the life he was so eager to begin with the baby. Oh God, he thought.

The baby. It was too terrible an option to consider, but what if the baby Myrtle was pregnant with was not his?

He slid to the greasy floor, leaning against the Chevy that he couldn't seem to fix, no matter how many tactics he tried. He could not unknow this knowledge, could not unsee the word. His wife was having an affair, and everything that he thought was settled was ripped out of place. The contents of his life may as well have been stuffed into a bag and thrown from a window of a train. Scattered, missing, gone—he finally understood how life can change in an instant.

The baby. Our baby, he thought. *My baby, my baby, my baby.* We were so close. So close to the finish line. How could she have gone and done this?

The easiest emotion for human beings to process is not sadness or grief. It's anger. Looking for a way out from under the incredible pain that filled him, George shifted to anger. To rage. To hatred for his wife and the careless way she'd decimated all he'd believed they'd had.

What a vile woman to have let another man touch her. And not just touch her, because he knew how these things went. She'd let him fuck her, had let him stick his penis into the depths of her that should have only been for him and ejaculate his sperm so that this other man, this other depraved, humiliating man, could create a new life inside her. All of these disgusting, unbearable things had gone on inside her. Inside of his wife.

The heat of his blood matched the heat of the mercury in the thermometer hanging on the wall. Just above the new box of whiskey. Everything looked so different now to George. He closed his eyes because blackness was all he could stand to look at.

Hadn't they been happy? Hadn't they lived the type of life that everyone wanted to live? They had everything they were supposed to have—a home, a steady income, a peaceful marriage. Soon they'd have a child. More couldn't be the answer. Enough should have been the answer.

George felt sick, victimized, but fueled by his anger. He felt he'd trusted the wrong person with his life, and it wasn't until he'd articulated this thought that it hit him—why had he trusted anyone else with his life?

If it was another time or culture or man, George might have considered the possibility of divorce. He may have abandoned Myrtle right then and there and let her fend for herself. She'd caused this with her decisions and actions; she could live with the consequences. He wanted her to suffer. He wanted her to suffer as much as or more than he did, but his marriage to Myrtle was as permanent as his own body. Only an act of physical warfare—not emotional—could sever their relationship.

They would remain married, he knew, but she'd have to sacrifice—if not their marriage, then he'd take other things that had more value to her. He'd destroy this man, whoever he was, and he'd destroy any delusions Myrtle may have been holding onto of her own goodness. He'd make her hate herself as much as he hated her.

George was done with the silence. He had no need for it anymore. He'd lived it for years, and it had brought him here, to the trapdoor of his marriage that had just opened up beneath him. It wasn't that he was braver or stronger now, he was just so damn hurt. He was so hurt and so angry, and all he could think of doing was transferring that pain to Myrtle.

Upstairs she was making lunch, so upstairs he went. He was oddly calm creeping up the stairs—and creep he did, because he didn't want her to hear him coming. He was still oddly calm opening the door, slowly, so as not to cause friction between the hinges sliding against one another, building the creaking sound it nearly always made. The calm went away when he saw her, buttering bread as if this were any other day and she hadn't been fucking someone else and hadn't just razed the comfortable life they'd led. The calm was gone, and there was nothing left inside him except fury and emptiness.

"I know what you've been doing. I know!" He didn't need her to confirm what he now felt certain of, but still, perversely, he wanted to hear her say it.

"What are you talking about?" Myrtle asked, fearful of this intensity she'd never felt from him.

"Who is he? Who've you been cheating with?" He grabbed her roughly by the arm, their faces so close they could kiss.

Myrtle didn't know how he'd found out, but George knew. She would never get the opportunity to confess or to end the affair on her own and make it all go away. She'd thought it had all been within her control, and now it was taken away from her.

"I don't know what you're talking about!" she yelled back, scared of what George might do next.

"The phone calls, the dog collar, going round all the time. I know, you little whore, just say it!"

"There's nothing to say! I'm not cheating!"

"Just say it! Just tell me the fucking truth!" George slapped her hard across the face. "Say it!"

His eyes were crazed, so full of hatred that Myrtle didn't recognize them as George's. This wasn't the man that drove someone who was down on his luck to a job interview, the man she didn't think capable of murder. This man was full of rage beyond anything she'd ever seen in him. And yet, this man was still her husband.

"Keep hitting me," she said. "Keep hitting me, George. Does that make you feel better?"

"I knew it. I knew something wasn't right with you. But I didn't think you were capable of this. I didn't think you'd stoop so low. How could you have done this?" George was screaming so loudly now that he disrupted the conversation among the short-skirted, bare-legged trio of women loitering outside Michaelis's restaurant.

Myrtle didn't speak.

"How could you do this?" he asked again. Then he hit her again. "Answer me!"

Myrtle still didn't speak. He hit her again, harder, and again, harder than that. Her silence enraged him further, and he forgot all about the baby that would never be. Needing a witness to her betrayal, he yanked her through the bedroom door and dragged her to the window.

"You might fool me, but you can't fool God," he said, pointing to the billboard bathed in the ginormous blue eyes and yellow frames of Dr. T. J. Eckleburg. "God knows what you've been doing, everything you've been doing. You may fool me, but you can't fool God. He sees everything."

George was acting insane, and she feared for her life. But looking into the eyes of Dr. T. J. Eckleburg, the orbs that had looked over her for so long, she gave in. She'd been found out for exactly who she was. She would accept the consequences. She would make it so they could go on living above the garage, beneath the gaze of those gigantic blue eyes, just as they always had, and, she thought, as they always would.

"What do you want to know?" she asked quietly. "What can I tell you that's going to make you feel any better?"

"Who is it?"

"No. I won't tell you that." He smacked her again.

"Is it someone I know?" George demanded.

"No."

"How long?"

"Months. But it's over. It's been over."

"The baby . . ."

"I don't know," Myrtle said.

He started to cry, and she continued to cry. Each of their pain, so different, mirrored in the other's tears.

"How could you do this? How could you do this?" George cried desperately.

"I don't know," Myrtle said, the bats flap, flapping in her stomach. She hated herself nearly as much as George hated her.

"You don't know," he said.

"I didn't plan it; it just happened. I've felt so bad, George. I'm sorry. I'm sorry. I don't know what to say. I'm sorry."

"You're sorry."

"I am."

"So sorry that you kept doing it, over and over, for months."

"Don't say it like that."

"I'll say it however the fuck I please," George said. "You don't run the show around here anymore, Myrtle. You're done."

"I'm sorry," she said again. Except she wasn't, and she was conscious of just how un-sorry she was each time she said that she was. Myrtle was angry too. She was angry for the years she'd tried to connect with George but was met with silence. She was angry that he chose alcohol, again and again, over her. She was angry that he'd given up his dreams—which had become her dreams—and she was angry that he could beat her without guilt or regret.

"I want to know why this happened," George said.

"So do I," Myrtle replied.

He pushed her down onto the bed. "Don't give me lip. Tell me why you did this."

"Are you actually going to listen to me?"

"I've been listening this whole time."

"Oh really? Because I don't remember you listening all those nights I tried to talk to you when you were passed out drunk. I don't remember you listening to me for years, actually. I have tried, George. I have tried to make the most of our situation here. I was okay with moving here when your dad got sick—when it was a temporary situation. I supported you, I took care of him, and I did not complain about it. But then it wasn't temporary anymore. You stopped listening to me and what I wanted. Everything we'd planned—you just threw it out the window. We were going to move west, you were going to paint, I was willing to go to work and do what I could to get your painting up and running. We were going to live the kind of lives we *wanted*, and then you just stopped. You gave up. We stayed here, and I begged you to get us out of here, but you wouldn't listen. You never listen to me. So funny that now you tell me you've been listening this whole time."

"It's been so hard for you, right?" George yelled. "Being taken care of. Not having to lift a finger all these years."

"I've been miserable all these years, and who do you think makes all your meals and cleans the house and keeps everything going? Yeah, but I haven't lifted a finger. It was supposed to be different, George. Our lives were supposed to be *different*. We were supposed to get out of here. You didn't used to want this. You didn't want to work in a garage like your dad did. You hated the thought! But here we are, and I've been miserable and you didn't want to see it and so yes, when I had another opportunity, I took it."

It was a strange time for him to rethink his past decisions, or rather indecisions, and it was amazing that his burning, furious mind could open up enough to allow in the idea that maybe he did play a role in creating this wreck. Maybe stagnancy wasn't a synonym for peace after all. Maybe what he'd thought of as tranquility was really the paralysis of their lives rotting away.

"An opportunity," George said. "That's what you call it. You fuck someone else and go against the vows we made before our families and God, and you call it an opportunity."

He had to continue disparaging her because it's what she deserved, the absolute minimum punishment he felt her crime warranted. He was justified, he believed, in hurting her in every conceivable way. But he heard her. What she said or how she said it or because she'd started a relationship with someone else—one of these, or a combination of these things, reached the version of him he'd been when they'd first met fourteen years ago. Moving far away seemed like the only answer to the question of how they could ever forget that this had happened. Pure and simple, they'd have to run away from the problem.

"I'm going to get you away from that opportunity," George decided. "We're leaving. You're never going to see him again. We're getting out of here."

"It's too late," she said. Myrtle had gotten what she originally wanted—an escape from her life above the garage, where she waited for George to fix what was broken. But she'd already escaped, and now George could not fix it.

"This is what you wanted," he continued. "We're moving. As soon as I make arrangements here, we're moving. Until then, you're not to leave this room."

"What, are you going to keep me locked up?" Myrtle asked.

"Until we move. You are not leaving this room."

"You think moving is the answer now? This is your reaction? It's too late. You can't recapture the past."

"Of course not," George answered. "But we can start something new."

"We're too old for new; we've been through too much. You spent years talking yourself out of this—you can't just undo that. You can't undo all the bad things we've done to each other."

"Done to each other? I'm not the one who had the affair. I'm not the one who lied and cheated."

"I did," Myrtle said. "You're right. I did a horrible thing and believe me, I'm ashamed. But you abandoned me years ago. You gave up. And now you're blaming me because I finally gave up too. I hung in there for years, George. I was fighting for us when all you could do was get so drunk you couldn't even function, let alone keep up your half of the marriage."

"Yeah, you're the victim here. With your cushy life and freedom from responsibility—freedom from everything—you're the victim. You're too much, Myrtle. You're too fucking much. Such a spoiled little bitch."

"I'm grateful for the—"

"Shut up!" George shouted. "You've said enough. Start packing, we're leaving as soon as I get things squared away here."

"I'm not going anywhere." You can't live forever, she thought. You can't live forever. If only that hadn't crossed her mind then, or months ago on the subway. Everything would be different; everything would have been the same.

"The hell you're not," George answered.

"I don't want to go with you," Myrtle said firmly.

"I don't give a fuck what you want anymore."

"You never did."

"Don't you tell me what I thought," he said, the anger mounting again. He caught Dr. T. J. Eckleburg's sinister eyes as he turned to beat her. Eckleburg approved and encouraged. As men, George thought, they were in this together.

Except for the man who caused this. Her "opportunity." George thought of this faceless man and punched Myrtle in the eye. He'd take out on her what he couldn't do to him.

"You won't fuck up this family," he said. "I won't let you."

Myrtle started to shout that the family wasn't his to begin with, but her pity toward George was stronger than her fury. She wasn't so cruel a woman that she'd give words to the knife she'd already stuck into him.

Out of the corner of his eye, George glimpsed the fading yellow of the doctor's glasses. He backed away from Myrtle and the decay of their marriage. Both husband and wife knew that this was the end of something, but what? They would go on together, had to go on together. They would beat on, boats borne ceaselessly into the current and wherever that took them.

On his way out of the room, George ripped out the door-knob, locking Myrtle inside. He listened to his wife's cries, her frantic pleas. To him. She was pleading to him. He spent several moments in the darkness of his shuttered eyelids before grabbing enough courage to walk away from her, down the stairs to the garage that had held them both hostage for too long.

CHAPTER 17

Density. Density is why hot air rises. Hot air is less dense than cold air, and so all that heat floats upward, as if trying to escape the confines of the normal, everyday air below. As temperatures climb, molecules get restless, zipping around faster and faster, expanding mass and lowering density. And so it rises, all that stifling heat, so stifled already itself.

By the time the hottest day of the year arrived, Myrtle had been locked upstairs with all that heated-up air for two days. Both of them—Myrtle and the ascending air—were wretched and cramped, wishing to break through the collection of molecules that entrapped them.

George's patterns over the past two days more or less mirrored those of the air molecules. He zipped through the garage, packing up this, throwing away that, essentially eliminating the lives he and Myrtle had led over the past decade. He would erase it all, and maybe then their original feelings for each other would find the room to come back.

But Myrtle didn't see George's zipping; she only heard the sounds of boxes thudding and tape ripping and trash barrels scraping the cement. The sounds that punctuated chapters, ending what had been and economizing what was about to be. He'd said, over and over, that they were leaving, and yet she didn't fully believe it. She'd known the entwined lives of Myrtle and George as living there, above the garage, among the ashes, for so long that it didn't seem that any other way was possible. What was possible had been the exclusive domain of her imagination for each of those years, and it never escaped the collection of molecules that made up her brain.

He'd beaten her the most the previous night. She'd focused her stare on the cloudy streaks of tissue paper on her bureau. The sheets that had held TJ's collar, which now seemed like an archaeological relic of another time and culture, and not an accessory of the affair that seemed so chimerical, so illogical, so not her own. Her face was once again bloody and swollen, and she thought that maybe that would be enough for George, for her wounds to be formed by his hands this time.

Looking at her, you might think she'd resolved herself to her husband's possession and will. Her lack of movement, her hollow eyes, they could have easily been mistaken for signs that she'd given up. Inside, though, her molecules zipped faster than the hottest air, darting furiously through her, beating against the thin film of what was left of her sanity.

Not long ago, Tom had said he'd loved her. Yet here she was. Some moments, she thought it was where she deserved to be. In others, that *more* that Myrtle strived for would rear its uncomplacent head, fueling desperate attempts at an escape. She'd ripped out the window screen, but while she could endanger her own life, she couldn't risk the other's inside her. When George entered the room, he'd pass through a door-frame scratched by clawing fingernails. The efforts hurt her, exhausted her, but led her nowhere.

For Myrtle, time was measured by the suffocation of the heat. When the barely detectable breeze chilled the beaded sweat on her arms and legs, awakening her from her hard-earned sleep, that meant it was nearly dawn. When the heat transcended atmosphere and became a dimension, a full-body bandage so thick and sultry that it drowned the pores, that meant it must be late afternoon. It was somewhere in the middle when George entered the room, passing through the clawed doorframe, looking like the ghost of his father before he died.

"Soon," he said. "I'm getting it all together. If you want those clothes of yours, you'd better pack 'em."

"I'm not going anywhere with you," Myrtle said quietly.

"Yes you are, and we're getting out of here soon."

"I'm not going."

"It's not up to you. You're my wife and you're going where I go."

"You look terrible. You need to sit down and rest and think about this."

"I've thought about it plenty," George said. "We're getting away from here and you're going whether you like it or not."

"I'm not afraid of you, you know."

"I don't care what you are anymore, or what you aren't. But we're going together all the same."

"You don't care that your wife doesn't want to go with you?" Myrtle asked. "That you have to force someone to be with you? We don't love each other anymore. What's the point?"

"You don't love me?" he asked, sounding like the child they never had, would never have. He'd already been so hurt by

Myrtle, so thoroughly beaten down in every way by her but physically, and yet he still felt the sharp pang of her insult. "You don't know what you're talking about anymore."

"I know exactly what I'm talking about, and all I want is to get away from here, away from you. I want to leave, but I'm not leaving with you." She'd grown to hate him. The slow-brewed indifference had fermented into hatred over the past two days. A potent hatred that couldn't stand the sight of the ghost of the man who she was tied to.

"It ain't up to you," George said.

"My life isn't up to me?"

"No, you lost that privilege, Myrtle. I gave you too much freedom. I let you run around all you wanted, and look what happened. You turned into a little whore. You won't do any more running around, I'll tell you that."

"I'd do it again," she said. "I'd do anything to get away from you."

He made the familiar motion of slapping the palm of his hand across her face. He tried never to touch her stomach, the baby he still hoped was his. "You'll watch your mouth is what you'll do. I've had it."

"Just keep hitting me, George. It's all you know how to do."

"Fuck you, Myrtle. We're leaving day after tomorrow."

"I'm not going," she said.

"It's funny, the way you think you have a choice about anything."

He turned the latch from the other side of the door, the one with the torn-out knob on the other side of the scratched frame. He shook with anger and grief and sickness, and no one looking at him would be able to tell where one ended and the other began. He was one large shaking blob of anger and grief and sickness.

George picked up the phone in his office, the one Myrtle had used to call Tom so many times. He called the same numbers as she had, not knowing that the sequence had been called before. He had no reason to think that the invisible connection between the mouthpiece in his hand and Tom Buchanan's home, wherever that might be, had been made so frequently, if ever.

"Buchanan residence," said the voice Myrtle had heard so many times.

"I'm looking to talk with Tom Buchanan," George said. He waited in embarrassment. He didn't want to feel like a charity case, didn't want to ask for a handout, but he needed money now. Tom had what he needed, and George would beg if he had to.

"Hello?" Tom answered irritably.

"This is George Wilson, down at the garage. I've been waiting on that car for too long. I need it now; can you bring it down this afternoon?"

"You're interrupting my lunch to inquire after my car? I'll sell it to you when I'm good and ready."

"Listen, I need it today," George said, his voice cracking. "I need to fix it up for something. I've got a buyer, and I need it now."

"Now isn't happening."

"Dammit, Tom! You said you'd sell me that car months ago!"

"Very well, then, I won't sell you the car at all." It took much less for a man like Tom Buchanan to take his ball and go home.

"You gave me your word!" George shouted.

"I'm under no obligations to you at all."

"We had a verbal agreement. I've had the money here for weeks, waiting on you."

"Well you're going to have to wait even longer now, aren't you? And as for your bothering me about it at lunchtime, I won't stand that at all!"

"I need the car, Tom. What good is it to you anymore, anyway?" But there was no use; Tom had already hung up the phone, leaving George in the familiar position of not being listened to. Both he and his wife were desperate for more from Tom than he could give. Or rather, what he could give, but refused to.

Upstairs, Myrtle leaned back against the bed's headboard. Even though her movement had been limited for the past few days, she was exhausted. It felt good to relax the weight of her body against the solid wood, allowing it to absorb the pressure of her tissue and bones. She wondered how she'd lived so long with such a tattered bedspread. How had she never noticed the tear in the corner? The gauzy batting was leaking out of it, and she'd never noticed. Where had she been, she thought. How had she spent so many hundreds—no, it must have been thousands—of nights under a bedspread whose batting was leaking out without ever giving it a second of thought? She was angry at herself for wasting so much time dreaming of what never would be when there was leaking bedspread batting to contend with.

From her position on the bed, she was watched by a single eye belonging to Dr. T. J. Eckleburg. It was not the other way around. She did not watch him; he watched her. It was a strange sensation, to be stared at by a flat, painted-on eye, and although the billboard had stood for years, the eye, at least the single one slanting its gaze upon her, felt lascivious and alive in a way that felt different from his usual passive judgment.

After several minutes of staring each other down, Myrtle felt a tinge of excitement at being watched. Someone was seeing her; never mind that that someone was a faded painting of a doctor in Queens. She leaned forward, lying on her stomach, still flat enough to conceal what she carried inside, still meeting Eckleburg's gaze. She liked the feel of the mattress beneath her, and she rubbed herself against it to make the feeling grow. She just wanted to feel good, to escape the pain and defeat. Just let her feel good again.

Dr. T. J. Eckleburg watched her rock forward and back, faster and faster, that single blue eye unblinking and wooden, but still, it was all that she had to watch her. She kept her eyes open and on his, until she couldn't any longer. She fell forward into the obscurity of her shut eyelids.

Downstairs George drank from a bottle that he'd half-hid in a cupboard Myrtle had reason to open. He drank to provoke his thirst. He drank and he packed, drank and packed. All the while his body burned with a fever that he pretended was not there. It begged him for rest, but he kept going—if he stopped, he thought, the distractions would cease. Nothing seemed so terrifying as a life free of distractions.

A little while later, a huge, creamy yellow Rolls-Royce pulled abruptly into his lot, beige dust inflating like a tent behind it. George recognized two of the three people congested into the front seat. Tom drove, and the man who'd accompanied him a couple months ago sat in the passenger seat. A pretty young woman sat wedged between them, but the fever kept him from recognizing her as pretty.

"Let's have some gas. What do you think we stopped for—to admire the view?" Tom said sharply. He didn't want to be there right then, but the car was nearing empty, and this was the only stop for gas for miles. He didn't want to think about or see his own mistress, as he'd just caught on that his own wife loved another. It was preposterous, that she could love another. And yet she did. "All that money for flamboyant parties and the man can't keep his tank even a quarter full," Tom muttered under his breath.

George stumbled over to Tom and the new car he was driving. "You changed your mind about the car," he said weakly. "I'm sick. Been sick all day."

"What's the matter?" Tom asked.

"I'm all run-down."

"Well, shall I help myself? You sounded well enough on the phone."

George stepped into the blinding beam of the sun, which illuminated his pitted, sallow skin and the dark, drooping bags under his eyes. Tom was shocked by the change in his appearance.

"I didn't mean to interrupt your lunch, but I need money pretty bad, and I was wondering what you were going to do with your old car," George said, reverently unscrewing the gas cap on the Rolls-Royce.

"How do you like this one? I bought it last week," Tom lied. It was not his car.

"It's a nice yellow one."

"Like to buy it?" Tom asked. He liked to play with his prey, and right now he was desperate to attack someone.

"Big chance," George said. "No, but I could make some money on the other."

"What do you want money for, all of a sudden?"

"I've been here too long. I want to get away. My wife and I want to go west," George said, regaining some life through peeks at the car's green leather interior.

"Your wife does!" Tom's efforts at self-control cracked. He couldn't lose both Myrtle and Daisy. He couldn't lose.

"She's been talking about it for ten years," George continued. "And now she's going whether she wants to or not. I'm going to get her away."

"What do I owe you?" Tom asked, looking almost frantically up at the window. Where was Myrtle?

"I just got wised up to something funny the last two days. That's why I been bothering you about the car."

"What do I owe you?" Tom repeated, eyes still darting up toward the empty window.

"Dollar twenty."

George could not have known that he and Tom were linked by identical discoveries. That Tom had just detected that Daisy was in love with another man—the Gatsby with the swans in the pool, in fact. George looked how Tom felt, and the bigger man, the privileged man, took pity on his rival.

"I'll let you have that car," Tom said gently. "I'll send it over tomorrow afternoon."

"Thank you. I've got the money for you already. This is going to help me out—I'm going to be able to get her away."

George didn't surmise, then or ever, that Tom was the impetus for his desperation to move away. He hadn't identified Myrtle's lover, but men like Tom seemed as out of reach to people like him and Myrtle as the wispy clouds in the sky. As it had many times before and would many times again, Tom's money shielded him from suspicion.

The bedroom window above the garage stared wide open, like an eye, and Myrtle was the pupil. She saw Tom, this new car, and Nick, the man who couldn't possibly live next door to Gatsby. But the figure that riveted her in jealous terror was the pretty young woman seated in the middle. The woman who Myrtle was certain was Daisy Buchanan. She would never know that the woman was not Daisy, but was Jordan Baker, a friend of Daisy's who Nick had been seeing.

Myrtle had thought a lot about Daisy, feelings that jumped from extreme compunction to reckless envy. Those feelings had all been very real, but not as real as seeing Daisy—or at least the woman Myrtle believed to be Daisy—in the flesh. Now she felt madness.

There in the car was the body—never mind the soul—that kept Myrtle from her desired destination. Her own body, so throbbing with life that it housed two human beings, seemed too shallow a vessel to hold the intense jealousy that crazed her. Myrtle wanted to leap out of that window, to pounce onto Daisy and become her. She wanted to fold herself into that picture-perfect little body and feel what it must be like to possess everything one could desire.

Her own eyes remained glued to the eyes of the window. Too stunned to move, Myrtle just stared. Her indecision, once again, cost her.

Tom saw Myrtle come to the window, but it wasn't her he longed for then. Her presence only amplified to him how badly he needed to be somewhere else, with someone else. Scared of losing his wife to a man he viewed as an unworthy opponent, Tom looked away from Myrtle and turned the key in the ignition. He chose Daisy.

The car inched out of the lot, sped onto the glowing, menacing street and disappeared into the clouded, impassable horizon. The woman, the would-be Daisy, vanished, but she'd gained a physical presence in the already rattled walls of Myrtle's imagination. Except now she wasn't left to the imagination. Myrtle no longer needed to employ her talents of invention and conjuring; Daisy had surfaced, revealing her true form. Myrtle saw the beauty of her opponent, and its certainty set free a murderous appetite for ownership.

And Tom; Tom had left. He'd chosen Daisy, as he always would, over her.

While on the outside she remained motionless, that boundless interior life we all underestimate raged through the halls of fury and anguish. Her molecules zipped faster and faster, lightening her obligation to sanity, creating a hot, vibrating mass of a desperate woman.

Myrtle's next precious hours were lived in that state of anxious, hopeless energy. It knotted and threw itself against her mortal body, and somehow she contained it. Somehow we contain in our vulnerable bodies all the emotions that drive the world forward and back, that create the euphoria, and inevitably destroy it.

At the exact moment that the heat broke, when the temperature climbed to its pinnacle and, seeing that the view from up there wasn't that great after all, decided to recede, Michaelis strolled over to the garage. He didn't find George out front or under a vehicle or probing a toolbox. He walked to the back, caring as much about his neighbor's privacy as his concern about his restaurant's recent clientele, where he found George bent over his desk.

"George, my friend! Are you all right?" Michaelis asked.

George looked up at Michaelis, sweaty, pale, and shaking. "I'm sick," he said.

"Yes, that is obvious. There's been a lot of noise over here lately. I try to mind my business, as they say, try to look another way. But there's a lot of yelling, George."

"It's nothing," George said.

"You look like a, like a—what's the word? What is the word for a body that is no longer alive? The word for a dead body? That is what you look like."

"I don't know."

"A . . . a cops? No, that is not it. It is not a cop, like a police officer, but it is a word that sounds very similar. Similar to cops. Corpse! You look just like a corpse, George!" Michaelis was so pleased with himself for snatching the word. "Like a dead body. You are so white, even whiter than usual."

"Well I'm sick. I'm not feeling myself."

"No," Michaelis said. "No, no. You need to go to your bed right away. You cannot be out here in this heat like this. And maybe you don't yell as much. Maybe you take a rest."

"Can't, I'd miss too much business."

"No one cares about the business, George! Not like this. You look terrible. Really, really terrible. I didn't want to say this, but George, you scare away the business looking like that! You hear? You go up to your bed and go to sleep and come down when you are better. Then the business will still be here."

"I need the money," George said weakly, gripping the chafing, rough edges of the desk. The money could get them all out. The money would make him better. The money would take him out of the only life he'd ever known and spit him somewhere, anywhere.

"The money!" Michaelis said, pronouncing the word like *moan-ee*. "The money! We all want the money, of course! Who doesn't like the money? But the money, it waits. It will wait for you when you are healthy and then you can grab at it all you want."

George had been speaking quietly, almost at a whisper, which made the noise coming from above seem that much louder. Myrtle was yelling, stomping, pounding the walls.

"Help me! Michaelis! Help me! Get me out of here!" Myrtle yelled and banged, trying to get Michaelis's attention. She had to get him to let her out. He'd see what was going on and help her. He was her last hope.

"I've got my wife locked up in there," George said nonchalantly, as if he'd always been the brutish husband who would cage his wife. "She's going to stay there till the day after tomorrow, and then we're going to move away."

"George, what has happened?" Michaelis asked, unnerved by the animal-like sounds coming from above. "What is going on? This is not the kind of man who you are."

"She's not the wife I thought she was."

"Michaelis!" Myrtle shouted. "Help me get out of here! He's got me locked in the room. You've got to get me out!" She threw bottles of nail polish onto the concrete below, splattering bloodred puddles over greasy shadows. She threw shoes, she threw the dog collar. She threw whatever she could get her hands on to convince Michaelis, or maybe her husband, that she warranted saving.

"You have a fight," Michaelis said nervously. "Fights happen. Maybe you let her out and you talk about it. You both be more calm and talk about the problem and then everything is good again."

Myrtle's yelling for Michaelis tipped off George that Michaelis was one of the only men they saw regularly. Meaning that he was one of the only men that Myrtle saw regularly. The Greek didn't look as helpful and friendly anymore.

"Hey," George said, standing straighter and speaking louder. "What were you doing last Thursday afternoon?"

"I was working, George. I am always working. Why are you asking me this?"

"There's been funny stuff going on," George said. "You may not think me a strong man, you might think I'm stupid, a push-over. The stupid husband who don't know what his wife's been doin'. But I know. I'm wised up now, and I know. I'm going to take care of this and whoever's responsible."

"Okay, George. I don't think you are stupid. You are a good man. A very, very good man. I don't like to see you like this. You and your wife, you are my neighbor. Been neighbors for years. I do not like to see the fights and the shouting. I like to see you happy. Maybe you will get to sleep and you feel better, yes?"

"I'm gonna take care of this," George continued, eyes darting around the garage. He wasn't looking for a weapon, though. He wasn't really looking for anything at all. He just needed to keep searching, keep scanning what was there and what was not.

Some workmen walked past the open garage door, their laughter booming its way back to the office.

"I have customers," Michaelis said. "Slow down, George. Take a break. The business and the money, they will wait."

"Michaelis!" Myrtle yelled out the bedroom window as Michaelis walked back to his restaurant. "He's gone crazy! He's got me locked up in here!"

Michaelis had already chosen a side. Simply by being a man, the woman would have to lose.

"It will be fine, Mrs. Wilson," he said. "Your husband is sick. He is in a bad way right now, but he will feel better and everything will be fine."

"It's not fine! You've got to help me!" she shouted.

"I have customers now. I will be over later and things will be better." He turned his back to her and caught up to the workmen, patting them on the backs and joining in on their booming laughter.

Myrtle couldn't think straight. She could only see the yellow car and the tanned brunette woman she mistook for Daisy. Her capacity for calm, for ponderment, was driven out by confusion. Only to her it wasn't confusion, it was certainty, and it drove her panic forward until she was controlled by a hysteria cloaked as reason.

The window would be the portal to her escape. Of course. She'd lost the ability to assess danger, to see how her hasty decisions could cause her future to wane. She'd lost the ability to process time, and she was glad for that. Her tears rolled like minutes, as she lost the remainder of the time she couldn't process. Myrtle waited, staring out the window she'd jump through, hoping that somehow Dr. T. J. Eckleburg could extend invisible arms and catch her. The blue eyes, the yellow frames; it was so easy to be him.

Her baby was less real to her than those billboard eyes. Less visible, and less taunting. Myrtle had forgotten that there were two of them, that she'd replicated like inherited behaviors. The baby inside her had become just another blind spot.

She was swollen with despair when she jumped. It wasn't far. Just a single story; enough to jostle her body but not break it. George saw her figure drop from the sky, like a wingless angel who'd given up on the impossible idea of heaven. He ran to her out of instinct, habitually hoping she wasn't hurt.

"What are you doing?" he yelled to his wife, who stood up with renewed purpose. She was free now.

"I'm getting away from you," Myrtle said, limping backward. "Don't you come near me."

"Get in the house, Myrtle," George coaxed, inching closer.

"I'm leaving you!" she shouted. "I'm going away!" *Away*, she thought, was a beautiful word. Away, away, away. It was not here; it was away.

"Where are you gonna go?" George asked, slowly approaching her.

"You hit me. You locked me up inside my own house."

"Get back in there, or I'll do it again."

"Beat me!" she yelled. "Throw me down and beat me, you dirty little coward!"

"Myrtle, get in the house."

"No," she said firmly. The bats flapped within her, but she welcomed them. She'd take them away with her. She'd let them propel her forward, away.

"Get back inside our house," George said, more gently. He still believed there was a chance they could recapture their past lives. He still believed their little family would actualize. He still loved her.

"It was never mine to begin with," Myrtle said. "I see it now. I see it all now, and none of it was ever really mine."

Even during the final moments of golden sunlight, the yellow flash was hard to miss—the creamy yellow Rolls-Royce Tom had driven earlier that day. Except Myrtle had it all wrong. It wasn't Tom's car, it was Gatsby's, and it was no longer Tom driving it. A woman she'd never laid eyes on now drove the car. The woman who haunted her, tormented her, held her down. Daisy Buchanan drove the yellow Rolls-Royce, but, for so many reasons, Myrtle couldn't have known that.

Using the only power she had left, her own futile body, Myrtle ran into the street, waving her arms, desperate to stop Tom in the racing yellow vehicle. It was her final effort to wrest Tom from his favored, ruling-class life and pull him down into hers. Without a thought, without a fear, she ran determinedly into the street. There was nowhere else for her to go, anyway.

But Tom wasn't even there. Tom was so untouchable that he wasn't even in the car she ran out in front of.

For a second it hesitated, and everyone who witnessed the tragic accident of irretrievable love thought that maybe the speeding car wouldn't hit the woman. Maybe it wouldn't strike her, fling her, and tear open her body. It did.

Myrtle's deep red blood pooled on the dusty asphalt, just beneath the pitying stare of Dr. T. J. Eckleburg, who looked, strangely, as if he'd seen this coming all along.

The shiny yellow car kept on driving.

You can't live forever. You can't live forever.

Acknowledgments

Obviously, this book would not exist without F. Scott Fitzgerald's masterpiece. *The Great Gatsby* is the first book I read to both of my kids as newborns when I brought them home from the hospital. It was the first required reading book in high school that I loved enough to read again (even without a book report due). It's the book I compulsively buy whenever I walk into a bookstore, because who doesn't need forty-plus copies of *Gatsby*? Fitzgerald's words have inspired me and countless others, and they will continue to for generations to come.

My biggest thanks goes to my agent, Jacklyn Saferstein-Hansen, who, even though she represented me for sardonic cookbooks, took a look at this not-sardonic-cookbook and got it out there into the world. Her support, encouragement, and brilliant edits made this book so much better. She is the number one reason you're reading this book today. And thank you to Alan Nevins for guiding my guiding light.

Barbara Berger at Union Square & Co. is next up on my people to be incredibly grateful for list. Besides her thoughtful edits and enthusiasm for the book, her attention to detail is just incredible. (I now know what a 1920s bra looks like!) I don't know how she does everything she does, and I cannot imagine a better editor for this book.

Thank you to all the experts that turned my hand-scribbled manuscript into a beautiful, readable book, namely project editor Alison Skrabek, interior designer Christine Heun, cover designer Jared Oriel, art director Patrick Sullivan, production manager Sandy Noman, and copyeditor Hayley Jozwiak.

And of course, thank you to my children for giving me the greatest love of my life.

Topics and Questions for Discussion

1. Even if you're unfamiliar with *The Great Gatsby*, you learn in the first chapter of *Mrs. Wilson's Affair* that Myrtle will die. How does that knowledge impact how you view her and take in the rest of the book?

2. We're witnessing two romantic relationships here—Myrtle and George, and Myrtle and Tom. One relationship has existed for more than a decade, while the other is just beginning. More than once, Myrtle considers how feelings change and how love, so powerful at first, seems to settle over time. "Isn't it the scariest thing in the world that love changes?" she asks. Do you agree with her assessment? How does love change? Is it a certainty that it will?

3. There's an imbalance of power between the genders in both *Gatsby* and *Mrs. Wilson's Affair*. How does Myrtle try to grasp power? At one point the narrator in this book says, "It was women who suffered most for men's sins." How is that true in *Mrs. Wilson's Affair*? Both novels take place in 1922. How have things since then changed or stayed the same?

4. Myrtle wants so badly to be a part of Tom's world, where she can buy a new dress, live in a nice apartment, and eat lunch at fancy restaurants. Tom is clearly from old

money—how does his powerful position in life affect his relationships? Is Tom taking advantage of this power with Myrtle and other women? Discuss what Myrtle might represent to Tom. Do you think Myrtle would have had an affair with a man closer to her own working class?

5. Myrtle and George both expected to be parents, but they weren't able to have children together. Do you think their relationship would have changed if they'd had a baby? How does the expectation to be a parent affect someone? How does family play a role in the book?

6. The apartment scene in chapter 12 is truer to the original *Gatsby* text than any other part of the book—the arc and some of the language is taken directly from *The Great Gatsby*. With the author more confined to Fitzgerald's text and portrayal of Myrtle, does the character feel any different in this chapter compared to the rest of the book?

7. So much of *The Great Gatsby* is about the American Dream. *Mrs. Wilson's Affair* is a very different book, without the big parties and glamour of Tom's, Daisy's, and Gatsby's world. How does the American Dream feel different from Myrtle's and George's point of view?

8. One of Myrtle's happiest relationships is with her younger sister, Catherine. What lessons do you think Catherine learned from Myrtle? And Myrtle from Catherine?

9. Discuss Myrtle's many forms of escape: from her imagination, to romance novels, to men. Why does she need these escapes? What do they give her?

10. Is there a villain in *Mrs. Wilson's Affair*? If so, who do you see in that role and why?

11. Myrtle believes that her and George's love has evaporated, saying that George doesn't arouse any passion or interest for her, and she believes he feels the same about her. "How can one care when feeling is gone?" she asks. Is the feeling really gone between Myrtle and George?

12. At one point the narrator comments, "She doesn't deserve sympathy anyway, this cheating woman. Does she?" Does Myrtle deserve our sympathy?

About the Author

ALLYSON REEDY is a fiction writer, food journalist, and restaurant critic. Her work has been published in a number of newspapers and magazines, including the *Denver Post, Bon Appétit*, and *5280.* She is the author of several cookbooks, including *50 Things to Bake Before You Die* and *The Phone Eats First.* She lives in Denver, Colorado, with her children, husband, and pug.